Prismland

Johan Adkins

Bon Nuit Publishing

The names and human characters in this book are fictional and are amorphous amalgams, and only some of them bear some resemblance to real friends and family of Johan Adkins. I won't say the Rainbow World creatures and Fairies are fictional.

See the author's web page at http://www.johanadkins.com

ISBN: 098275891X
ISBN-13: 9780982758915
Library of Congress Control Number: 2010904609

Fiction/Visionary fiction and Metaphysical

Bon Nuit Publishing
1740H Dell Range Blvd. #142
Cheyenne, WY 82009

Printed in USA, First Printing 2010.

If someone told you that you must help save another dimension, and without your help, Earth would die too, would you believe them? Could you afford not to?

Prismland is the story of a group of healthy and flawed people who live and work in Cheyenne, Wyoming, and on ranches in Granite Springs and Table Mountain in Wyoming, and someone is telling some of them that very thing.

Rainbow World sits one-half dimension off Earth and is dying from Earth's pollution. It is home to some surprising and varied creatures. Many are present on Earth as well, but they are only visible to some, and outside of perception to most.

Elf Class Shamans called Walkers have worked on Earth for millennia. Rainbow World is also home to the pink, light bodied ethereals called Lemp who are responsible for keeping the secrets of all the known worlds and universes programmed in Record Keeper crystals.

The Record Keeper for Rainbow World itself was stolen by young Walker Initiate Temujin, who escaped to Earth by misusing it. Generations of his family hid the crystal, but eventually it was "recovered" on Earth. Tazman Khan is the last descendant of Ogodei, The Great Khan, who was the third son of Walker Temujin known on Earth as Genghis Khan.

Tazman Khan will stop at nothing to get the Record Keeper crystal back.

A Dragon named "Sentinel" has sent the oldest Walker Bearer to Earth to protect the crystal and to find the human destined to help save their world. Only this human can unlock the secrets of the Rainbow World Record Keeper crystal. This person must use the Record Keeper to find eleven more people to help.

If these twelve are found in time and are successful, they may save Earth as well.

. . . Time is running out.

Special thanks to Patricia Landy, Editor.
"Cum Aenea"

Also by the Author, Johan Adkins

Prismland

✢

Earth 1 (Sequel to Prismland)

✢

Spirit Speaks, the Transformation Connection

Table of Contents

Temujin – Rainbow World, Earth Year 1165

✡

Temujin – Rainbow World, Earth Year 1165

"Temujin! Pay attention!" Walker Saduffsan grabbed the young Elf by his pointed left ear. "If you can't keep all five balls spiraling in the air, how do you expect to help keep entire planets in their orbit?"

Temujin squinted his eyes and hissed through his teeth. Walker Saduffsan was not oblivious to the disrespect. He sighed and said quietly, "I weary of your lack of self control. Go now to the seclusion room in the Lemp Tower and meditate about what you really want."

The Shaman Walker instructors were all becoming unbearable in Temujin's estimation. As a Rainbow World Initiate Walker, he had three more years to endure to become a Novate Walker. After that he had twelve more years of even more grueling shaman and warrior training to become a Walker. It felt like his whole life would be spent in the confining discipline of school, although he knew that wasn't really true. He would have at least a thousand more years or more to live if he chose to.

He had already been through three years of Initiate training, and he knew more than most of the instructors. He was bored. No, he was more than bored. He was fed up.

He batted at a Fairy hovering near his head. "Pest!" He was bitten for his insolence, and the tiny Fairy shook her fist at him. He walked slowly towards the Lemp Tower of History. Overhead the Minervan beings, who resembled colorful spinning disks with a million tiny legs, worked in pairs to create a constant array of "moving pictures" in the sky with the cloud formations. The vastly huge Rainbow Beings, who were recognized by their flowing multicolored robes and very slanted eyes, flew above too, zipping through and around the cloud art weaving color and three dimensional densities into the constant art show above them. Usually, he stopped to admire the view, which was a favorite pastime of everyone in Rainbow World, but not today. He surged ahead, watching his feet and mumbling under his breath. He paced back and forth like a tiger in a cage.

As mad as he was, it was not in his conditioning to disobey a Walker. They were powerful and magical beings that inspired a begrudging awe, even in one who felt totally oppressed by their authority. The scope of Walkers' abilities extended far beyond keeping planets in their orbit. The Walker Elite were scattered throughout many Universes, living secret, exciting lives that only a few in Rainbow World would ever know. Some Walkers chose to stay on their assigned areas permanently to monitor their assignments more closely. They did what was necessary in the view of the Rainbow World Elder Council. At the very least, they helped move the interplay of universal energies in magical ways that were unseen and would be unimaginable to the inhabitants of the planets they protected.

Walkers could also "assume" any form and blend in to indigenous animal forms, plant forms, or the populace if they chose. They could extend their energy into another and just "walk-in" and share or take over their body. That's why they were called Walkers.

Temujin was practicing "assumption" at night when everyone else was asleep. It was usually not taught until sixth year Novate Walker training, but he could do it with ease. He particularly enjoyed entering one of his sleeping enemy's bodies and putting him on the roof of the dormitory where they all slept. It was hilarious leaving him to wake up wondering how he got there. He had to be careful doing that though, he might be expelled from the Walker program if he got caught. Being expelled wasn't an option. He wanted to know the secrets they kept, secrets so big even the Walker Elite wasn't privy to them all. He understood he had to stay in the training he was being offered and that it was an honor. He just didn't think he had the patience he needed to trudge through it all day after dreary day. He knew most of it already and just wanted the process to speed up.

He wanted to be a Walker Bearer, the leader, not just a nobody shuffled off to some obscure planet in the Outer Rings. The Walker Bearer named Prime was the undisputed ruler and keeper of the Holy Secrets. He was ancient beyond time and could actually bend the matrix of the Universe and travel outside Rainbow World with a thought. He would give anything to be able to do that. Anything.

He wanted to go to Earth; that's all he ever wanted to do. Go to Earth and ride the horses he watched so often in the seer globes. Ride free and wild with the wind blowing in his hair. They didn't have anything like that here. He had to stop processing this way; it caused a physical ache in his stomach knowing he might never see Earth.

He passed a group of tall, delicate Lemp beings. Their bright translucent pink bodies were actually painful to look at for him. Looking directly at them always gave him a headache. They were so beautiful, but their bodies were shifting, ethereal, and wraithlike. Their voices, however, rang like bells and calmed and soothed his jangled nerves a bit. The group stopped and sat together by the clear water fountain that jetted balls of shimmering turquoise water that giggled at the ride. He sat on the opposite side of the fountain and just listened to the Lemp group laugh and talk together.

He knew better than to strike up a conversation. They were historians of everyone, everything, everywhere, and loved to talk. Usually, he didn't really listen to anything other than the sing-song of their tones, but today, he made himself listen because they were talking about something that interested him very much…very much indeed.

"Just how do they propose to move the Record Keeper crystals from the West wing of the Lemp Tower to the secret place?" asked the young Lemp female named L'Nalde.

"There will be only a short window of time this evening when the energies protecting them will be down, and we will be able to move them then," replied Dar'L the older male.

"So, we will have adequate numbers to help? There must be thousands and thousands of crystals and each will have to be cataloged?" L'Nalde queried.

L'Nei, the older, long-haired female replied, "No, special task work units worked all night last night, and they are already labeled. We will just have to make do. We'll have to work in shifts and move them as we can. We can't afford to misplace even one. If anyone knew they could be used to travel through the matrix portals to other worlds, the Record Keepers might be at risk."

Dar'L admonished, "Shhh. Lower your voice please."

They went on talking quietly, and Temujin left discreetly. He went over the hill and doubled back toward the Lemp Tower from another direction. His brain was working overtime. He had a plan.

Chapter One
Thursday on Earth, June,
Modern Day Wyoming

☆

Ariane Selph

Ariane didn't want to take a bath. She was in a strange grouchy mood. She was hardly ever grouchy. Even though it was almost time for bed, she just wanted to get away from her mother and escape to her tree house. It was her very own secret, private sanctuary where nobody ignored her, or worse yet, bossed her around. She would rather be with her Fairy friends in her tree house in the middle of a grouping of pines that made up a magic circle in the woods.

She would *not* take a bath. She would just sneak out and no amount of pleading by her mother that she smelled like an old sock was going to change her mind. "I *like* to smell like old socks, especially week old ones." That being bravely said aloud, she poured in the bubble bath, stripped, and slipped into the hot water.

"Wonder if anyone ever died of inhaling bubbles?" She tried to inhale them and found that was just boring, so she pretended she was an alligator hiding among the bubbles waiting for dinner. If dinner did come along, it would make the bubbles bloody and red, so that particular pretence was given up. She just floated and allowed herself to relax.

Could Fairies get through the windows and the doors to visit her here? Would they visit her here, do you think? She watched the ceiling and imagined herself in another place. She often imagined herself in another place, just any other. Mom usually wasn't home this early in the evening to bug her. Wonder what was up?

Mom's name was Joanna Vanderlin. Poor, pitiful, recently widowed Jo Vanderlin who didn't even take her husband's last name when they married. Now her dad, Brian Selph, was dead. She and David, at least, had loved their dad. They had his last name.

When her dad was killed, her mom had barely cried. She just sold all of his stuff and almost everything else they owned, packed her and her brother David up, and moved from Tacoma, Washington to the Wyoming sticks. Within three months, she had opened a shop downtown in Cheyenne called "PRISM." It was twenty miles away from where they lived, twenty miles away from her kids, but what did she care?

Ariane was growing to hate the store and everyone associated with it. Her mother obviously cared more about it than she cared about her. "What did PRISM stand for again? Personal Research in Stupid Mentals? No, Personal Research in Synergetic Metaphysics." Ariane knew perfectly well what the acronym meant. Her mother had drilled it into her enough times. Synergetic metaphysics was the personal study of everything to everybody of all things weird and out of the ordinary. This was the explanation that Ariane had come up with for herself to help understand some of the "weirds" that frequented the store.

She got a mental picture of some of the prime examples of the people she called "weirds." Mrs. Flannery was an astrologer and wore seven layers of mismatched clothes and always seemed to be in a rush to finish your sentences and talk for you. Ariane wondered how she ever made any money. Some people liked her. Ariane didn't. She didn't like the squelchy numerologist nerd, Jeremy Plattern, either. Seemed like he was always mumbling about nothing at all. "Letters equate to numbers. The good numbers to work with are 3,4,6,8,9; everything you do has to equate to these numbers. Add the compound numbers and it's the same; for example, the number 12 equates to simple numbers of 1 plus 2 which equals 3. So important, so important." Weirds.

Ariane had to admit that not all of them were "weirds." She really met some interesting and wonderful people there too, like Spero Zezas. She loved saying that name, Spero Zezas. Even David liked Spero.

Her mom seemed to accept all things from all people, no matter how unbelievable or outrageous their stories. Ariane remembered the old lady who came into the store in a tizzy and told her mother that she had a ghost who was demanding money to keep from haunting her house. Her mother had taken that case on personally and followed the lady home in time to see the neighborhood loony tune in a sheet ducking out of the lady's back door. So much for blackmailing ghosts. *That* incident was at least explainable and understandable. Some of the things that happened in connection with Prism were less easy to understand.

Her mom seemed to have patience for everyone and believed everyone, except her, of course. If someone said they were taken up by aliens, her mother would ask what the aliens looked like. Ariane fumed that her mother probably even believed her brother David over her, except that David rarely talked to his mother either. He barely talked to anyone anymore.

David was sixteen and would disappear as soon as someone else was around to take care of Ariane. He stuck pretty close to home if it was just the two of them to keep an eye on things, to keep an eye on *her*, but if she did try to actually have a *conversation* with him, he was usually just RUDE. He was getting weirder and weirder. Nobody seemed to care that she didn't have anyone to talk to anymore… any people anyway.

Ariane looked down and noticed the bubbles were gone. As her fingers had shriveled into hands that looked about eighty-years-old, she got out and dried off. As she was drying her long auburn hair, she looked at herself. She was ok looking, for a twelve-year-old with mal-formed nodules instead of boobs. She was shorter than lots of her friends. Her eyes were her best feature, deep brown, just like her dad's. She missed her dad. She seemed to be the only one who did. He didn't call her Ariane. He used to call her Ari and always used to come up to kiss her goodnight and tuck her in. He always said she was his "Elfling" and that a Fairy had stolen the ugly baby and left her just for him to love. Ever since she was little, she had loved Fairies for that very reason.

She felt her eyes tearing up again and decided just to put her pa-jamas on and go to bed. How long was someone supposed to cry?

"Stop, just STOP!" She stood there looking at her feet, forcing her-self to hold back the tears.

She stopped at the kitchen table to kiss her mom goodnight.

"Why do you always hate to get in the tub and then spend hours in there?" Her mom pulled her close and looked into her eyes. "You ok? Tired honey?"

"Yeah, I'm just going to read awhile and go to bed."

"Well, you smell better anyway! Sweet dreams."

Dreaming was Ariane's favorite thing to do; she could hardly wait to go to sleep every night. But, lately, she had been dreaming about the same place over and over. Her dreams were continuing from night to night, and they seemed to pick up where they left off from the night before. Too weird. She used to dream about unconnected things that didn't make sense at all and half the time she didn't re-member the dream when she woke up the next morning, but that isn't how she dreamed anymore. A few times she woke up suddenly, for one reason or another, and then the dreams would just keep go-ing. She would swear she was awake. One time when she woke up, her mother was sitting beside her bed and talking to her about the dream. She swore that really happened, but her mother had never mentioned it, so she assumed she dreamed that too.

Ariane tried to read, but she kept dozing off and losing her place so she gave up and turned off the light. She snuggled down into her comforter. It wasn't long before she fell asleep. She immediately picked up her dream.

She was in a dark cave with drawings all around, and there were other people in the cave all sitting in a circle. Then, it seemed they all went to sleep, and their heads would drop and a bright light would surround them, and something like ghosts would all drift away from the sitting figures up to the ceiling. She became aware that she was looking down at her body sitting in the circle.

The drifting selves were light and could float or fly and were brighter and surrounded by many colors that shifted around them. Everyone had different colors around them. When they were happy, the colors were bright and light, or if they were unhappy, the colors seemed muddy or dark. David was often there, and his colors were always a kind of muddy brown. She was aware that others were floating beside them, but she didn't recognize them.

The cave walls that the dream bodies saw weren't dark and solid. They were made of crystals, and colors seemed to dance across the faces of the crystals in every color of the rainbow. But the colors were lighter and brighter and so pristine they almost made you cry.

The drifting dream bodies would travel down crystal pathways that wound here and there, but she always made herself stay in a straight line. Sometimes, the side passages seemed like interesting places to visit, but so far she didn't have the courage.

At the end of the straight passage, there was a bright white light, and each night she always traveled toward that light. So far, she was only traveling, traveling, and the light never seemed to get any closer. She always went to bed thinking that this would be the night she reached the light, only it never was.

Her brother seemed to be with her this time and was enjoying her company for once. She noticed that when they flew together or soared high into the crystal caves, his muddy colors would get brighter and brighter and eventually be as bright as hers.

Her dream self decided that she would go down one of the side passages and see what was down there.

She was about to break away from the group...

POOUUMMMPH! She woke suddenly. Her cat, Miss Phit, had jumped in the middle of her stomach.

"What on Earth is the matter with you? You scared me! Why did you do that?" The cat was cowering and shaking, and Ariane pulled her close.

Miss Phit was a perfect name for her cat. She was all black and not friendly to anyone except Ariane. Miss Phit would hiss at anyone who even thought of being nice to her. One way for sure, to make her hiss at you is to call her "Kitty." She hated that.

Ariane got up holding Miss Phit and tiptoed down the hall to her brother's room. She knocked on the door and expected to hear the usual, "Screw off, munchkin," but instead she heard a quiet, "Come in, Ari." She quietly opened the door. The cat jumped down and immediately sat in the middle of the room, stuck her back leg straight into the air and started washing it.

David's long legs were stretched out under his computer table. His red hair was getting longer, and it looked like he hadn't combed it in days. He didn't even look up at Ariane. "Why do you always come to visit so late?"

"Why do you always tell me to go away?"

"Well, most of the time, I just want you to go away."

"I miss you David. I miss Dad, don't you?"

David turned toward her and looked at her for a long time and didn't answer. He was holding a crystal that mom had told him about and he had bought with his own money. "Ever see one of these?"

"One of what? A crystal….yeah lots."

"Not like this one. This one is called a "Record Keeper." See the tiny raised pyramids on the sides? This side has some on top of each other there are so many. Mom said that some ancient civilizations believed that each of these raised areas contained a map or secret information to the society or culture that placed information in the crystal. She said that the crystal would tell its secrets to many, but only *one* individual in space and time was capable of unlocking and understanding the secrets. This ONE person was the only one worthy of becoming a human "Record Keeper" for that society. Pretty cool, huh?"

David handed the crystal to Ariane, and she immediately dropped it on the carpet. Her eyes got big as she waited for her brother to jump down her throat and scream at her for maybe "breaking" his precious crystal, so she talked fast.

"David, don't be mad! It stung me!!"

David looked at her quietly and said, "What do you mean, stung?"

"I don't know, like walking across the carpet and touching a metal lamp. Stung!!"

"Try holding it again."

Ariane picked up the crystal, and it just felt warm, not SO tingly, but still tingly. She turned it around in her hand and looked at it wearily. "Did this ever sting you?"

As usual he didn't answer her directly. "What did you see when it stung you?"

She had to think about that because she did see something; she just wasn't sure what. She also wasn't sure she should share the weird "what" on the edge of her mind.

"I can see that brain working, Ariane. Out with it."

Ariane sighed, "I saw lots of "things" not people, but <u>like</u> people, and odd patterns of colors and strange images rushing at me in super fast motion and talking to me all at once in languages I didn't understand."

"What did the things look like?"

Ariane handed him back the crystal. "I don't know for sure. It's like I remember seeing some of them in dreams and things before, but I don't remember when or where."

"Did they seem like they were "bad" or mean things?"

"No, just different than you and me. It seemed like they were in trouble, and they were happy to see me, but too happy, you know, too "rushy," like they were scared or something."

David watched Ariane for a long time before he tried to hand her the crystal once again. "You keep this for awhile, and see if you see anything else. I want you to tell me if you do."

"I don't want it, David. You keep it."

"Shoulda known you were too much of a chicken to do an experiment with me."

"Yeah sure, the day I'm afraid to do something you would do will be the day!" With that, Ariane grabbed the crystal out of David's hand and left his room. Miss Phit looked at David with great disdain and marched out with Ariane.

David said to himself under his breath, "I could swear that cat is a clone."

✦

David Selph

David sat there for a long time after Ariane left and tried to sort through his jumbled thoughts. He ran his fingers through his red hair and for a moment felt like pulling it out. "Acchhh!" he said aloud. She did feel something with the crystal, so it wasn't just his imagination, and she saw exactly what he saw....the one and only thing he ever "saw." His whole family was so messed up.

"All of us are freaks, and I'm talking out loud to myself again." But his logic told him that at least the other freak kid saw what he saw, so that gave validation to what he did see. But what did he see? His perception was that they were somehow shades or shadows of forms he had seen in the skies. He could see through them, but still see them clearly at the same time.

David's favorite pastime was being outside observing nature and watching the skies. Sometimes he could swear that he saw faces with eyes and features that watched him and shifted into other forms, but still with eyes that watched him. Nuts...he was nuts.

One time though, he watched the skies for a long time and noticed two tiny white cloud spheres side by side. Small perfectly round dots were set equidistant from each other and got rounder and rounder until they disappeared. Then they reappeared a short distance away and did it again. They both got rounder and rounder and then disappeared. Once he noticed pairs of dots, he saw hundreds of pairs of them <u>all</u> the time. If he noticed them, why didn't anyone else?

Sometimes the dots seemed to create down sweeps of clouds that made the pair look like they had a beak, and sometimes he could swear that hundreds of pairs made up paintings with clouds just for him.

Yep, he was definitely nuts.

Since his dad died, he just wanted to be left alone. During most of his free time, he took his rifle and just walked in the woods outside their home. Wyoming still had bears, cougars, and badgers, especially in the area around North Crow where he liked to explore. It wasn't wise to be out there alone without some protection. He didn't want to kill anything but didn't want to argue about territory either and get eaten or mauled. He just wanted to be able to defend himself if he had to.

Last winter he did a lot of cross country skiing exploring the area. He and his dad used to cross country ski together in Washington. They used to do lots together and have long talks about everything and nothing. Now it was NO talks about anything to anybody. Suited him just fine cause he had nothing to say that didn't sound totally insane.

He felt himself getting mad all over again. It seemed like he was angry all the time, and he was just getting tired of it. Ariane said she missed their dad too. The little twerp hadn't said anything about their dad for a long time, but it had to be hard on her too. His mom wasn't around much either for her to talk to…or for him, for that matter. He was more than tired of his mom leaving everything for him to do. Seemed she only cared about the shop and everybody else. She barely made it home before nine every night. He didn't care that she had a bit of a drive to get to Cheyenne. Why did she have to work anyway? His dad left them enough money to live comfortably.

It wasn't like she was a terrible mom. She was just available to everyone except her kids it seemed. She usually cleaned house, and did their laundry, and had something cooking for them in the crock pot or oven, or brought home pizzas, but he had to be responsible for Ariane most of the time and that was getting old. He was sick of feeling responsible for her. Not that he was really mentally there for Ariane though. He made a mental note to try to be a better brother. The twerp was lonely, he could tell.

Chapter Two
Friday

☆

Jo Vanderlin

Morning so soon? Jo drove into town with the window down even though the morning was a little chilly. "What am I doing? – WHAT am I doing?" She was so tired she was afraid she would fall asleep at the wheel. It was 6:00 am, and the mornings were getting earlier and the evenings later. She had gone home early for once last night and both kids were off doing their own thing. They didn't seem to need her anymore. They didn't seem to care if she was home to be with them or not.

On some level, Jo knew she was kidding herself. She knew that they needed her *too* much, so they punished her when she found a few extra minutes to be with them. Bryan had just died eight months ago, but it seemed like an eternity ago. He had traveled the world most of their married life, but the long stretches he was at home used to make up for it. Well, mostly. The last two years he had been gone more than he had been home, and his job in public relations for "big oil" in the Middle East seemed to put him into increasingly more and more dangerous places. She wasn't over being mad at him for getting killed, and that's the last thing she wanted the kids to see. She didn't fully understand it herself.

She glanced off to her right and noticed the observatory. It seemed so strange to see a giant telescope tower in the middle of the prairie. Well, it was close to the neighborhood "watering hole," a restaurant/bar out in the middle of nowhere so "that explained it" to the locals. She was getting used to the idiosyncrasies of Wyomingites again. They have a quirky, subtle and playful sense of humor. Now she knew where she got her tongue in cheek inclinations. She had grown up here but left when both of her parents died when she was in her twenties.

The Sun turned gold against the "backbone" area, a vertical out-cropping of regal sandstone cliffs that wound up the hill. What kind of power could do that? What was the world like when it was turning upside down? Well, maybe it was kind of like what her world was like now.

Prism was more than her business, it was an escape from what *her* world was like now. She felt like a total failure at being a mother, but surprisingly enough, she was a good business woman. The community seemed hungry for what she was offering.

"Who would have thunk it?" Jo mused aloud. Rocks, incense, herbs, beads, cultural pieces, healing paraphernalia, great jewelry, pottery and art generated by local artists, and books, books, books. The library was growing by leaps and bounds, thanks to the generosity of so many who donated so much. She felt needed, and her regular customers seemed to be doing everything they could to help bring in business. She was constantly amazed that the pioneering spirit still existed in this day and age. Some of her customers would show up Saturday mornings to dust and sweep the floor for her.

She giggled when she thought of last Saturday's impromptu cleaning crew. It turned into a childish play session that had them all laughing so hard she thought she would start snorting. Jo only laughed so far and so hard and then always (well usually) stopped herself. If she really laughed, she'd snort and then keep snorting.

Bryan used to love that about her. He'd tickle her to *make* her snort until they were both rolling on the floor….well enough of that. It was her secret. She had so far been "snort free," and she was going to keep it that way!

Her thoughts sure went in strange directions now days. It seemed that the more she used her intuitive abilities, the more she was able to help people coming in with very strange and varied problems. All the years of traveling with Bryan all over the world when they were younger seemed to have culminated in a perfect blend of metaphysical "know how." She had learned at the feet of the best healers and spiritual teachers in the world so that she could bring different healing philosophies and techniques to bear to help others when she needed to.

And healers and teachers just showed up at the store, sometimes staying in the area for weeks to teach her. There were so many examples of that happening. Most recently, Little Fawn, a Medicine Woman, stayed in a tent in Vedauwoo and came into town every day to teach her about the healing power of stones. She demonstrated how stone circles could intensify certain aspects of healing with different colors and different vibrations coming from each type of stone or each grouping of stones mixed just so. Each teacher's training was an incredible and touching gift. It was as if the Universe was sending teachers to her now.

Her closest friends seemed to have a sixth sense of when to show up at the store. Spero Zezas was waiting for her as she drove up. He was an enigma. She wasn't even sure that was his real name. He worked as a janitor at the Cheyenne Family YMCA. He rode a bike everywhere and seemed ageless, but her guess was that he was probably 60 or so. He dressed like Brendan Fraser in the "The Mummy." Jo was constantly amazed at how he pulled that look off in today's world and looked so comfortable with it that everyone else looked dull by comparison. She wasn't really sure what his background or nationality was…Native American? Eskimo? Indian? He had long white hair that he kept in a neat ponytail and the greenest eyes she had ever seen. He seemed a living example of Spirit on Earth. He walked into a room and filled it with energy.

The first time she saw Spero, she was shocked at the instant recognition although she had never seen him before. She started crying and walked into his arms. He held her and said very softly, "When things come up against you, sweetheart, just dance with them." Then he danced with her across the store. It all felt perfectly natural, and pretty soon she was wiping away her tears and smiling again. He had been her best friend ever since.

"Whatcha know, kokimo?" He asked with a sly smile.

"You know, I don't think know ANYTHING. I believe a few things that may or may not be right."

"Well, then you have it licked, kiddo. You either know a thing to be true or it's not. Beliefs are luxuries and often mislead you into spreading strawberry jam on your cereal."

Jo laughed, "You're in rare form this morning, Spero."

"Yes, I am, because I want to propose an idea I had to you! I'm practicing my poetic turns of thought because I want to have a writer's group in the back room on Saturday mornings. Would that be ok with you?"

"Sure, sounds like fun. What would you call it?"

"How about 'Wordsmiths?'"

"Want to put an article about forming it in the newsletter?" Jo asked.

"Ahh…my first work of art for the famous group known as the Wordsmiths! Want to join in?"

"Love to, but not sure I can get the store covered, so I might be a Wordsmith of few words."

"Thanks! I love you, Jo."

"Love you back."

And he was gone. He often came and went like that, but every time he left, Jo felt better than she had before she saw him. Would anyone ever feel that way about her? She worked in the store alone because she just couldn't get over the idea that she had to be there constantly to keep it open and successful.

The kids needed more time than she could give them right now though, and she was starting to think she would have to hire someone to give her more time with her family.

"Ugggh. Who?" Jo mumbled aloud. She thought of the applications lying in the bottom drawer of the desk. Everyone seemed to have one area of experience. They were Christians, Light Workers, Angelic Realm Workers, Wiccan, Buddhist, Moslem, or Hindu. Jo was looking for someone who was open to many spiritual paths.

Some applications were obvious attempts to slur the store, and in their view, keep the devils out of Cheyenne by "exposing" Prism as "evil." Jo just didn't understand this kind of blind hatred in the name of God or Jesus.

She mused. Not all Christians were extreme. She knew that. She was a Christian, or used to think of herself as one, but now she wasn't sure what she was. She believed in something much bigger than herself as a higher power but just couldn't limit it to only God or Jesus. She didn't understand how the evil that had been done in the name of God could ever be construed as being a true Christian. Seemed like there was a lot of hate mongering in the world in the name of God.

The puzzle pieces that put together her particular spirituality seemed to make up a very large and varied picture of bits and pieces of beliefs from everywhere and the puzzle seemed to shift constantly. Why didn't people understand that because you believed in the power of nature and the elements as well as a higher power, or as part of the higher power, it didn't mean you had no respect or concept of ANY other religion's beliefs. Metaphysics didn't discount any religion; it only supplemented it.

Beliefs. Dogma. That was where we all failed as spiritual people in her view. Spero said once that when more than two people got together to decide what they believed in, the result was always corrupted by the act of deciding because it immediately became exclusive and superior. The more she thought about that, the more she agreed. Enough of this. She was off on a tangent and she was starting to feel down again. She'd have to start thinking whether or not to hire someone. She wasn't ambivalent, was she?

✬

Ariane Selph

Ariane was slow to wake up. The cat didn't even wake her like usual. She vaguely registered that mom had left really early. David must still be asleep too. She wasn't in any hurry to get up. All she did in the morning usually was just eat cereal and watch cartoons until he woke up. She had agreed a long time ago to stick close to the house and porch until David was up too. Boring. She was twelve for crying out loud.

"'Crying out loud'. That's a weird expression. Wonder where that saying came from?" Ariane mused aloud.

She had been thinking about the crystal. It was still lying on her bed stand. She didn't have the courage to pick it up again no matter what she had said to David. The images she had seen when she touched it kept going through her mind. She had no point of reference to explain or understand what they looked like, or why they seemed familiar. None of it made any sense.

Ariane rolled to her side and looked at the shelf under the window. All of her rocks and shells were glinting in the Sun. Mom knew what each rock was called, and where they were mined, and what their "healing vibrations" were, but Ariane didn't care about that. She liked each one for the memory it held. Dad had picked up her favorite shell on one of their beach walks and wrapped it up in kelp and gave it to her as a present. He spent the whole day with her once…just walking along the docks in Tacoma. They shopped at the open air market and bought Alder smoked salmon, bread rolls, and soda for lunch. They sat on the dock and threw tiny pieces of food in the air, and the seagulls caught the pieces in mid air.

Where was mom then? She wasn't working, but she wasn't with them on this outing either. Maybe she was with David, but Ariane couldn't remember a time when her mother spent the day just with her, or with David for that matter.

She rolled back to her back and put her hands under her head and looked up at the ceiling. The prism hanging in the window cast rainbow colors all over the room. She remembered the dream again and the rainbow passageways.

She decided to go to her tree house regardless of the rules. She was old enough not to be babysat anyway. She dressed quickly and slipped out the back. She slipped through the hole in the fence and ran toward the woods. The location of the tree house was a secret from every mere mortal because you had to cross over into the Fairy realm in order to find it. It was invisible, and she was invisible in it. She reached the circular grouping of trees that acted as sentinels to the magic kingdom and slipped between closely placed pines. In the center, was the magical Fairy tree, Ariane's tree.

Suddenly, she saw a metallic flash of movement just to the side of the trees. She stood very still and watched. She was barely breathing. All of a sudden she heard someone yell, "Stupid branch! Son of a …..Acchhh!!!"

Hidden within a loud commotion of branches breaking and gravel sliding, was a boy with an Aussie hat covered in aluminum foil. He rolled down a nearby embankment. Landing in a heap at the bottom, he was spitting mad and dirty from head to toe. It was hard to tell where the dust left off and the boy began.

He looked up and saw Ariane standing there. "Well don't just stand there like an idiot! Help me up!"

Ariane came down a way, braced herself against a root and stuck out her hand. The boy scrambled up to grab it to lever himself up. She yanked him up, and they both got to the top of the embankment.

"Uh, thanks. Sorry I yelled at you."

Ariane didn't reply, she was struck dumb. Someone had violated her secret place and then had the nerve to be rude to her. She looked around at her magic circle, and some of the magic was fading away. It was becoming an ordinary group of trees with an ordinary tree in the middle already. She turned around and started back to the house.

"Hey!" he yelled. "HEY YOU! I said I was sorry and you're just going to turn around like a big snob and leave! Go ahead, leave! Jerk, oh excuse *me, jerkette.* Leave!"

Ariane stopped dead in her tracks and counted to three. She turned slowly and worked up her best dirty look. "What are you... lost? What do you think you're doing on our property?"

The boy looked down shyly and kicked at the rocks on the ground. "This ain't your property. I've been coming up here all of my life."

"Yes, it is our property. We own that house over there, and this ground RIGHT HERE, and you don't have permission to be on our property."

Suddenly, David came crashing through the underbrush and grabbed her arm and twisted it back behind her back. "Ok, you little twerp, I'm going to lock you in the closet. What are YOU doing on OUR property?"

The boy looked a little nervous. "Hey, dude! It's ok! I mean....she didn't do anything."

David looked for the first time at the boy. He looked him up and down and settled on the aluminum hat. He didn't say anything immediately, just kept looking at the kid. Ariane was making little hurt noises, but it was mostly her pride that was hurt.

"I mean, if you're going to hurt her ....ahh...you'll have my brothers to answer to. Won't stand for no girl to be hurt around me."

"Your brothers, huh?" David arrogantly looked around him. "Where are they now?"

"Ok dude. You'll answer to me instead," and with that, he threw his aluminum covered hat to the ground and put up his fists.

David let Ariane's arm go and said, "No need to fight. I'm not going to hurt my own sister, well, too much anyway." He looked at Ariane and she was rubbing her arm and tears were rolling down her face. Dang, maybe he had been too rough. "Sorry, kiddo. Did I really hurt you?"

"As if."

David offered his hand to the boy. "I'm David Selph, and this is my sister Ariane. Who are you?"

The boy hesitated, and then shyly shook David's hand. "Peter. Peter Postelwaite. We live over the hill there."

David handed him his aluminum covered hat. "What's with the aluminum, Peter Postelwaite."

Peter looked a little embarrassed. He adopted an Aussie accent. "Ah, I'd tell you mate, but then I'd have to kill ya and eat ya."

"Fair enough." David glanced down. The boy had blood running down his leg into his shoe. "Looks like you've cut your leg. Why don't you come up to the house, and we'll clean that up, and I'll get you a bandage."

Peter thought about it for awhile. His four older brothers ranged around David's age, and all he ever seemed to get from them was a world of hurt and teasing. He didn't remember ANY time when he had been hurt that any one of them had ever tried to help him. This guy was definitely a mystery.

"Yeah, if you don't mind, but I'm really dirty; I fell down the draw a ways, so I'll just stay on the porch...if that's ok."

Ariane had been watching this interchange with curiosity. David had actually apologized to her and was being nice to a total stranger. She decided to check his room for hookah pipes and drugs.

The threesome walked toward the house, and Peter settled on the front porch steps. Now that she actually had a chance to look at Peter, he was blond haired and blue/grey eyed and actually not too bad to look at. He was wearing a dirty t-shirt and cut-off cargo pants. He seemed to be all legs though, as if his body had elongated too fast and outgrew his clothes. His build wasn't like David's. David spent lots of time outdoors and had bulked out over the last year. He ate constantly and looked almost fat compared to Peter. No, it wasn't that David was fat; Peter was really, really, skinny.

David was applying a dressing to a cleaned cut near his knee. One clean spot on a very dirty leg.

"There, think that'll do ya." David tilted his head and looked into his eyes and Peter looked quickly away.

Peter smiled and said, "Thanks....um...feels better." Ariane figured out that when Peter smiled, he was actually handsome. His whole face smiled. "Well, I'd better get back home before my father wakes up and finds me missing."

David stood up and stretched backwards, "Uh, I was going to make some breakfast for us. Care to stick around just a little while? Had breakfast yet?"

"No thanks. I've got to get back. Uh, thanks anyway though!" Peter tipped his aluminum hat and backed off the porch. "Ariane, right? See ya sometime maybe. You too, David. Thanks again."

Ariane watched him walk away and decided she had stepped into another world and the magical kingdom must have shifted away from her tree grove to the real world because she had never, in all of her life, seen her brother act like this.

After Peter was a speck on the hill, she turned to David. "Where is my brother, and what planet did you come from?"

"Didn't you recognize that kid from school?"

"No. Why should I?"

David just shrugged his shoulders and started walking away.

"No sir, you're not just walking away this time. What are you getting at?"

"It's just that I know his brothers, and they're a pretty rough group. He doesn't seem such a bad sort though. He actually was going to fight me to protect YOU."

Ariane was struck dumb for the third time in one day. This time, she gave *David* the dirty look and walked away.

✫

Peter Postelwaite

Peter stopped and took the bandage off and kind of smeared the dust around the clean spot. No way to explain what had happened and where the bandage had come from without admitting that he had crossed over into someone else's property again. He wasn't going to put himself in a position of getting a licking for that. He wasn't that stupid.

He liked to walk early in the morning before the rest of his family was up. It was his time of day. The only time he ever had any peace of mind.

The girl had found his special place and had been as surprised to see him as he was to see her. He honestly thought that the tree circle and tree house was his particular find and the cottonwood in the center his special, private place. It was pretty disappointing that she apparently knew about it too.

He stopped and carefully removed the aluminum foil from his hat and folded and molded it to the inner part of the head piece. Aluminum foil was hard to come by, but some camper had left about a half a roll of it in the bins near the lake. Peter usually went south toward the lake instead of north back toward the woods. He didn't usually catch it for going into public property. He knew every rock around Granite Lake. Every rock and every tree.

He had never been able to afford a fishing pole but enjoyed watching the other families boat, fish, and picnic together. His family would never in a million years do anything like that together. They wouldn't be caught dead having fun together in a family outing. The closest thing he had ever had to a family outing was at the Rocking C Ranch with Demy and the rest of the Cresenzos. He hadn't seen his best friend, Demetrius Cresenzo, the Demy man ...well, for a long time. He'd thought about calling him, but he knew there would be a lot of questions that he wasn't ready to answer.

He had to get his chores done before his father got up. They had lots of chickens and the meanest turkey you ever saw. He needed to feed them and get the coup cleaned out and the eggs collected for breakfast. Ma was already up and banging around in the kitchen, so he rushed the job and gathered what he could find.

He took his hat off and left it on a hook in the coup. It was safe from his brothers in there because they wouldn't be caught dead in the chicken coup. He actually didn't mind having that particular chore; he'd rather do that than split wood. His brothers sold wood cords to make extra money for the family. Father worked sometimes doing odd carpentry work but hadn't been able to work much this summer. Usually, the summers were the busiest time of the year for him, but he slipped the axe awhile back and really hurt his leg. Being laid up made him meaner than usual, and usual was pretty mean, so Peter tried to stay away as much as possible.

His ma was ok. Pretty quiet, really religious. He often thought that she was afraid of his father too. As far as he knew, his father only yelled at her but had never hit her. He took out most of his meanness on the older boys. His father had only walloped him once, but it was really bad, and Peter had to be hospitalized for a week. He didn't remember much about it. He just remembered that he was supposed to tell them he fell off the roof. His body was black and blue all over. They thought his liver was bruised.

The Family Service people had put him in a teen center afterwards anyway. They didn't believe the "roof" story. He was pretty screwed up mentally and physically for awhile. He had gone to school there until summer vacation started. After he got back home, he found out that his father had been laying off actually hitting anyone else since the "accident." If there was one good thing that came of that, at least his father just yelled and screamed, and sometimes punched holes in walls, but he didn't beat anyone anymore. Peter just didn't trust him not to though, so he still kept a pretty low profile. One thing he knew, he would never just take a beating again without running away or fighting back.

Peter took his ma the eggs and hurried into his bedroom. He got clean clothes and ducked quickly into the shower. He should have probably hosed himself off in the yard; he was really a muddy mess. He really enjoyed the feel of water cascading down his body. He turned the water on as hot as he could stand it. He just kept thinking about this morning. He couldn't get his head around the way that David guy had treated him. He didn't understand that kind of kindness from a guy. Peter didn't lie when he said that his leg had actually stopped hurting, and that didn't make much sense when it was screaming at him just minutes before.

The only older guy who had been kind to him had been Ryan James, a male counselor in the teen center. Peter figured maybe Ryan got paid for just acting like he cared. But David didn't just ACT like he cared. He was really gentle, and Peter felt how much he did care. Really care. Weird.

He cleaned the bathroom after his shower as well as he could. All he needed was to have the drains back up with mud. He ran extra water down the drain, and it seemed ok. With four brothers, the bathroom could be a real mess, but he always tried to clean up after himself to make it easier on his ma.

Sometimes, his ma would look at him and tears would well up in her eyes. He had a pretty good idea why she cried when she looked at him. She had watched her husband beat him and beat him and didn't stop him. Pete hadn't expected her to. His father was a big guy. His oldest brother, Jerry, had finally tackled his father and the other boys sat on him to make him stop. Sooo.... after thinking about it, he guessed his brothers did try to protect him after all. Funny, he had forgotten that. He'd also forgotten just what he did to make his father so angry at him that day.

✲

David Selph

David actually made good his promise to make breakfast, and for once, he and Ariane sat together on the porch and ate together. Bacon and eggs and toast. Ariane couldn't believe it.

David took his time eating too and then gathered their dishes and walked into the kitchen. Ariane followed him.

"Ariane, I guess I have to talk to you about Peter."

"What about him?"

"Do you think you might want to be a friend to someone like him?"

Ariane immediately got defensive. "Like him? What's that supposed to mean?"

"He's a little eccentric or different, don't you think? Aluminum hat and all?"

"What's that got to do with anything? What kind of snob are you?"

"Ok, poor choice of words, and that isn't really what I meant. I'm trying to figure out how to tell you something without telling you."

David took a long breath, "Ariane, do you remember when our old dog Buster got hit by the bus and got his leg crushed, and how he yelped, and whimpered, and cried until the vet gave him a shot, and he calmed down? Do you remember that even when the vet cut off the bottom part of the leg and the stump was totally healed, that sometimes Buster would lick in that area like it was still there? Peter is like Buster."

It was Ariane's turn to raise her eyebrow and look at David without saying anything.

"Ariane, I guess I've had a secret for a long time that I haven't understood myself. Lots of times I find hurt animals in the forest and try to heal them and make them more comfortable."

"Like the hawk?" Ariane asked.

"Yeah, like the hawk. But the thing is this, I usually find them because I can feel them before I see them, and I can feel that maybe something is wrong and something is hurt."

David had kept a hawk for a couple of weeks and taped its wing and fed it by hand until it could fly away. The hawk still came to visit once in awhile.

David was silent for a long time and then asked, "Do you have any idea what I'm talking about?"

"Yesss….well sort of. When dad died, I think I knew it. I started crying and crying, and we hadn't even heard yet, but I knew something was terribly wrong. I just didn't know what."

"Yeah, it's like that. We really are a bunch of mentals aren't we? Another point I have to make though is this. I don't want you to go anywhere near Peter's house. He's welcome to come here, but don't go there."

"Why???"

"Because I'm not sure you would be safe there, and I'm pretty sure Peter isn't safe there either."

✭

David had told Ariane more than he wanted, but she just looked into his eyes for a moment and said, "OK," and went off down the hall. She seemed to take it in stride.

He remembered the night she had screamed and cried and couldn't be consoled. They learned of their father's death the next day.

David had a lot of reasons for warning Ariane away from the Postelwaites. The four brothers had done everything in their power to make his life a living hell last year. They ganged up and tried to victimize everybody, but the four of them seemed to take great pleasure in picking on him relentlessly, taunting him in the halls, knocking food trays out his hands in the cafeteria, or body slamming him into the lockers. As far as he could figure out, the only thing he had done was come to school mid-year as the new kid. He figured he'd eventually have to take one of them on in a fight to get any respect.

He had actually come to Wyoming hoping it would be different, but he was always the odd man out. It was always the same wherever he went. He was really sick and tired of being taunted for having red hair and freckles. Like he could help that. When his parents used to buzz cut his hair when he was little, the taunting was even worse because then his ears stuck out too. The kids had always teased him mercilessly.

The odd thing was though, around Christmas, the brothers just started keeping to themselves and left everyone alone. They were usually loud and boisterous, but suddenly, they were trying to be invisible. One of the guys at his lunch table told him that there was some rumor that Nels Postelwaite, the father, had almost beat one of their younger brothers to death. Now he knew that rumor was true.

Peter was a pretty neat little kid. David had liked him immediately. At least, if Ariane did develop a friendship with him, she should be safe with him as long as she stayed clear of the rest of his family. Peter seemed to have lots on the ball. She really did need a friend, poor kid. She was getting twitchy talking to the trees.

David could hear music in her room, so knocked on her door. "Feel like a road trip?"

"Are you kidding?"

"No, let's go."

David had been able to drive a car alone for a few months now and although he had a '95 Subaru at his disposal, he didn't usually drive much. He made a couple of peanut butter sandwiches and threw a couple of sodas in a small cooler and as an afterthought grabbed a couple of bananas and some cheese. He jotted a note to their mom in case she came home and found the house locked and them gone.

He figured that he and Ariane would probably make it home before she did, but just in case they didn't, or in case they had car trouble or something, she'd know which direction they went.

"Someone told me about an area up at Happy Jack called "Hawk Point," and I'd like to try to find it. They said there used to be beaver ponds up there, and there is a small waterfall somewhere out there."

"No way! Really? A waterfall?" Ariane couldn't believe her ears.

"Remember to grab your coat and don't wear those sandals. Go change into jeans and your boots in case we have to climb." David gathered the picnic and decided to take a couple of blankets just in case.

He yelled, "I'll meet you out front!"

He put everything in the trunk and backed the car out of the garage. As soon as he reached the front of the house, he was surprised to see that Ariane was already there.

David smiled at her. "Wow! Good timing munchkin. Did you lock the door?"

Ariane jumped in the front seat and slammed the door. "Yep!"

David peeled out on the gravel and came to an abrupt halt at the gate. He always did that when he left by himself, but this was the first time he had ever done that with Ariane in the car. She squealed and laughed. David smiled.

David got out and opened the gate, and then drove the car forward.

"I'll get it!" Ariane jumped out of the car and closed and locked the gate and hopped back into the car and buckled up.

David headed west on Happy Jack Road. They looked toward Granite Lake, and the Sun was glinting off the water. It wasn't too hot yet and the prairie was really green. Blue lupine, red and orange Indian Paintbrush, and yellow sweet clover were starting to bloom. The large sage was everywhere, and the air mixed with pine smelled fresh and wonderful. The day felt like it was an adventure waiting to happen.

"Thanks, David. This is so cool!"

"Well, we might not find the waterfall, but let's see what we do find!!"

David drove along until they came to a dirt road cut-off to the North. "Let's get off the highway here."

The dirt road wasn't in just bad shape really, but it wasn't long before the roads started branching in different directions.

"What if we get lost in here?" Ariane asked.

"Well, we can't really get too lost. Things are either... north, south, east or west, and I have a really good idea which direction is which. Don't worry, even if it winds around a lot, we'll be ok."

Ariane decided not to worry and just to enjoy the rock structures and the trees. This area had a lot of rocks like Vedauwoo. Now that was a word. She had learned that it's pronounced Veed-a-voo. The rocks looked like great big...well, piles of poop. She turned red thinking of them that way. She couldn't help it! That's what they look like! She turned her head toward the window so David wouldn't see that she had embarrassed herself. She forced herself not to giggle like a silly girl.

David said, "You know, there's rumors that there are caves up around here. Wouldn't it be cool to see a real cave?"

Ariane stopped smiling immediately. Her hands felt sweaty.

David looked at her. She had suddenly gotten pale. He pulled slightly to the side of the road and stopped the car. "What's the matter? Are you sick?"

"No, it's just weird that you mentioned caves. I keep dreaming over and over about a cave."

She spent a long time explaining the dream in detail to him.

"The thing is, David, I think the cave and the light world are real places, and it feels like I'm supposed to find them. The other thing I just realized this moment, is that I remember where I saw those Record Keeper creatures before. I think I've seen them in those caves in the light at the end of the tunnel."

David didn't say anything, just turned the car back onto the road. "It's just a dream, Ari."

He hardly ever called her Ari, now he had called her Ari twice in just the last couple of days.

"Well, if it's just a dream, why does it happen night after night? Even if I wake up sometimes it just keeps going, but I never get closer to the end of the tunnel?" Ariane asked.

"You didn't happen to bring that crystal with you, did you?"

"Yes. I've been trying to make myself touch the crystal more, I just don't like to."

There was a Y turn coming up. David pulled off the road and stopped. This time he turned off the car. "Want to try an experiment with me? Let me see the crystal."

Ariane got it out of her back pack and handed it to him. David reached across her and opened the glove compartment and took out some string.

"Come on, let's go over to that grouping of rocks over there." They reached the rocks and David climbed up to a flat surface of one of the larger rocks. The Sun was shining on the rocks, and it felt wonderful. Ariane was quick to follow. David sat cross legged and Ariane sat across from him.

"Ever heard of a pendulum before?" David asked.

"No, what's that?"

David demonstrated. "You take something from nature, like this crystal. Tie it to a string and suspend it in midair and watch how it moves."

Ariane looked at him suspiciously.

David held the crystal very still and held his hand very still and pretty soon the crystal started moving in circles.

"You're doing that!" Ariane accused.

"Here, you do it if you think I am." He handed the string to Ariane.

She mimicked what she had seen David do and held her hand still. The crystal again began to move in circles. She grabbed it quickly with her left hand and almost threw it back to David.

"Whoaaa....here you take it."

David took it from her and started again. The crystal immediately started moving in circles again.

"Now here is the freaky part." He spoke in a quiet voice. "Please show me a movement that means 'yes.'"

The crystal stopped the circular movement abruptly and then moved back and forth instead of around and around and then stopped again.

David mused, "The crystal moving like that just broke a law of physics called perpetual motion."

He smiled and continued, "Please show me a movement that means 'no.'"

This time, the crystal twisted slightly on the string.

"David, we're actually talking to the crystal, aren't we? Looks like it's shaking its head. This is too weird!" Ariane was mesmerized!

David resumed. "Please show me a movement for 'I don't know or I can't answer.'"

The crystal just sat still.

"Where did you learn how to do this, David?"

"Remember that lady named Little Fawn that came to mom's store and camped out here somewhere? She said she was a Medicine Woman? She taught me. She said that we had to be respectful of the Stone People and ask direct yes and no questions using computer logic."

"What?" Ariane looked puzzled.

"Like, you can't say, for example, 'Can you tell me if Sonya likes me?' because it would say 'yes.' That doesn't mean, 'Yes, Sonya likes me,' it means, 'Yes, I can tell you.' Get it?"

"Well, how would it know if Sonya likes you or not?"

"Little Fawn said that it reads our energy and the energy of anything and anyone around us. She said that even if you had a picture of the person or something they had touched, the Stone People could read an energy signature from that. The pendulum can tap into universal energy which is connected to everything and everybody and answer any question."

Ariane was so happy that David was actually talking to her. She made herself pay close attention and not talk. To talk to David, you had to listen and wait in the quiet pauses for him to finish getting his thoughts together about what he would say next. If you interrupted in these quiet pauses, he would just stop talking.

David continued. "Oh, and she also said there is an element of the pendulum being a tool to our inner knowledge and a way to tap into our own subconscious and bring what is inside, outside."

"Whoaa….it can do all that?"

David was really animated, and he was smiling and happy too, for a change. "She said it could do much more than that. It can read a person's health in their hand, or if you take it over the body it can show you where there are problems. It follows the energy pathways or meridians and looks for blockages that keep the person sick."

He interrupted himself to ask her, "Do you know what meridians are?

She shook her head "no."

"Meridians mean lines, you know, like those oriental charts that show lines all over people's bodies for acupressure or acupuncture?"

He paused for another moment, and Ariane waited patiently. "Anyway, Little Fawn said that the pendulum could be a tool for helping the healer, and the person being healed, to unblock the energy. Once the body's natural energy starts to flow freely through all the meridians then the body would seek health again."

Ariane wondered if this was the way that David was helping the animals.

David was excited about this subject. Ariane could tell. David squinted his eyes and looked off in the distance like he was trying to remember everything. "Oh yeah, and she said placing colored stones over major chakras…do you know what those are?"

"No, not really," Ariane smiled. This was the David she loved and missed.

"They're like tiny tornados where two lines meet. They meet all over the body but the seven major ones are at the top of the head, the forehead or third eye, the throat, the heart, the solar plex, the abdomen, and what is called the root chakra, at the base of the spine."

He was on a roll, apparently, but Ariane was loving it!

"Anyway, if you put colored stones there or crystals, then the healing process is sped up and the body is even more open to universal energies to be healed."

"Rocks can do that?"

"Lots of cultures from a lot of different countries believe in the power of stones, not just for healing, but for other things. The Bible mentions stones and gems in lots of places. Even the Christian culture talks about the stones as being good, as being gifts from God. The Cornerstone was said to be a gift from God. Did you ever read about the twelve tribes of Israel? God stopped the waters during a flood. They crossed safely and were told to gather one rock for each tribe to build an altar in remembrance of God."

"The ancients even named two holy stones the Urim and Thummim that were supposed to be worn over Aaron's heart in something called the breastplate of judgment. It was to be worn when he went before the Lord bearing the judgment of the children of Israel on his heart. It's in Exodus in the Old Testament somewhere, I think. Many scholars think that the Urim and Thummim were one white stone and one black stone. White for 'yes' and black for 'no'. You know…like yin and yang."

David said, "It's my belief that it isn't out of the realm of possibility that Jesus used stones." David lay down on the rock and put his hands under his head and looked at the sky.

"Whoaa," said Ariane, and she lay down too, mirroring his position.

"All through history in lots of cultures and even today, sometimes stones were put in skin bags worn around the neck called amulets. There was also a box called a "phylactery" that held personal objects. The box had straps that tied around the head and was either worn at the top of the head or worn on the psychic center or 3rd eye I was telling you about? Somehow the stones inside help them weigh all the aspects of a problem and come up with solutions."

Ariane giggled, "I'm trying to picture this."

"Jewish people, even today, use something similar called a tefillin. They are small boxes that something can be put in, but it's my understanding that they put torah passages in there and not stones, but it's still a fascinating concept. They tie really long leather strings to the sides of the box and have a certain way to place the box between their eyes, on their 3rd eye, or on their upper arm for the straps to go around their hands."

He was quiet for awhile and then he continued, "Maybe they have reasons to do this that we don't know about, but what I've read is that they believe when they pray that it binds the commandments to their hands and between their eyes. Sorry, I'm kind of getting off the point. It's just really interesting to me."

Ariane just keep looking at David. This was the longest speech he had ever made to her. The first long speech was about the crystal. She was happy just to listen, and besides that, it really was interesting.

David sat up straight and got back to business. He started holding up the crystal and watching it move around in circles.

Ariane sat up too and quietly asked, "What are we trying to ask the crystal?"

"Where your cave is."

✡

Demetrius "Demy" Cresenzo

Demy was bored. He was beyond bored. He was bored, bored, bored. Last summer he and Pete had spent practically the whole summer together and had a blast. It had gone by so fast that they were both shocked when school was about to start. Then, halfway through school, Pete just disappeared. Demy heard the rumors and had no doubt that they were true. The few times he had been around Pete's family, he couldn't believe how scary it was, how rough they all treated each other. Pete spent most of the time hiding out from his father and big brothers. Demy might be bored, but at least the Cresenzo family loved and cared about each other. His family were more than ok; they were fun too.

Demy lived at Rocking C Ranch on one hundred twenty sections of land near Table Mountain with lots of ranch hands around that were like extended family. Not as though there was a shortage of extended family around either. His great, great and maybe another great grandfather had homesteaded here, and when the other homesteads failed or they just flat gave up, all of his line of grandfathers would buy their land.

The family formed a corporation that actually owned the land so that everyone "on the board of directors" had to agree what was to be done on the ranch. His dad, Martin, as the oldest family member active in the ranch, was president of the board and the ranch manager. His two uncles, Mario and Jack, and their families lived on the ranch and were the other major shareholders. When the children of all the families were twenty-one, they were given one hundred shares of stock and a place on the "board" and then had a say in the ranch activities as long as they stayed at the ranch.

There was always something to do, but he knew if he complained he was bored, his dad would put him to work fast enough. He was just tired of just working all the time and not spending any time having fun with someone closer to his own age.

"Demy! Where are you?" His dad yelled at him from the yard.

Rats, he'd been found. "I'm here, Dad," and he came out from around the barn.

"Do the Postelwaite boys still have their tree cutting business? Do you have their number? I'd like them to clear that patch of woods by the north pasture for the hunting lodge. I'll pay them for their time, and they can keep the wood."

"Sure, I'll get it for you. But Dad! Would you mind if I call so I can invite Pete too? I haven't seen him in a long time."

He replied, "Sure. But you two steer clear of where we're working today."

Demy was thinking about the hunting lodge. His family had allowed friends to hunt in the area for a long time and had decided last year that they might as well make some money at it and open a lodge for them to stay in. More and more people had been asking for permission to hunt. The deer and antelope had to be kept thinned down anyway. They ate what the livestock ate and Rocking C had always had to deal with them one way or another. The natural predators of deer and antelope in this area were coyotes, bears, and mountain lions. But the predators were moving further away to get away from humanity so the herds weren't thinning that much anymore. The Cresenzos blamed the ranchers that had "sold out" and subdivided their land and parceled it off into small acre "ranchettes" which were springing up all around them. Dad called the influx of people wanting to live in the "country" them "danged yuppie cowboy wannabees."

It was inevitable, though, that his dad would think of some way to cash in on the way the world around them was moving. Martin Cresenzo had made so many jokes about how he thought they might end up being a "dude ranch," that he gave himself the idea to become one. The hunting lodge could be expanded out of hunting season to a dude ranch. Well, it was one way to get help during round up and branding time and the dudes would basically be paying the family for the privilege of working instead of the Cresenzos paying for extra hands.

The Cresenzos were always looking for ways to make more money. His dad's brother, Jack, had even talked the family into having a flock of sheep to expand their profit base. Cattle people were *not* normally sheep people, but the world was changing. Demy's dad wouldn't even consider it for a long time.

The only way he would agree was if he'd never have to deal with sheep personally. So the family hired a Basque family of sheepherders to deal with all aspects of keeping them. They lived in sheep wagons with the flock. The ranch sectioned off land specifically delegated to the sheep who tended to graze closer to the ground. The cattle people called sheep "Range maggots." His dad took a lot of flack from his fellow ranchers about new wool coats and socks and things, but his dad would always counter with, "Yep, those coats are lined with gold boys, and they are so soft! They just make me warm all over."

✫

Peter Postelwaite

Peter had just finished talking with Demy and hung up the phone. Well, that wasn't so bad after all. He and Demy just picked up their conversation where they left off. He felt sorry that he hadn't called Demy.

The only thing that Demy had said that was a little uncomfortable was that he missed him. Well, he didn't say that precisely; he said his **dad** missed him and wondered if he could come along to keep Demy out of his hair for the day cause he was sick of Demy following him around asking, "PPPPLEASE play Fantasy Kingdom with me." Wow, it had been a long time since he played that!!

Demy was the funniest, most popular kid in school. He had black hair that was always getting into his blue eyes and a really cocky way of acting and walking. Peter always teased him about his "John Wayne walk," asking him if he had something in his pants that was biting him or something. It was always a bit of a surprise and shock to Peter that Demy wanted to be friends with him. Demy always said that Pete was so cute in his aluminum hat that he got the girls' attention so Demy could get the girls. Yeah, like he'd know what to do with one if he actually got one!!

Peter asked his mother if it would be ok for him to go over to see Demy and if his brothers could help out at the Cresenzos. Mr. Cresenzo needed some land cleared and had offered to pay them all for their time and offered the wood they cleared as additional pay. Peter always talked to his ma about this kind of thing and she talked to his father. Peter hadn't spoken to his father since his "accident" and his father hadn't really spoken to him much. The chances of ever getting an apology about the "accident" from his father was nil. He could always justify hitting people "for their own good."

His ma settled that the boys would take the truck and flatbed and go that morning. Peter gathered his things to go along. His father limped in to the kitchen and saw him getting ready to go too.

"Where do you think you're going?"

Peter's mom came up beside Peter and put her arm around him. "I told Pete he could go too. He hasn't seen Demy for a long time." She had emphasized the words "for a long time." She looked very deeply into her husband's eyes, but Peter noticed she was shaking a little.

His father looked sharply back at his ma and turned his back and walked back toward the living room. "Get him out of here, then. Protect your little baby from the big bad man."

Peter looked up at his mother and she smiled. "Have a good time!"

He rushed off before they changed their minds and jammed himself in the cab of the truck with his brothers. In thirty minutes or so, he'd be with Demy. He felt great.

☆

Jo Vanderlin

Jo was really having a rough day. One thing about owning a metaphysical center was that the clientele tended to be pretty sensitive. They would walk in the door, decide the energy was "off" today and turn around and walk out.

Jo decided to smudge the store to clear away any negativity and cleanse the air, so she locked the door and turned the sign around that said, "Out to lunch" and turned the little clock hand up an hour. She rarely closed the store, but truth be known, she needed some personal time. She chastised herself for the luxury of one hour alone but decided if anyone actually knocked on the door, she'd open it up.

She walked back into the office/storage area and unlocked the door. She learned the hard way that she had to actually lock up anything and anywhere that she didn't want customers to get into. She was a little surprised that they would actually open a door and walk in. This place was a mess. She had to force herself to do necessary paperwork, and the desk was strewn with, well, probably pretty important stuff. She saved the paperwork for Sunday when the store was closed. This really wasn't the best idea because she didn't really even have one day off a week.

She gathered her smudging materials, sweet grass braids and sage, and went into the little room she used as a meditation room. She placed the herbs in a large incense burner and lit them. She blew softly on the flame until it caught the smudge, and then she blew out the flame leaving a cinder that smoldered.

She sat holding the smudge and set it on the small stone altar she had built in the room. Lots of good it would do to smudge the store when the negativity was in her. She moved her hands in a circular motion in front of her body, bathing in the smudge and asked Spirit to cleanse her body and mind of negativity and to help prepare her to cleanse the store of the same. She tried to clear her mind and think of nothing, but that wasn't working today.

"What is wrong with me?" she said out loud.

Suddenly, she heard a soft knock on the door. She doused the smudge and approached the door. She tried to remember if she had seen the man before. He was about 6'4", dark complexion, with long dark hair pulled neatly back. His eyes were slightly slanted and so brown they appeared almost black…bedroom eyes. He was really dreamy looking but a little slimy looking at the same time. No, he was someone new. She pointed at the sign showing she was closed, and he yelled, "I need to talk to you."

She unlocked the door and stood in the doorway blocking his entrance. He inhaled briefly, "Smudging?"

"Trying to. I didn't get very far before you knocked. Just felt like something I needed to do."

"Yes, I can see why," he said arrogantly.

"You can?"

"Yes." He started to say more, then he tilted his head slightly and visibly pursed his lips. He suddenly looked very uncomfortable.

Jo waited for more of an explanation and none came. Finally she broke the silence, "You said you needed to talk to me?"

"Yes, I'd like to know why I had to quit a perfectly good job, making lots of money in Boston, Massachusetts, to walk into a store in Cheyenne, Wyoming and offer you my services, probably for minimum wage if you can even afford to pay me anything."

This time, it was Jo who was silent. She just kept looking at him expectantly.

"Ok, let's start over. It's pretty apparent that you need some help, and I'm apparently here to help you, so what can I do?" said the man.

Jo said in a rush, "I'm not in any position to hire anyone right now, and quite frankly, I don't know you and I wouldn't hire someone I didn't know and trust. I'm not sure what kind of game we're playing here, but I'm not very good at them, so you can cut through the bull and tell me what you really want."

"A lady after my own heart. I learned a long time ago to listen to my intuition, and my intuition was telling me that I was needed here. Haven't you been trying to decide whether or not to hire someone?"

"Well, yes. Someone part-time, but that particular 'vibration' could be explained away by the fact that I'm a new business and new stores often start out with just the owner for a time."

"True, true, but that isn't the case here. I go where I'm led, and I was led here. There is no reason in the world for you to accept what I say at face value. You don't know me, but unless you give me a chance, you could be passing up a gift that the Universe is offering you. I'll give you some of my time for as long as I can afford to do it without being paid, and you decide if you should pay me. Fair enough?"

"Look, I'm not comfortable with the way this whole thing has gone. You could be anyone. You could be casing the place for all I know. I'm sorry, but I'm not prepared to take you up on your offer." Jo tried to close the door, but he blocked it with his foot.

"I don't really blame you, but in case you change your mind, my name is Tazman Khan. People call me 'Taz.' I'll be staying at the Nagle Warren Mansion Bed and Breakfast for a few days. I'd like to have the opportunity to change your mind before I have to leave to get gainful employment somewhere else."

After the man left, Jo shuddered. She felt suddenly cold. She couldn't believe how rude she was to someone offering to help her. She shut the door and walked back to the office like she was a sleepwalker and got some poster board and promptly wrote, "Prism will be closed for the next few days due to family commitments. See you all Monday."

She checked to make sure the smudge was cold, turned off the lights, got her purse, taped the sign to the door, walked out of the door, and turned and locked the store. She was in her car driving home before she even realized what she did.

☆

Tazman Khan

Tazman chastised himself. "Well, that really didn't go according to plan." He went around the corner of 17th Street to Central Avenue and looked for the Nagle Warren Mansion Bed and Breakfast. It was a historical treasure. They had really done a lot of renovation but tried to keep the old world charm alive. It would suffice as home for awhile.

He tried to think what his next move would be. This would have all gone a lot easier if he could have worked closely with her. There was just something about her. His obvious strong reaction to her was still confusing him.

After he registered, he went back out and found a coffee shop and ordered an espresso. He was sitting in the window enjoying the sun when he saw a man go by that shocked him into spilling coffee in his lap.

"Spero," he said under his breath.

He drank the rest of his coffee in a hurry and followed the man down the street. Spero stopped in front of Prism and stood there gawking at the sign with a worried expression on his face.

Tazman walked up behind Spero. "Glad you can still read. Anything interesting?"

Spero knew that voice, he responded without turning around. "What are you doing here?"

"What I always do, I'm following you."

"This is really getting boring. What precisely do you think I know that you don't know?"

"What a silly, silly question. You stole the crystal from me, so who knows what you know. Where is it?" Tazman almost spat the words out.

"Safe from you, safe forever, and you don't have to hang around here to try to find it. This is the last place I would hide it. I think this conversation is over." Spero turned his back and walked away.

"IT'S NOT OVER UNTIL YOU GIVE WHAT IS MINE BACK TO ME!!" Tazman yelled after him.

✡

Spero Zezas

Spero didn't respond. He walked around the corner to where he parked his bike and began to unlock it. He was fumbling with the lock and cussing under his breath. "His. Yeah, it's his. My eyes!" He got on his bike and headed home. Spero had managed to stay away from Tazman for months, and it was finally feeling like he might be able to settle in Cheyenne for a time in peace. He was mad at himself for showing obvious concern at Jo's sign that the store was closed. He needed to find out what her family commitment was. She and her family were too important to risk.

He needed to warn her against Tazman, who could be quite charming and persuasive if he wanted to. He'd seen him manipulate women time and time again. Tazman was wealthy beyond measure; it was too bad he didn't use his wealth to do good or to enrich everyone's knowledge. Spero knew he certainly had the resources to do just that.

"What a strange double life I lead," mused Spero.

He wished he could be totally honest with Jo, but experience had taught him that was impossible. The fact that he wasn't from around here, from anywhere, or anytime, around here, was always a hard pill to swallow for people. It was too much of a jump for them to accept that there were dimensions or worlds outside of what was accepted as reality, where all kinds of creatures, even some like himself, lived. He was a "Walker," a being from another dimension capable of shifting anywhere on Earth, or between dimensions and worlds, by secret means known only to the Elite Shaman class of his world. The Walkers were human in appearance except for one thing. Their ears were slightly pointed as were their Elfin descendants.

✩

David Selph

David and Ariane traipsed all over the Hawk Point area. David found the beaver ponds. From the looks of things, this was a really popular camping spot. He was impressed with how well Wyoming people took care of places like this. It was a really secluded, sweet grassy valley surrounded by aspens. High rock structures and active beaver ponds were only a short walk away.

David spread one of the blankets under an aspen tree and laid out their picnic lunch. "Champagne for madam?"

"Oh yes, sire. Just a touch," Ariane responded in her best snobby voice. David handed her a soda, and they downed sandwiches, bananas, and cheese slices in nano seconds.

Ariane had rarely felt so happy. She lay back on the blanket and looked at the Sun and the sky through the fluttering, shimmering aspen leaves. "I wish we could stay here forever, don't you?"

David lay down beside her. "That would suit me just fine. Wake me up in an hour or so, would you?" He promptly rolled to his side and dropped off to sleep.

Ariane sat up on her elbow and listened to him snore. She whispered, "Man, I wish I could sleep like that." She lay back down and listened to the wind. That was one thing that she loved about Wyoming. The wind was always moving. Lots of times it moved violently, but the fact that it moved made everything around feel so fresh and alive. She yawned and just closed her eyes for a moment. Just for a moment.

When David woke up, it was getting dark. "How did that happen?" He shook Ariane awake. "Sorry, kiddo, we have to get going."

She looked around her in a confused way. "Whoa. Time warp!"

They gathered the blankets and lunch stuff and cleaned up the area, taking their trash with them, and got into the car. They buckled in, and David stretched and adjusted mirrors and the seat.

He yawned, "We'll probably beat Mom home, but it might be really dark before we get there. I'd like to get back to the main road while there's still a little bit of light. Hey, what happened to wake me up in an hour?"

"How long did we nap?" Ariane asked sleepily.

"Few hours. We must have needed the rest. All those late night excursions into caves must have made you tired too."

"I'm actually really glad we didn't ruin everything by looking for one. I have to admit though, it doesn't seem like I'm really resting much. Usually I sleep like a log all night long. A train wouldn't wake me!!"

Just then, they heard a loud pulsating scream that sounded like it was coming from every direction. It seemed to bounce off the rocks.

"What on EARTH was that!" Ariane jumped and yelled.

David started the car and turned on the headlights. He locked the doors with his master control. "Ariane, give me the flashlight in the glove compartment." Ariane handed him the flashlight, and he turned it on twisting quickly back and forth, sweeping the area around the campsite. Neither one of them saw anything.

"I've spent lots of times in the woods around here, and I have NEVER heard that before. Let's get out of here."

"David. Was that a woman screaming?" Ariane asked.

David could tell she was really afraid. "No, if I had to guess, I'd say it was a mountain lion."

"Would he eat us, do you think?"

"Well, aren't we just meat on legs, really?" David smiled over at her mischievously, but backed off deciding she was scared enough without him helping it along. "I think they're probably more afraid of us. They tend to run away from people. More of them stay alive that way."

David was more shook up than he let on. That was NOT a mountain lion, and he didn't have a clue what it was.

✡

Jo Vanderlin

Jo came home to an empty house. It was only 1:00 in the afternoon. She noticed the note from David and smiled. She was really glad they were doing something fun and getting out of the house for a change.

She dropped her briefcase next to the kitchen table and stood in the middle of the kitchen. She couldn't even remember the last time she had been home alone in the middle of the afternoon…or early evening for that matter.

She was exhausted. She could barely stand. She kicked off her shoes and shuffled off into the master bathroom. She ran a hot tub and as a treat added some lavender oil. She stripped and sank into the steaming water.

"I needed this." She closed her eyes and for once the quiet was restful instead of terrifying. She realized that she had been avoiding having any time to think, because if the hustle and bustle of life suddenly stopped, she'd have no excuse not to give in to her grief. She was terrified that if she ever started crying she wouldn't stop. The tears welled up in her eyes, and she lay there quietly crying. Quietly crying was about all she had been able to muster since Bryan died. She cried off and on more than she cared to admit and usually it was over silly things. The other day she started crying on the way home because a hawk seemed to be tracking the car, and she noticed and remembered a similar incident with Bryan.

She was pretty proud of herself that she had stayed strong for the kids. Last thing they needed was a blubbering idiot for a parent. She had to be both mom and dad, and it was mentally and physically exhausting. She started asking herself just what that was supposed to mean because it was painfully evident that she was a total failure as both a mom and dad. She finally gave into to a good self pity cry.

She couldn't put off hiring anyone anymore. Her family was falling apart, and she was falling apart. David had a right to a social life too, and right now he had absolutely none. Ariane was having nightmares and talking in her sleep. She began to process the strange incident of a few nights ago. Ariane's dream was so specific. She had seen enough visionary experiences to understand that there was something going on there. What kind of a twelve-year-old dreamed like that? Visionary, trance states were usually reserved for the old.

Aspects of the dream were very alarming. It sounded like astral projection, and if that is what it was, that could be very dangerous.

Sometimes a bit of the soul leaves the body and travels outside the body, but when it does, it puts the body at risk of a drop in body temperature. Breathing becomes more shallow, and the body's overall metabolism could drop. She really needed to figure out what was going on.

Jo got out of the tub and put her thick terrycloth robe on. She looked at herself. Petite frame, short, strawberry blond, messy hair, good complexion in spite of not taking care of it very well, green eyes and a good figure still. She was still young, and she could be happy, couldn't she? She dried her hair and gave herself the luxury of a facial. She realized she really hadn't been taking very good care of herself. Her face was all red and puffy. She glopped more night cream on so that all you could see were two red eyes and a round mouth. "There, now I'm beautiful." She walked out on the porch and sat in a lawn chair and put her face to the Sun. Her new life really was good. She reminded herself to count her blessings. It was really quiet and beautiful out here.

When Bryan died, all she could think was that she had to get home to Wyoming. Her mom and dad were both dead, but she had grown up here, and this was home. It had been a really good move. This was a good place to raise kids. It was a fresh start from places where they had had a life together. She started crying again and went back into the house to wipe the goop off.

She decided just to dress for bed and run around in her bathrobe for awhile. She went to the kitchen and tried to think of something special to make for the kids. Boy, would they ever be shocked to see her home! She settled on making spaghetti and meatballs. Always a hit, and she couldn't remember the last time she had made a dinner that required a few hours to cook.

It was really relaxing cutting up the mushrooms and onions and gushing her hands in the hamburger to make the meatballs. She always thought of her mother when she made the sauce. Nobody could top her mom's spaghetti sauce. She remembered when she lost her mom, how her dad had gone into a deep depression and cried almost constantly. He was the strong mountain of strength in her life, a man whom she had never seen cry before in her life. He died a year later. She was convinced he died of a broken heart. Her parents were best friends and lovers. Throughout their life together, they had held hands and kissed and been really affectionate with each other and with her. She had a really wonderful childhood.

She just remembered how insecure she felt to see her father grieve like that. Even though she was in her twenties, she was afraid that if her dad didn't stop crying, he would die too. And he did. That's just what he did.

She turned a Loreena McKennitt tape on and tried to change the mood. It wouldn't do to let the kids see her cry.

She put the sauce on low simmer and went and lay down on the couch. It wasn't long until she was fighting sleep. The sauce would be ok for awhile. She would just close her eyes, just for a moment.

She woke up suddenly, hearing the sauce boiling away. "Oops, hope it isn't burned." She jumped up and rushed into the kitchen. She lucked out; it was just a little burned. Mom always said that made it taste better anyway. Well, they'd see.

It was 7:30. "Wonder what the kids are up to?" She said aloud.

She got a loaf of French bread out of the freezer and put it into the microwave to defrost. She decided to make garlic bread, so as soon as it was thawed, she split it in the middle and spread butter and garlic salt on it and wrapped it in aluminum foil and put it into the oven. She decided not to cook the spaghetti noodles or warm the bread until they got home.

She walked back into the living room and flipped on the TV. She always did that so she could turn it off again. She couldn't remember the last time she had actually sat down and watched a whole program. She and Bryan used to make a regular date of watching a movie. After the kids were in bed, they would pop popcorn and drink beers and snuggle up on the couch together. The thought crossed her mind that she probably had been avoiding watching a movie alone. Then she had a brainstorm. She decided to have a movie night with the kids instead.

She checked the pantry. "Popcorn, check. Uh, beers? Uncheck. Soda? Check! Movie…" now she was in trouble. What did her kids like? Oh well, she'd let them choose.

Just then she heard David's car pull into the driveway. She breathed a sigh of relief. He pulled it into the garage, and they both came in through the mudroom.

"Mom? What are you doing home so early?" David asked.

Ariane looked worried, "Mom are you sick? You're in your pajamas and robe! Have you been crying?"

David just stood there and looked at her.

Jo quickly interjected, "I'm fine. I was tired, I think. But I've been taking a long bath and nap and burning your dinner."

"I smell spaghetti! Mom, are you kidding! Is it really burned?" Ariane rushed into the kitchen and lifted the sauce lid and looked disappointed.

"Burned to perfection. My mom always said that was what made good spaghetti sauce great! We'll be ready to eat in about a half hour. I was also wondering if we could have a popcorn and coke movie night after dinner? Would you guys choose a movie?"

David and Ariane stood there with their mouths open. David finally spoke. "Uh…sure. Mom, we need to get cleaned up a little. Um…we've been climbing rocks and stuff."

"OK, see you in thirty minutes." Jo yelled down the hall, "Put your pj's on and we'll have a spaghetti …**and and** garlic bread…**and and** popcorn and coke pajama movie party, ok?"

Ariane practically skipped down the hall, smiling all the way. All David could think was that his family was weird, just weird, but he couldn't hide his smile either.

✡

Spero Zezas

Spero was pacing. He couldn't stand it anymore, he had to make sure Jo was all right. He did something he rarely did. He picked up the telephone and dialed her home number.

The stereo was going full blast in the kitchen, so Jo apparently didn't hear the phone ringing.

David answered on the fourth ring. "Hello. David Selph here."

"David, this is Spero. Is everything ok?"

"Mom being here, you mean? Yeah. She just seemed to need a day off. She's ok. We're ok."

Spero tried to sound light. "I'm so glad to hear that. Hey, your mom said you bought the Record Keeper?"

"Yes."

"Take good care of it, and don't let anyone outside of your family see it, ok?"

"Sure, but what's going on?" David asked. Spero's tone sounded strained.

"We'll talk more later, just you and I, ok? No need to let your mom know I was worried. Enjoy your evening."

David hung up and decided that was one of the strangest conversations he had ever had.

Spero stood looking at the phone after he set it down. This isn't the way it was supposed to work. When he first met Jo, he felt for sure that the crystal might be for her, but when he showed Jo the crystal and told her the story about the Record Keeper's properties and then actually handed it to her, she had not reacted to the crystal. Spero had explained that the Record Keeper, in the hands of the person it was destined for, would issue a slight electrical jolt which would pass the information contained in the crystal. Whatever information or knowledge that had been placed in the crystal would then be permanently imprinted into their brain.

There was no need to fear that the information or transference would be harmful, because by virtue of their nature, a pure crystal would only pass true and pure information. Many might receive the slight energy surge or jolt, and the information would pass to them, but the true human Record Keeper would be the one who could unlock the transference and tell others the full story of the civilization that placed the information in the crystal and the secrets within it.

As a favor, Spero asked Jo to show her children the Record Keeper and tell them about it. He asked her to give it to whichever one of her kids could feel the energy from it but not to let on who had given it to her.

Jo had related that when David was working in town with her one day, she had handed it to him and he had definitely responded to its energy. He seemed to zone out for a time before he very simply said, "Wow. I've read about being able to feel energy from a stone, but I've never experienced anything like that...ever!" He was so fascinated with the Record Keeper mystery that he asked if he could buy it. She sold it to him but stressed that it had been a precious gift to the store and to safeguard it, as it was very, very rare.

Spero knew that if either David or Ariane were the true human Record Keeper, they would know to search him out and be able to describe what they saw. If they were not, he would "recover" the stone as he had "recovered" it countless times before. It would simply disappear from the owner as if lost. After all, nobody could truly own any stone person. The stones would stay as long as the relationship was mutually satisfying. The crystal belonged to everyone and no one.

Spero reflected on Tazman Khan and wondered just how far he would go to recover the crystal. He hadn't wanted to scare David, but somehow had to stress the importance of keeping the crystal safe.

Spero also had to make sure Jo and her family were kept safe from Tazman Khan.

✫

Tazman Khan

Tazman Khan's paternal ancestor was not of this world. He began his training as a young elf named Temujin as a Walker Initiate in Spero's "sky world," better known as the Rainbow World. Before the deeper secrets of his shamanistic training could be revealed, Temujin was dishonored and was outcast from further training.

It was suspected that he stole a master Record Keeper, and for that he was shunned. It was a holy relic stolen from the Lemp Tower of History where all of the secrets of all of the known worlds and dimensions and Universes were locked into Record Keeper crystals. It was believed that the crystals were safe. Theft, even the concept of it, was almost unknown in their world. Temujin never admitted that he removed the crystal and therefore would not reveal where he had hidden it.

An opportunity to escape Rainbow World presented itself, and Temujin recovered the crystal from its hiding place. With it, he was able to shift dimensionally into this plane of existence, on Earth, through a vortex portal or door that was sealed after he used it. He could never go home. Temujin had abused the use of the crystal to escape permanently to Earth. He had visions of gaining power and having dominance over others. Self aggrandizement and personal gain were other concepts alien to the Rainbow World.

He "landed" in Mongolia. He looked like a child to humans and was adopted into an influential family who had no children. He would rise to power by making himself appear to be "magic" and mystical. He had knowledge and skills they could barely conceive of.

By 1206 in Mongolia, Temujin would be elected Universal Ruler, which translates to the name he would be forever, Genghis Khan. He lived his life in war and strife and gathered great wealth, but he also became an incredible statesman. He united great groups of warring tribes into a unified group governed by simple and non-traditional rules. He honored women, and he honored and rewarded individuality and free thinking men.

By 1225, Genghis Khan conquered four times the land that Alexander the Great did, and he did it in a twenty-five year period. He ruled everything between the Caspian Sea and Beijing.

The Mongols had always considered their mountain ranges and steppes to be at the center of the Universe. It was their belief that Genghis was not only *favored* by the gods, but he was, in fact, considered holy. He was known as the Holy Warrior.

Mongols worshiped the eternal blue sky and the golden Sun. They believed God was too great to be held in a small place or building. He needed the sky. This fit into Genghis' view of things, having come from the sky world of Rainbow World.

The Mongols believed that upon death, their spirit resided in their spirit spear banner or "sulde." Genghis Khan embraced this concept and attached great magical power in two shafts of spears, one with his favorite black horse's hair adorning the spear of war, and another with white horse's hair adorning the spear of peace.

He planned to place his soul in one of them if his Earthly body was damaged beyond repair. Walkers could live for thousands of years in their dimension. The Walkers of his world could assume an Earthly body from their ethereal form when they crossed into heavier energies. He thought he would never truly die, but something on Earth had to be the repository.

The white spear of peace was passed through his family throughout time. The family believed it was the true repository for his soul because they believed his true nature to be peaceful. The white sulde was now in the possession of Tazman Khan.

In the 16th century, the black spear of war, believed by the world to be the repository of his soul, was guarded by one thousand Yellow Hat Sect monks from Tibet in a high mountain monastery established by one of his descendants, Buddhist lama Zanabazar.

In 1938, Stalin had all the members of the monastery slaughtered in Central Mongolia along the River of the Moon near the great Shankh Mountains, and Genghis Khan's black sulde was lost forever.

Genghis Khan was eccentric and would not allow anyone to capture his image because he never appeared to age. Tazman speculated too, that his Elfin appearance was another reason.

He was reputed to be the greatest Shaman of his time and worked with telepathy, vibratory tones, dreams, divination, and the spiritual power of nature. Mongols believed in the power of Earth and sky. They believed that the soul of the Earth flowed in her waters and the Sun was sacred. All of their beliefs fit in nicely with his Walker training. There was power in the sky.

Genghis always returned to Burkhan Khaldun, or "God Mountain," to gain strength from the mountain and rest, but always there was another reason. He continued to go there to search for the means to return to the Rainbow World. He never found it. Burkhan Khaldun was considered sacred by all Mongols because it was close to the sky. It was also sacred because Genghis' portal originated there. He sealed areas of Mongolia from all foreign travel and encouraged Mongols to hold to their traditions by keeping others out and to always honor the sanctity of their land.

Genghis' journals frequently mentioned the importance of music and vibration as a means to heal and clear energy. Mongols would hold their palms upward to the sky and sing. Mongols participated in throat singing which involves sustained low notes that allowed the singer to split the tones and sing two tones at once. Drums and vibrations along the lower bass line opened the meridians and moved energy in the body and cleared the aura. Song was a tribute to their ancestors' and nature's spirit, and the deep tones frightened their opponents. Genghis knew that song was more than that. It healed their bodies and it healed their land. It kept the land free of negativity and kept the feeling of open free space clean and clear.

In the course of his lifetime, Genghis Khan became a great leader and turned into a great man. He established a government based on the individual's merit and not on the aristocratic, feudal, tribal system that governed, or didn't govern, vast numbers of people. The international law that he created was for everyone, including him. No one man was above the law, but individual loyalty and achievement was what was important.

He was a fierce warrior, but he was, in many ways misunderstood. He would not abide theft, arbitrary raids, or assassination or murder and those acts brought swift and lethal justice.

He actually was a "Robin Hood" for his times, redistributing vast wealth to encourage free trade and commercial endeavors. He encouraged literacy and supported and rewarded educational activities. He even went as far as offering no taxes to priests or holy or greatly learned men and to those who pursued or accomplished a high education. He would not allow the holding of hostages, and ambassadors were to be given safe passage always. He would not allow torture or the kidnapping of women. His wife, Borte, whom he loved dearly, had barely escaped kidnapping, and it was thought that was the reason he abhorred it so.

He allowed everyone they conquered to retain their own religion and spirituality, but the Eternal Blue Sky was the supreme law to all he conquered. He made great effort to safeguard holy documents and the magical secrets and practices that were gathered from the learned and holy men from the lands he conquered. Those men were never to be killed and remained under his and his family's personal protection. He wanted to know what they knew and was a voracious seeker of knowledge...and magic.

Genghis' body fell off a horse. To the Mongols, he died in 1227. Mongols did not bury their dead, they left the bodies in the open to return to the land and believed their souls resided in their sulde. To give them honor, the sulde was supposed to remain in the open air. Genghis left instructions for his third son's family to hold the white sulde within the family always.

He was a man far beyond his time and his system of governance ultimately kept years of peace.

He had the foresight, however, before he "died" to appoint his third son, Ogodei, to succeed him. Ogodei showed the most Elphin gifts and was a strong leader. This decision was backed up by a great Mongol council assembly, and in 1229 Ogodei was to be known as the Great Khan. He extended the Mongol conquest into Russia and Northern China.

The Record Keeper crystal was passed to him along with a personal journal that revealed the secret of Genghis Khan's Elfin lineage and his association with Walkers. The journal was written in a family code language that only Ogodei's family could understand, in order to keep it safe. This resulted in a treasure which was passed to future generations and included not only his Rainbow World secrets, but the magic gathered from all the shamans and magicians of his time.

Societies have searched for this book for centuries, and it was generally thought to be a myth. It was not a myth; Tazman Khan was in possession of it. He learned to read it from his father, as his father had learned from his father. Someday Tazman would have a son, and he would teach him to read his family code language and pass the vast family wealth and the wealth of knowledge to his son, along with Genghis' soul, in the form of the white sulde.

Many of the other documents left to the family were written in an ancient Mongolian text of letters which ran up and down the page like Chinese. This text was used throughout his subjugated land to unite the different myriad cultures so that they could communicate using one understandable text. Mongols had traditionally passed their information down verbally, so a written text was extremely progressive. Genghis Khan even established a postal system for quick delivery of instructions to his vast troops.

Other documents were gathered by Genghis Khan. Each captured area's knowledge added to the bank of knowledge already available. Genghis Khan, unknown to most of the world, invited scholars and spiritual leaders from everywhere he conquered to join his personal retinue under the holy protection of his family. These men had lifetimes of knowledge to impart and Genghis Khan had a particular wish to understand techniques of war, science and math, and astronomy.

Genghis Khan's primary obsession was accumulating knowledge on this world which revealed deeper secrets of magical and shamanistic power. Tazman shared that obsession.

Genghis Khan had hundreds of such men traveling with him constantly, writing extensively of what they had learned so that this knowledge could pass to his descendants. The documents that Tazman inherited filled a large room. As time passed, it was the task of the Khan family to translate and preserve a treasure beyond measure. Ancient historical documents and accumulated knowledge thought lost forever were locked in the Khan family vaults.

Tazman Khan was the last of Ogodei's pure blood direct line and had therefore been entrusted with the family legacy and the Record Keeper crystal by his father. Tazman had spent his life reading every translation he could find and had practically memorized the ancient documents left by Temujin about the Rainbow World and its varied creatures. The other creatures of Rainbow World, except for the Walkers, were considered on the whole to be gentle, and therefore weak, by the great Genghis Khan.

Tazman knew that these documents could expose the Rainbow World and all aspects of their world and he felt that gave him powerful leverage to get the crystal back.

Taz was obsessed with recovering the Record Keeper, yes, but his obsession was greater than that. He wished to rule not only the Rainbow World, but all the other worlds whose secrets could be unlocked by the thousands of other Record Keepers in the Lemp Tower of History. Genghis had revealed the secret of his theft and the means to access the other crystals. Tazman would not conquer land on Earth like Genghis and Ogodei and Kublai, but worlds upon worlds and gain their wealth.

Tazman only knew for sure that Spero stole the crystal from him, but he suspected much more. Tazman suspected him of being a "Walker Bearer." A Walker Bearer was the leader of the elite warrior Shaman class considered by other Walkers and the Rainbow World to be sacred repositories of the highest secrets of their society and Holy messengers to other worlds and dimensions. They were great healers, and there were, at the time of Genghis' writing, only three of these men in Rainbow World history. It was rumored that they lived thousands of years and aged very slowly.

If this was true then, Spero didn't require a Record Keeper to pass from one place to the next on Earth, or one world to the next, or one dimension to the next, or even one Universe to the next.

With Tazman's ancestor's Elfin genes, if Spero was in the near vicinity, he could sense the presence of Spero's energy and had been dogging him through every move Spero made in an attempt to recover the crystal. He could also sense the energy of the crystal, and he knew that somehow it was associated with Jo.

Tazman would never harm Spero because he knew the information he needed was from Spero, but Tazman would stop at nothing to recover the Record Keeper crystal. He would use anyone or anything to get it back, and Jo was definitely someone he could use. Spero cared about her, that was evident.

Tazman intended to track Spero to the portals through which Spero moved from dimension to dimension and worlds to worlds. Portals weren't just doorways where points in the vortex system of the matrix of the Universe intersected between dimensions and worlds. They were gateways to anywhere. Even the matrix could be manipulated by a Walker Bearer. He didn't need portals to move from place to place.

Taz hoped that with the crystal, he would be able to travel as Spero traveled and go anywhere on Earth and in the Universe that he wanted to. The crystal was indestructible. It was meant to survive even the death of the Rainbow World. Taz was counting on it.

The Mongols believed Genghis would rise again. Tazman's secret was that he thought he was the reincarnation of Genghis, and now his dream was to rule many worlds and carry on in the great name of Khan!

☆

Postelwaites

The Postelwaite boys all came home in great spirits. They had loaded up the truck and flat bed with the wood for sale and still maybe had another two or three loads to bring in. They all had dollar signs in their eyes. It had been a lot of work, and the guys from the ranch who were helping them gave them the wood they cut too.

Peter had such a great time with Demy, he just couldn't stop smiling. They had played Fantasy Kingdom all afternoon and then just horsed around with the horses. His favorite horse, Apple Pie Annie, seemed to miss him too! She whinnied when she saw him and paced back and forth looking at him as he crossed the corral to get to her. She nudged him so hard that when he finally reached her he fell over. She reminded him of a cat. She kept rubbing up against him like she was trying to hug him. Peter loved horseback riding better than anything in this world.

They walked into the house. Their mother was sitting very still at the table looking out of the window. She had a full cup of coffee that appeared to have gotten cold and had not been touched. She motioned for silence and indicated that they should follow her to their "talking" place behind the chicken coup.

When they rounded the corner, Jerry couldn't hold in their good news. He hugged his ma. "Ten cords, Ma, we've got an extra ten cords for sale. I think the Sorenson's will take three, and it won't be hard to get the other ones sold." The other boys crowded around her, patting her back and hugging her.

"I'm so pleased." A tear rolled down her cheek. "Really pleased. But I want to talk to you all while your father's napping. Please just let me talk quickly and get what needs saying, said, ok? Your father is going to want to talk to you about what you plan to do with the money from today and those ten cords and the cord money you sold so far that you kept. You boys have been really fair about giving me most of the money for what you do, and I appreciate it. I told your pa that, but he feels like you should all pay your weight around here and give it all up to the family. I don't feel that is entirely fair, and I tried to talk to him about it before he started getting himself so worked up."

The boys all looked alarmed. "Don't worry, he didn't hit me," she interjected. "But I stopped talking so that he would settle down some before you got home. I wanted to tell you one thing for when you talk to him. If it gets ugly and he goes for any one of you, I want you all to do what you did for Peter and stop him from hurting any one of you."

"We can do that Ma, no problem," interjected Ernie. "We can all tackle him again. That did work last time for Pete, a little late, but it worked!"

"Ok, Ernie, thanks, but please let me go on?" She looked at them pleadingly. "It's so late in your lives for me to say this, but I wanted to tell you all too, I'm real sorry I ever let him hurt any of you. EVER. I don't have any excuse. I should have stopped it long ago, but I'm stopping it now. You all have my permission to protect yourselves and each other."

She pulled a nylon rope cord out of her apron pocket and showed it to them all. "I'm keeping this rope in my pocket, and I'll pull it out and hand it to one of you if I feel we need to use it. I would rather you take this rope and hog tie him down than hit him or hurt him, because then, we're just like him, aren't we? If he goes for one of you again, he will be gone from this house. I've told him that so he knows."

All the boys looked at her, and they were dumbfounded. It had taken a lot of courage for her to say that to their father.

"You all talk among yourselves and decide what is fair. I know you try to do what you have to do to keep him from getting ornery, but this time, I want you to decide what is fair for all of you too, and tell him what you are all willing to do, and stick to your guns with him. You're not little boys anymore for him to boss. This is your business, and it will be your future business, and it is not his to tell you what to do anymore. But it is his truck and flatbed, well actually, half his and half mine, so figure out what you all would like to do, as grown up businessmen."

Their ma and Peter went in, but the boys all stuck around the chicken coup to talk. They had already been hatching a plan for a long time with secret meetings and a lot of whispering in the nights. They had saved most of what they had kept and put it into a pot. With the money they earned today, they would have enough to offer to buy the old flatbed and truck outright. Ernie, who was seventeen and the second oldest was the bookkeeper of the outfit. He had been researching "fair market value" for the truck and the flatbed trailer, and they all decided to offer their pa a little more than that. They all agreed on the price and elected Jerry to talk to him.

Jerry was about the only one of them who ever had any luck talking to him. At eighteen, he was the biggest of them, almost as big as his pa. They figured out that if their pa wouldn't sell them his rigs, they would pay a two hundred dollar rental for the day and use the rest of the money to buy something else. They figured too, that if what Ma said was true and he expected them to pay room and board or something, they'd agree to do that at one hundred dollars a month each. They figured they'd get the four hundred covered somehow and that would be really the best deal for them so they didn't have to justify everything they did, or didn't do, to their pa anymore. Jerry was out of school now and could start working at generating business while they were in school in the fall.

Jeff, the third oldest, was fifteen and rarely talked, but whispered to Blake. Blake, who was fourteen nodded in agreement and said, "How about this? We'll offer dad the two hundred for the daily rental and one half of the value of the truck and the flatbed, and the other half will go to Ma?"

Jerry narrowed his eyes, and dropped his head, and put both hands on his forehead, "Echhhh. We're in for it for sure if we do that."

They all looked from one to another silently for a long time, and then suddenly there was agreement in all of their eyes. They all knew what they were going to do, and they knew what would happen. Enough was enough.

The Postelwaite boys came back into the house and thought their pa was still sleeping. They explained to their ma and Peter what they had decided. She was sitting with her hands flat on the table. The only thing she said was, "You all talked it out and made your decisions, so stick to them."

Nels Postelwaite had been listening out of view behind the kitchen door. He walked around the door into the kitchen and stood there with his fists balled.

"Peter, leave the room, now please," Ma quietly said.

Peter fled quickly through the kitchen door and ran to the coup.

Nels Postelwaite was ominously quiet. "You all decided. You *all* decided. What a joke. You don't decide; I decide, and I've decided that you won't keep one dime. You hand over what you made today and go get that pile of money you've been squirreling away and put it right here." He slammed his fist on the table in front of Bette. "And beings you think your ma has rights over me, I'll be taking over the family accounting from now on."

Jerry tried to explain that their father wouldn't have to do the heavy lumbering, he could take only the carpentry jobs he wanted, and they would handle the harder work, the lumbering end of business themselves, paying him four hundred a month for their keep.

That's when his father said, "You ungrateful prats!" His fist shot out so fast that Jerry couldn't duck it.

The boys reacted with lightning fast agility and had their father on the floor with his arms pinned behind him.

Ma walked over to Ernie and handed him the rope. "Didn't have to be like this, Nels, but now it is done, and you are done hitting our boys. I warned you what would happen."

She picked up the phone and dialed the number for the Sheriff.

Nels was screaming at them all, threatening to kill them all.

"Put something in his mouth, I've heard all of that I will ever listen to." Ma's tone was angry.

Jeff, the silent one, put a clean kitchen rag in his mouth. He said gently, "Father, don't make it worse on yourself."

The Sheriff showed up and talked to them all for a short time before they hauled their father into the patrol car. Ma told the deputies that he wasn't welcome back.

She turned to the Sheriff, "I'll sign that form to keep him from us. He crossed a line when he hit Jerry and threatened to kill us all. I won't have him back here, and I'll be filing for divorce. Would you please wait for just a moment?"

Ma walked back into her bedroom and pulled down the old suitcase and packed Nels' clothes and personal belongings. She called the boys in. "Please go get the two hundred and all of the money you offered to pay for the truck and flatbed and put in my share too. I'll give him that."

When Ernie came in with the cash, she put it in an envelope and sealed it. "I'll get the titles." She crossed over to the desk drawer and pulled them out and put them in another envelope and sealed it too. She marked one envelope,

#1 Titles to be signed off by Nels Postelwaite, and the money envelope was marked,

#2, Money to be given to Nels Postelwaite if he signs the titles and leaves them with the Sheriff.

She and the boys walked the suitcase and the envelopes out to the car. Ma privately asked Jim Riggs, the Sheriff Deputy, to have him sign off on the titles before they gave him the second envelope. "If he won't sign, he'll only have what's in his pocket to get him by."

Jim tipped his hat, "I'll get both envelopes back to you Mrs. Postelwaite if he doesn't sign. Don't worry," he promised.

Nels was looking daggers at everyone but didn't say a word. He hadn't spoken to the deputies either, other than to say, "Ain't talking without an attorney."

As the patrol car drove off, Peter came out from behind the coup. "Is he really gone?"

"Really gone, honey. Life is going to be a little different around here now," his mother promised.

"What about the house and land Ma?" Jerry asked.

"Well, we'll have to talk with an attorney. My family homesteaded this land, and Pa always hated Nels. Before we got married, he made Nels sign an agreement that he understood the house and land were mine and would pass to our kids and not to him." The boys looked at their mother in wonder. "I think my pa knew it would come to something like this someday. He tried to warn me but I thought if I loved Nels enough, I could gentle his temper. Obviously, I was wrong."

"Ma?" Peter injected.

"Yes, Peter?"

"Mr. Cresenzo told me you two grew up together and were friends all your life? He told me to tell you that if anything ever happened, and if Father ever hurt anybody again, that he would pay for the attorney himself if you need one. He says he has a good one."

She patted his head. "I'll have to call him then and thank him for his kindness."

☆

Martin "Marty" Cresenzo

Martin Cresenzo just put down the phone. He just couldn't resist a little dance and yelled, "Yes!!!" Bette Postelwaite was finally free of a virtual monster living among them. He gave her the name and phone number of his attorney.

Martin decided to call his attorney right away himself to let him know that he was to give her anything she needed and to bill him. He dialed the number and got his attorney's voice mail. He left a message so that was taken care of. He was happy to be able to do something for her. He'd lay awake lots of nights worrying about her. He had wondered about Peter himself. He'd heard the rumors too. Poor Bette Postelwaite, she'd been through it. That sorry sack Nels

Postelwaite should be shot. The locals were more than upset over the whole thing.

He wasn't sure how Bette's family was going to get along financially, but she was a survivor, and they would probably manage fine. He'd offer the boys whatever work he could throw their way. They were hard workers, and he knew they'd do a good job at whatever they took on. Bette had said the boys had saved to buy the old man's truck and rig, but they were waiting to see if he'd sign off on the titles and accept the cash. In the meantime, the waste of space was in jail, and he would be there for awhile. After he got out in between court dates, if that happened, there would be a restraining order in place. His attorney would see to that.

The boys would at least have the truck and flatbed for their timbering livelihood for a time. They still had four cords or so to pick up, so every little bit would help. He was genuinely touched at how grateful the boys were of the extra wood. They helped him; he was happy to help them. Happy to help Bette.

Bette used to be his best friend when they were kids. He really got a kick out of watching Demy and Pete. They reminded him of how he and Bette used to be when they were kids.

Martin met his future wife, Lynne, when they were in high school and they were inseparable from the day they started going steady. She was the love of his life. Bette, surprisingly enough, started running with a rougher crowd and then hooked up with the school bad boy. He never understood it. Nels was always ready to fight and was a whole lot faster with his fists to settle an argument then he needed to be. He was sure a good looking guy though, and his boys were all nice looking boys. Martin didn't realize until Peter was hospitalized that he was brutalizing his family all these years. If he had known…. well, let's just say it was a good thing he didn't know.

He decided to talk to Demy and his wife before the rumor mill hit and tell them what happened first hand.

Demy's reaction floored him. He started crying and roughly washed the tears out of both eyes with his fists. Martin could honestly say he had not seen his son cry since he was a baby.

"Ok, son?"

"Man, this is stupid!" Demy laughed and cried at the same time and pretty soon he had them all in tears and laughing too. "I've never done <u>this</u> before," but he couldn't stop it either.

Martin held him tight and Lynn came and put her arms around them both. "Thank goodness," she kept saying, "Just thank goodness."

Demy blurted out, "I wanted to go over there and kill him for hurting Pete! And then Pete went to that school and even when he came back, he didn't call me. It was like he died or something, and it felt like I was...well...part of me was dying too. When he came over the other day, he looked really, really scared. I figured we wouldn't talk about it, we'd just have fun. We had so much fun, Dad!"

"Guess what, Demy?" Lynn said gently, "I bet you're not done having fun. It's just the start of summer! I bet he'll be here, or you'll be there a lot!"

"Do you think so? His brothers are still pretty mean."

"I have a feeling they won't be nearly so mean now. They've all been going through an awful lot for a really long time. They've been treated mean, but now they won't be," Martin said gently.

"Pete used to say that Jerry and Ernie always got the worst of it, and they would stand up for their mom sometimes even though they knew they would catch it."

"Do you know if Nels used to hurt Bette too, son?" Lynn asked.

"Pete said he never saw it, but always thought that he must."

"I'll promise you this son, Bette and her family are in for much better times, and they all have all of us as friends and a lot more besides. Nobody is going to hurt them again if we all can help it!" Martin promised.

"Yeah, dad...right on!! Can I call Pete?"

"Let's give them a little time; let him call you, 'cause I bet really soon, he'll want to invite his best friend to his house." Lynne smiled, and Demy hugged her.

Chapter Three
Saturday

✹

Vanderlin/Selph Family

Jo slept in the next day until almost 11:00. It was Saturday, and it felt absolutely heavenly. She must have really needed the rest. She and the kids had a great time last night. She lay in bed for a few minutes, and the house was totally silent. If the kids were up, they were being awfully quiet this morning.

She got up and walked down the hall and checked the bedrooms. Both of them were gone.

She checked the kitchen table and didn't see a note; she checked the garage and David's car was there. She was starting to panic when she noticed them coming through the hole in the fence. They had been off together exploring.

David came in the back door very quietly, "Shhh, she might still be asleep."

Jo popped around the corner. "I'm up guys. Thank you so much for letting me sleep in. I guess I really needed it!"

"Well, we were all up pretty late watching movies," David quietly said.

"What do you guys have planned for the day? Can your mom be included?"

David and Ariane were shocked that their mom was actually going to spend the day with them, and faced with that, they didn't have a clue what to do with her. They looked at each other and shrugged their shoulders.

"We didn't have any plans really...Is there something you would like to do?" David asked.

"The weekend is ours. I've closed the store until Monday. I've decided I'm going to hire someone for the weekends, and I'm going to try to get them hired next week so we can have some time as a family. I'm also closing the store by 6:00 p.m from now on. I decided to use the fourth bedroom as an office so I can do paperwork and whatever at home instead of there, so I can be home more."

Ariane walked over and hugged her. David just looked at her and didn't say anything.

"I'm really sorry, guys. I realize I haven't been there for you, and we haven't had time to talk. I have to tell you, I've been a little afraid that we were growing too far apart. I know you've been mad at me, but the business is set up now, so we can spend more time together. You guys are the most important thing in the world to me, and I think it's about time we start being more of a family. Agreed?"

David was silent for a long time and then finally said, "Mom, did you love our dad? You haven't even cried, not really."

Jo looked at them for a long time and decided that they deserved the truth. "I'm sorry you didn't get to know my parents. They loved each other so much that when my mom died, my father grieved horribly. He fell apart and stopped caring about anything or anybody else. I was twenty years old, and I promised myself that I would never make my kids feel as helpless as that made me feel, even as a young adult."

Jo continued, "When your dad died, I was afraid that if I started crying, I would never stop either, so I tried to be as busy as I possibly could. To give myself a chance to keep myself together, I selfishly decided to move here, where I was happy as a child, to get away from places where your dad lived with us."

She was obviously on the verge of tears, so she took a few minutes to regroup her emotions. She was trying to decide just how far to take her "truth." And then she decided it was time for them all to get everything out.

"I *have* cried, lots, just not around you guys because I wanted to be strong for you. I didn't want you to go through what I did. When my mom died and I needed to cry, or when I was sad, I couldn't show it. Because it would have hurt my dad even more to see me suffer too, I just held it inside. I was trying to give you both time to grieve your dad in your own way without feeling like you had to take care of me. I didn't want you to see me cry."

Ariane touched her shoulder, "But mom, crying washes your soul clean just like the rain washes the Earth."

Jo smiled and hugged her daughter. "I never thought of it like that. When did you get to be so smart?"

"When I had to cry by myself and nobody would cry with me. I had to make myself feel better somehow. Mom, you should have told us about grandpa, and then we would have understood better. It just seemed like you didn't love Dad, or…" Ariane hesitated, "or us." David nodded in agreement.

"I'm so sorry. I didn't know you both were feeling like that." Jo pulled David closer and put her arms around both of her children.

Jo looked at them, and tears filled her eyes. "I don't know how to make this up to you guys. I don't even know where to start except to say, I'm so sorry. I…am…so sorry I ever made you doubt my love for your father or for you two."

David turned to his sister, "Well, I didn't make it easy for anyone either. I've just been mad, really mad for a really long time, and I'm still trying get over that. I haven't cared much about other peoples' feelings either."

"I'm glad you said that David," Jo interjected, "because that's exactly how I feel, only I'm mad at your dad for dying, and I still don't understand that. I thought you guys would hate me for it."

"No, I understand it," said David, "but I'm not mad at him as such. I'm just selfishly mad at the world because I lost my best friend."

"We all did," Ariane said.

This was the first time they had talked together about Bryan's death. It was good to get their feelings out.

Jo brushed a tear away and said, "I'm so glad we all talked. I think it was finally time, huh? I'm going to have to remember you guys aren't little children and that I should just tell you both the truth. It would have been easier on everybody all the way around if I had told you sooner. I'm really sorry that I bungled things so badly. Please forgive me and let's start again?"

David and Ariane nodded "yes."

Let's try to enjoy the rest of the weekend. Anybody got any ideas what to do with a whole two days?" Jo asked.

"Do we have to stay in town? A Celtic Fair is going on in Colorado this weekend. It's outside Denver somewhere. I think it's about a three-hour drive," David suggested.

Ariane squealed, "Mom, can we really go?"

"Sounds absolutely wonderful. We'll stay in a hotel tonight in Denver and swim and eat junk food until we puke! Then we'll spend tomorrow at the fair. Sound like a plan?"

"Pretty cool, except for the puking part. Do we have to do that?" Ariane asked half seriously.

They all laughed.

"Mom, I forgot to tell you; Spero called to see if everything was ok," David interjected.

"When?"

"Just before dinner last night. I told him we were fine. He asked about the crystal I bought. Why would he do that?"

"I'll call him before we head out. I know it's the first time we've been together for awhile, but would either of you mind if I invited him? I don't think he gets out of town much." Jo added, "No is a perfectly acceptable answer."

"Mom, would you mind if Ariane and I talked this over and then we can let you know what we think?" David asked.

"No, not at all. I'll go get dressed, just let me know what you decide."

After Jo had gone down the hall, Ariane confronted David. "David, why do we have to talk about it? If another adult comes, Mom will just be talking with him the whole time. I like Spero too, but for a whole weekend?"

"Stop and think, Ariane," David interjected. "We've barely talked since Dad died. We just said most of what we've been needing to say. What are we going to say to each other stuck together for two days constantly? We'll still be with Mom, but Spero and she can talk while we swim or shop. Plus, is mom really going to want to spend hours looking at the Fairies?"

"Fairies?"

"Yes, I read in a brochure about the Celtic Fair that there is a booth with nothing but Fairy paintings, figures, and even life-size Fairy wings."

"Oh, David! Really?"

"Yep."

"I think you're right. Spero should join us."

"Be sure to take that crystal in your backpack. He wanted to talk to me about it."

Ariane just looked at him quizzically.

David shrugged his shoulders, "Don't ask me, but I could tell from his voice that something is up with it."

"David, that thing freaks me out. You take it." Ariane went to her backpack and took it out and handed it to David.

"You haven't seen anything more?" He asked turning it over and over in his hand.

"No, but I had the dream again last night. Guess what? In the circle of people that I didn't know, I recognized two people there beside me and you."

"Who?"

"Peter and Spero."

"And who else?" David asked.

"Still people I don't know. There were twelve of us, though," Ariane replied.

"How do you know that?"

"Because we were sitting in this." Ariane drew a Star of David. A six-sided star. "Six of us were sitting within the point parts and six were sitting between the points and there was a circle of stones all around us."

"Maybe you should talk to Mom about your dream, Ariane," David said. "She really does know a lot about this kind of stuff."

Oh, I already did." Ariane skipped off down the hall to ask her mom to invite Spero.

David just stood there looking at her, shaking his head, and said under his breath, "Weird kid. She's a very weird kid."

☆

Jo called Spero and was actually surprised that he answered. "Spero, David said you called last night?"

"I was just concerned. Your note said you had a family commitment, and I was worried that something was wrong."

"No actually, there's something a lot right. I'm taking the rest of the weekend off to be with the kids, and we've all agreed we'd like to invite you to spend the weekend with us. We're heading for Denver this afternoon and then tomorrow we're off to a Celtic Fair in Colorado. Are you game to join us?"

"Are you kidding? Is the Pope Catholic? I'd absolutely love to," Spero cried.

He was so relieved that he might actually have enough time to warn Jo against Tazman, and it would be a wonderful opportunity to get to know the kids better. He should be able to tell by the end of the weekend what was going on with the Record Keeper. He had planned to ask David to give it back for safekeeping.

"Oh, Jo, do me a strange favor please. I'll explain further later. Please ask David to bring the Record Keeper?"

"Sure, no problem. We'll pick you up in an hour? At your place?"

"Can't wait!!!"

The mood getting ready for the weekend was festive. Even David couldn't hide his excitement. Everybody packed a night bag and there was a lot of running around with Ariane panicking every two seconds.

"Mom, I can't find my other sandal! Mom, do you know where my swimming suit is?"

"David, be sure to take the crystal; Spero asked that you do."

They all finally got everything packed along with a cooler for water and pop. They decided not to pack their own food so they could restaurant it all weekend. The pit stops along the way could be at convenience stores for the requisite "puke food." Mom's comment had started a trend. David thought that now he would always think of junk food as "puke" food.

They drove into Cheyenne and pulled up to Spero's house in their van. He was waiting on the side of the house, ready to go. The minute they saw his happy, beaming face, they were all very glad they had included him.

The trip to Denver went fast. It was wonderful to see the Poudre Mountains around Ft. Collins. David pointed out that here, the mountains were on the west, so it would be easy not to get lost. Ariane smiled, remembering her concern in North Crow.

"Hey Mom! When David and I were picnicking at Hawk Point, we heard a long, like outer space scream that seemed to come from everywhere and nowhere. We thought it might be a mountain lion. Do they sound like that, I mean, does their cry echo off everything all at once?

"I don't really know, honey. Spero, are you familiar with what that might be?"

Spero was trying very hard not to show any emotion. He knew what the scream meant, and it wasn't good news. "Where exactly is this Hawk Point?"

David explained where it was and how to get there.

"David, would you mind showing me the area? Maybe Monday? Sorry to ask that it be so soon, but I'd like to see the area where you heard the weird noise."

"Yeah, sure. So, do you think you know what it was?"

Because Spero wasn't ready or able to tell them all what it was, he hedged the question. "I've heard tell of Prairie Apes, sounds like it could be one of them there elusive Prairie Apes." Everybody laughed.

"It did sound like a great ape come to think of it. Are these apes any relation to the jackalope?" David quipped.

"I think they sometimes abduct antelope and rabbit babies and experiment with their genes."

Jo was laughing so hard, she thought she might be in danger of snorting!!

David was so happy to hear his mom laugh, he realized he had not heard her laugh for a very, very long time.

In no time at all they were in Denver. They decided to travel on through and stay closer to fair. The area turned from prairie to woods and mountains, and they were really glad they had made the trip already. They pulled into a hotel in Castle Rock that was nestled against rocky hills and had an outdoor pool.

Spero paid for double occupancy with two twin beds for his room and turned to David. "Would you mind bunking with me in mine, and the girls can have their own space?"

"No, that would be just fine." David actually looked forward to a night away from the women in his family, and Spero had said he wanted to talk to him.

"Everybody change and meet you at the pool?" Jo asked.

"Last one in is a rotten egg!" Ariane laughed and rushed off to their room.

The group swam and played until almost 7:00 and decided to clean up for dinner. They met at the car at 7:45 and went in search of a good restaurant. There were so many choices, but they ended up in a great Mexican restaurant. They all ordered something different and passed the choices around to share.

"Oh man, I'm stuffed. I feel like a nap," said Jo. Ariane was practically falling asleep at the table. David nodded his head that he was ready to head back to the hotel too. They were "good" tired from the sun and the swim.

"Couldn't agree more. Want to make it an early night?" yawned Spero.

✡

Spero Zezas and David Selph

When David and Spero got into their room, David crashed on his bed and almost immediately went to sleep. Spero was a little disappointed that he missed a good opportunity to talk with David alone but knew he had to check something out. He slipped the Record Keeper out of David's backpack.

He ducked out of the room and softly shut the door. He looked both ways down the hall and tried to think where to go to have total privacy. He opted for the woods nearby.

The hotel was rather nestled among rock structures and trees, so he went back a way into the tree line.

He saw a rock grouping that had a rather large space between the stones that would be blocked from all view. He gathered a group of twelve stones and placed them in a circle. He drew a Star of David in the earth with a stick, then sat at the center of the circle and pulled out the Record Keeper crystal. He rolled the crystal in the dirt and bathed it in some of the water from his water bottle and then mumbled a few words and sat very still. He seemed to be in a trance state. Gradually, the crystal started to glow.

David had just been dozing when he realized that Spero had slipped the crystal out of his backpack. He followed him silently into the woods and was watching him.

Spero sat for some time and the light from the crystal became brighter and brighter until David could no longer look at it. He shielded his eyes and at the brightest point, Spero and the crystal simply disappeared.

David stood there for a moment and then he had to sit down. He knew what he had seen. He just didn't believe what he had seen.

He got up and moved closer to the area where Spero had disappeared and looked at what he had drawn in the earth. It was the same structure that Ariane had explained from her dream. The exact same one.

The area inside the circle started to get lighter and David stepped back to where he had been hiding. It got brighter and brighter, and at its brightest point, he noticed that Spero and the crystal were back.

Spero got up and scattered the stones and swept the Star of David away. There was no remaining evidence that something strange had happened, no burned earth, nothing.

David stepped out from where he had been standing and confronted Spero. "What did you just do?" he demanded, "I followed you because you took the crystal, and I watched the whole disappearing act."

"I know," Spero said quietly. "I was aware that you were there. I thought it might be the easiest way for you to swallow what you and I need to talk about if you saw for yourself that I'm not a nutcase."

Spero looked straight in David's eyes, and David noticed for the first time, how different Spero's eyes were. They were deep green and slightly slanted. He had really dark eyelashes and eyebrows, but white, white, hair. David had noticed when they were swimming that Spero's ears were slightly pointed and wondered about that.

"You're not from around here, are you?" David asked.

"Now that's a question. I have spent a very great period of time "here" in your dimension, but no, I'm not from here as such. I come in peace. I mean you no harm," and he signaled to David with the Vulcan hand signal from Star Trek.

In spite of his confusion and fear, David laughed. "I'm... I'm speechless. I don't even know what to think or do."

"Well, the obvious question might be to ask me where I went," said Spero matter of factly.

"I'll bite. Where did you go?" asked David quietly.

"I went to Hawk Point to see why they were calling me from home. 'ET, phone home.'"

"So, that was what that screaming was? A phone call?" asked David.

"As close to one as it gets. The area must be a natural vortex, and you must have had the crystal with you, huh?" Spero asked.

David nodded.

"Your mom said you felt the energy from the crystal. Did Ariane too?"

"Yes. I just felt strong energy. It actually shocked Ariane," David answered.

"Do you begin to understand what this means then?" asked Spero.

"That Ariane is the Record Keeper, I suppose."

"That you both are, and one or both of you must have been receiving some kind of transmissions in dreams?"

"Yes, Ariane has. She actually dreams the same dream over and over." He related the whole dream to Spero. "She drew that structure that you sat in when you disappeared and told me that there were twelve of us in the structure and that she and I and you and Peter were part of the group, but she didn't recognize yet who the others were."

"Mind if we sit down?" Spero asked. "Disassembly takes a lot out of me. Who's Peter?"

"A neighborhood boy we both just met, Peter Postelwaite. Wait, go back. Disassembly?" David asked.

"The breaking down of heavy energy to transfer lighter energy from point to point. It's the way I travel when I'm not riding a bike. Because I haven't figured out how to take my bike with me yet, and it would really come in handy sometimes," Spero mused. He actually sounded a little sad about that.

David couldn't stand it anymore; he had to ask the obvious question.

"Spero, who are you and what are you?"

"Now that, my friend, is a very, very long story." Do you want to hear it here or back in the warm hotel?"

"The hotel, I guess. But answer one question for me now, please. I assume the crystal is yours?"

"It belongs to nobody and everybody. When we get back to the room, I'll explain."

✫

Postelwaite Family

Peter's family was recovering from the shock of the incident with their father and his arrest slowly. It was dawning on them all that there would be life without their father, and it could be very, very different.

Their ma reacted very strangely to beginning their new life. She had them take out all of the furniture and wash floors, walls and windows and clean carpets and furnishings. She had been washing all their clothes, the dirty ones and even the ones in their drawers. The washer and dryer had going almost constantly night and day.

She didn't seem to sleep at all the first night, and she and Jerry had sat at the table and talked almost until dawn. That act in itself was so very unusual.

She had them take everything that could remotely be construed as belonging to Nels and put it on one side of the garage. She had thrown out, not recycled, but thrown out, lots of perfectly good bedding and curtains and rugs. She seemed to be purging the house of anything that had bad memories. Lots of weird stuff apparently had bad memories. Peter was really unsure what the curtains had done to her.

It soon became apparent what she was doing. She was making a dark, dingy and cluttery unhappy house a clutter free and changed house that let in the light and shone with cleanliness.

The mood of the boys was one of total freedom and exuberance. Peter had never seen them laugh and smile so much. Peter was beginning to think that for once in his life, he could actually have a happy home. His brothers weren't fighting much, and when something did seem to result in a tiff, Ma was right there and sat whoever was disagreeing down and had them talk it out together quietly and without even verbal violence, like a real family should.

She called a "family meeting" and sat them all down in the kitchen. She stood up to talk and told them she had always understood why they had been so mean and unfeeling toward each other, but that wasn't going to fly anymore. They would learn to behave "civil" and treat each other with kindness. It was a new day and one that the Lord had blessed, because they no longer had to live in fear of anything. She stressed that everyone in the family, no matter how old they were, deserved equal respect.

Ma told them all seriously, "That means that I will not be getting any calls from school about disrespectful behavior and bullying from anyone. Those days are over. It was just that kind of behavior that made your dad mean, and I won't stand for it in my boys."

Ma continued, "There are lots of ways to handle things that allow you to respect yourself and others. If you can't solve something without your fists, you are no better than your father. You are no better than the lowest of the low."

She had started crying and her voice was breaking up, but she continued on. The boys all got up and crowded around her. "I know you weren't taught better, and that's my fault, but I'm trying to teach you now. We are all Christians are we not?" The boys all nodded "yes."

"We will resolve together to live in the image of the Lord our God and will not raise our voices and our hands to one another. We will all try to practice love, and kindness, and forgiveness, and turn the other cheek. Won't we?" The boys all nodded "yes," in shock, mostly.

She was really sobbing now. "We all watched your father live in hate, and I cannot live like that anymore, I just can't. Am I very clear?"

The boys were humbled because Ma rarely cried. They would hear her crying late at night sometimes when she thought they were all asleep, but to see her cry and actually sob, they realized how much she must have been holding in all these years and how unhappy she must have been. They all hugged, kissed, and patted her.

They had never heard their ma go off on them like that. Their father had always handled the punishment when they got in trouble at school and Ma had never said a word. The most she ever said was that she was disappointed in them. That was worse than taking a beating from their father.

She sat down and blew her nose and calmed herself down. Jeff had made them all tea and got six tea cups and saucers down. After he laid out the tea things, he went out to the yard and picked some wild flowers growing there, and brought them in, and handed them to her. She calmly got up, and got a glass, and put water in the glass, put the flowers in the glass, and sat it in the middle of the table. The boys all sat around the table, and she held out her hands to Peter on one side and Jerry on the other and they joined hands around the table to pray.

"*Bless this house and this family who loves you, and help us all to make it a happy house and give us the courage to keep it so. Please help us, Lord, and give us strength to be a real family and to find the joy you have given us with each new day. Please help their pa to walk in your grace. Amen.*"

The boys all said, "*Amen.*"

Their ma looked around at all of them, smiled, and raised her hands to the ceiling and looked up and said,

"*And thank you, dear Lord and Jeffrey, for finally giving me a tea party with my boys.*"

Ma smiled one of her rare, sunshine smiles that showed how pretty she was once and still was to her sons.

They all started snickering and chuckling and pretty soon they were laughing so hard they were practically rolling on the floor.

✡

Spero Zezas and David Selph

Spero and David sat up talking most of the night. Spero told David things that blew his mind.

Spero began by explaining that he thought Ariane might be the person he had been looking for, for a very, very long time. He had searched the globe for the person who would be able to translate what the Record Keeper had shown so many. Most, whose minds had been imprinted by the Record Keeper, were not able to "download" the information and take the extra step of really seeing and understanding and relating what was passed. He mused that it was probably because everyone else was too old; they weren't tuned into the lighter universal energies the way children were.

He said too, that the human Record Keeper might be both of them. With Spero's help, David may be able to open up too.

Spero gave David a little bit of his background. He was a Walker Bearer in his dimension, which was one-half a dimension up from Earth. He admitted that he was of Elfin lineage and had special gifts of telepathy, healing, and dimension traveling or "shifting." Spero said that his people had once had physical form on Earth but evolved up to the dimension of his world, the Rainbow World, in what he called "transformational states or light bodies."

He claimed that many Walkers had lived alongside humanity throughout all time in Earth's dimension and had protected people, where they could, who were at risk of persecution or death at the hands of those who misunderstood their gifts. He said that his kind and few others could travel back and forth from their dimension to Earth and assume physical form on Earth. Spero said that many from his dimension help guide those who had reached transformational states in ours.

According to Spero, humanity was beginning to evolve to transcend their body and join them in the higher dimension. He said that many forms of life existed simultaneously on Earth and in the Rainbow World, like dolphins, whales, manatees, jellyfish, salmon, and trout in the water and the Minervan Wind Beings that made the round dot pairs in the air. The Wind Beings were actually transformed beings from another planet who helped the Air Elementals, Directional Beings, and Rainbow People of the Rainbow World safeguard the ozone layer around the Earth, which was literally half way into both of their dimensions.

Spero explained that the health of Earth's atmosphere affected their world even more because the beings that tried to clear the air of pollution were often harmed or made ill. He said that they could easily see each other on the Rainbow World just as we did on Earth, but an Earth person viewing them from this dimension would not see them as having solid physical forms. When Rainbow World creatures came to Earth or worked in the skies, their forms could be discerned by us and each other with something he called "Fairy sight." Some people on Earth had Fairy sight and could see some of Rainbow World's creatures.

David immediately wondered if Ariane really did see the Fairies she loved so much.

Spero said that most people have experienced Fairy site in their lives and have taught themselves not to see. If they were really look-ing, they should see shapes and shadow forms in trees, or the sky, or in water, or in grass on the plains, or discernable patterns in anything that were changeable. All they have to do is to look in the sky and at the clouds and they would actually see forms. David admitted to Spero that he was always able to do that and had not lost that ability but always chalked it off to an overactive imagination.

"No, you're really seeing what you think you see, or at least part of what you think you see," Spero smiled.

Spero further explained that most people weren't that lucky. In order to even conceive of Fairy sight, they had to re-train themselves to look at something elusive from the corner of their eye to catch movement, shadow, and form. Spero used the example that it was like looking at someone through a glass with petroleum jelly smeared on the glass thickly. Something would be there, but the shape and the form would be mostly indiscernible.

Mirages were glimpses into their dimension. They could certainly be explained away by scientists, but science often fell behind spiritual understanding, finding perfectly sound explanations for what many people had known or suspected all along.

"Either that, or scientists, metaphysicians, and otherwise religious or spiritual people are patently misguided, sometimes in the same direction and sometimes in different directions," Spero said." Lots of human understanding is half or part truths accepted as absolute."

Spero pointed out that ancient peoples sometimes understood what scientists and modern religions did not. For example, the matrix of the Universe is made up of the Metal Element, just as the ancient Chinese said. It is the filament that holds Universes, planets and eve-rything, even people, into discernable forms. It is called the Vortex system.

"How did those ancient people know that?" Spero pondered.

Spero went on to explain that the vortex network is like a multi-layer, multi-dimensional spider web that encompasses not only our solar system, but the whole of the known Universes. The ancients drew its concept in mandalas.

The Vortex system is alive and has a lot of responsibility. It gives form and direction to the grouping of atoms comprising the light body form at the center of our physical bodies and gives physical aspect to humans and every part of the Earth by condensing the atoms or spreading the atoms out. This basic principle guides also the ability to assemble or disassemble.

"Disassembly and assembly is what you witnessed," explained Spero.

The ability to touch, sense, and taste was all based on the vortex supplying our atoms with heavy enough energies to group sufficiently to enjoy physicality. The trees, the plants, and the mountains all had form because of that.

Because human beings are, at the source of their existence, light bodies too, some of their souls are like a light that never goes out. They are just transformed from lifetime to lifetime into different forms. We are all basically made of the same "star stuff" and are part of the universal energy.

When anyone from lighter dimensions comes to Earth through intersecting doorways, or portals in the vortex, that form entering Earth can have heavy physical form. This is part of what gave rise to Earth's mythology of "Fallen angels." Some of the Rainbow World's lighter forms, and those of a higher dimension still, choose to take permanent physical form and may choose to never go back.

This long explanation absolutely blew David's mind. If what Spero said was true, and he was pretty sure it was based upon what he saw with his own eyes, nothing was like he thought; all of his beliefs were turned upside down.

"So God doesn't exist? Heaven doesn't exist? Is your world heaven?" David asked.

"Oh, we most certainly KNOW that God and heaven do exist, just probably not in the exact way humans believe. But that is true of every belief system. Everybody has one, but knowing is the thing. KNOW a higher power exists, in whatever form you can conceive of it, and walk your talk. Living in the light, in the best and highest parts of your faith, whatever your belief system is, that's what impresses what I call 'Spirit.' But that is certainly another discussion, or many other discussions for another day because I have something very important to tell you."

"I don't know if my brain can take much more, Spero."

"This is important. There is a man on Earth who is possibly dangerous, and he wants that Record Keeper. He thinks he can use it to travel as I do and exploit the dimension I come from of its knowledge and wealth and exploit other worlds of their wealth."

"Can he do that with the Record Keeper?"

"No, he will simply die if he tries to go back through the vortex to Rainbow World with it. He will be permanently disassembled. The Record Keeper's energy can only come through the Rainbow World to Earth's portal one way. It was designed like that to protect it in case my dimension is at risk. It can't go back.

It now is supposed to be in the hands of the human Record Keeper when the person is found by the Walker Bearer so that it is kept safe forever and the secrets within it are told."

"Do you know this 'possibly' dangerous person? Could you explain it to him like you did to me?" David asked.

"No, I can't explain anything I told you tonight to him. I'm not supposed to explain it to your mother either, and I have longed to so many times. This information should only be passed to those who have had Record Keeper imprinting. Others, generally, are not capable of accepting what I said as truth. I would just be chalked off as totally insane and committed to a mental institution faster…well, faster than I have in the past a few times," Spero mused with a sly smile on his lips.

"Well, one thing about that, you could escape easily enough, right?"

"Yes, I can." They both laughed.

"David, you and I are faced with a real problem. The man who is obsessed with the crystal is in town. He has already met your mom and knows the crystal is somehow attached to her. "

David started to panic. He said quickly and loudly, "How does he know that?"

Spero shushed him so they didn't wake Jo and Ariane next door and lowered his own voice. "Because his grandsire, Genghis Khan stole the crystal from our dimension, and escaped from our world into yours. He was a Walker in training, and his descendants have some of the Elfin gifts of reading energy patterns on Earth."

He told David the story of Genghis Khan and his ancestors.

"I stole the crystal back from this man named Tazman Khan many years ago. He knows that I took it, and he knows a lot about my dimension. He is the last of Genghis Khan's third son's line and so inherited all of Khan's massive library and personal documents and knows how to read them."

Spero went on, "I suspect that he suspects me of being a Walker Bearer. I haven't always been careful to move from place to place by air or bus. Plus, I keep trying to lose him, but he shows up sooner or later wherever I am. I'm sure he believes with every fiber in his being that the Record Keeper rightfully belongs to his family."

Spero looked deep into David's eyes. "I took it to safeguard the crystal and pass it to the human Record Keeper because it was now time. But also, I took it to keep Tazman Khan from trying to use it, and in doing so, lose his life in the process."

David asked, "What do you want me to do? How are we going to protect Mom and Ariane? Would this guy try to hurt them?"

"More likely he might try to use him to get the crystal. David, I'm going to ask you to give it back to me so that I can keep it safe and get the energy signature away from your family. I'm guessing that I'm going to have to be very scarce for a long while, but I will be back when I can. I want to enjoy every minute of our day together tomorrow, and then when we get back, I'm going to try to lure him away. He and I have been playing this game for a long time. He will follow me, as long as I have the crystal."

"What if he doesn't?"

"Then, if anything happens, all you have to do is set up the circle Ariane described with the people she finds, and Ariane will know what to do and I'll come to you. Save room for me in the middle!!"

"Spero, are you and I going to tell Ariane about this?" David asked.

"No, if she is who I think she is, she'll tell us. Your job is to be on the lookout and help keep her and your mom safe. Try to guide her in discovering her abilities without outright telling her what I've told you, if you can help it. The things I've told you seem like a lot for a young person to accept, but I think you'll find she already knows them."

✡

Demy Cresenzo

Demy was jumping out of his skin. He just couldn't wait any longer to call Pete. He decided to risk it.

He dialed and Peter answered. "Peter Postelwaite, here."

"Demetrius Cresenzo, here." He made his voice sound very formal and official. "I wonder if you could give me just a few minutes of your valuable time to answer a few poll questions?"

"OK, shoot," Peter said, playing along.

"First question. When did you first start wearing your aluminum hat?"

Peter knew where this was going. "When I first realized that I was invisible in it to nosy poll takers!!"

"Second question. Have you always been invisible to nosy poll-takers?"

"No, only since I started wearing the hat."

They both started laughing. Demy said, "Dad told me what's going on. Are you ok?"

"Just a minute, I need to ask my ma something." The line went mumbly. "I'm back. Well, why don't you come over and see?"

"Are you kidding? When?" Demy's voice got loud.

"How about Sunday afternoon? I mean, tomorrow afternoon."

"Yeah, I'm sure I can. Wow, Pete."

"Yes, wow. Wait till you see, wow. Bow wow, see you later." Peter hung up.

Demy was shocked. He ran out to the barn to talk to his Dad. "Dad, Pete just invited me to come over tomorrow afternoon. Can I go?"

"Yeah, that would be fine." Demy started to rush off when his Dad stopped him. "Hey, tell me what you think of this idea. I thought we'd activate the Fire District hot line and invite all the volunteers and their families to a surprise party at the Postelwaites. It will be a Christmas Tree Farm Party and everyone can take a small live evergreen over to the Postelwaites. Each family can plant what they bring. They can also bring a carry-in-dish to feed everyone and show our support to their family. I thought we could all help them start a Christmas Tree Farm for the off season." Martin smiled; he was pretty proud of his idea.

"Could everyone get it organized by tomorrow afternoon? That's pretty quick," asked Demy.

"Your mom can organize anything. Go inside and ask her to get busy! When we take you over, we'll all come too for a big surprise party. How does that sound?"

"They'll love it, I think! Won't they?" Demy wasn't sure.

"If I know Bette, and I do, she will really appreciate it. She needs to know we're all there for her."

Demy rushed in and slammed the door. His mom rounded the corner like she was going to be mad, but his happy, breathless news deflated her from yelling at him for slamming the door.

Lynne got on the phone and called three people to explain what she was asking them to do. Those three people called three each and so on. The area Fire Fighters used this same system to call in the volunteers in case someone needed them right away.

Martin came in to get a drink of water and rest a bit.

"Marty, should we call Bette and forewarn her?" Lynne asked.

"Nope. Demy has a date with their family tomorrow afternoon, so she's already expecting company."

Demy had never experienced a day going so slowly.

✶

Jo Vanderlin and Ariane Selph

Saturday night, when Jo and Ariane got back to their hotel room, Ariane barely got her pajamas on before she climbed into her bed and went immediately to sleep. Jo was also tired, but decided to watch a movie. She chose one from the pay selections that looked good. She hadn't been to a movie for so long, so she hadn't seen any of the new runs, and there seemed to be some good choices.

When the movie was over and she started to turn off the lights to sleep, she noticed that Ariane was mumbling and tossing in her sleep again. She went over and lay beside her daughter and touched her forehead and arms and hands. Ariane was ice cold and her breathing was shallow. Jo, tried to wake her and couldn't wake her. She was afraid she knew what was going on.

Jo was careful not to touch her anymore, but spoke aloud and said, "Ariane, it's Mom…. Where are you, darling?"

Ariane didn't open her eyes but spoke in a panic, "Mom, I'm lost! I can't find anyone! I've been searching for so long…'m tired. Mom!"

Jo tried to calm herself down. She was afraid of this. Inexperienced people who practice astral projection often find themselves out of their body too long and then they lose their way back to their body.

"Ariane, stop moving. Look around you and tell me what you see?"

"It all looks the same Mom! I can't find you!"

"Stay in one place and try to calm yourself. Picture your physical body, where is it?"

"Sitting in the circle," Ariane replied.

"Ariane, I want you to close your eyes and concentrate on your body sitting in the circle. Do you see yourself clearly?"

"Yes."

"Now look at that Ariane's belly button."

"But I have clothes on, Mom!"

"Look where your belly button should be. Can you imagine that?"

"Yes."

"Good, keep looking at your belly button and imagine a string of bright light, like a light rope that you see at Christmas? Imagine something like that going from there, traveling, traveling to your belly button where you are now. Keep one end attached to the circle Ariane's belly button."

Jo waited for a short time before asking quietly, "Is it working?"

"Ok. I'm trying mom."

"Close your eyes; that will help."

After a short time, Jo said, "Pretty soon the light rope will come toward you. Do you see it?"

"Yes!"

"When it gets to you, to the floating Ariane, let it attach to your belly button and keep the rope attached to both belly buttons, ok? Then you float back the way the rope goes. It will just get shorter and shorter until you find your body. When you find your body, move the floaty Ariane back into it. Ok?..... Are you on your way?"

"Yes."

"Keep going, and tell me when you get there."

After some time Ariane said, "I'm there mom. Thanks!"

"Go back into your body, Ariane"

Jo gave her a little time. "Now, wake up please."

Ariane's eyes fluttered, and she turned and looked at her mother.

"Mom, you found me." Ariane looked at her with her eyes wide.

"I'm so glad. Are you OK?"

"I'm really cold."

Jo got in bed next to her daughter and wrapped herself around her to get Ariane's body temperature back up as quickly as possible. After a short time, Jo noticed Ariane's skin was getting warmer and her coloring was better.

Jo hugged her daughter tightly. "Ariane, please tell me what happened," Jo asked as they snuggled together comfortably.

"Did I tell you about the cave dream the other night, or did I dream that too?" Ariane asked.

"No, you told me about it."

"Well, it was that dream again. Only this time, I decided to see if I could find a short cut to the light, so I went off away from the rest of them, and then I got lost for the longest time, and then I heard you talking to me, and then I got back."

"Ariane, do you have any idea why you keep having these dreams?"

"Oh yes. We have to help the light people. They're in trouble."

Jo held Ariane's face and turned it so that they were both making eye contact. "How do you know that?"

"Because they told me."

"Do they talk to you?"

"Yes and no. I just know."

"How is that you know, do you think?" Jo asked.

Ariane looked at her mom and was trying to decide how to answer, and then she decided to tell her what she thought. She sighed, "Because I figured out that my dreams must have started when David bought the Record Keeper in the house. I think when it stung me it was telling me something, all at once though, and so fast I couldn't understand, but I'm understanding more now. I don't have to be afraid of it; that's just how it had to talk, well, when it talks with its voice anyway. It talks other ways too," Ariane said matter of factly.

"What other ways?" Jo asked.

Ariane looked thoughtful, "Well, in dreams for one, and another way that David showed me. He tied a string around it and asked it questions. We're going to work with it to find the cave."

"You and David have been looking for a cave? The one in your dreams?"

"Yes, because it's somewhere out by where we live, I just know it."

"What will you do if you find the cave?"

"I told you mom; we have to help the light people. Twelve people in the circle have to help all at once. I think if we really do it, it will really help them."

"Who are the twelve people you are talking about?"

"I don't know them all yet. I only know a few of them." She counted them off with her fingers, "David, Spero, Peter, and me."

Jo was taken aback for a moment when Ariane mentioned Spero, but asked, "Who's Peter?" Jo had never heard of him.

Ariane told the story in a rush of words, "Peter Postelwaite. He wears a cowboy hat with aluminum foil on it. He was at the Magic circle and I got really mad at him, and then he fell, and David came and twisted my arm back…and it really hurt…and then Peter tried to fight with David, and then David healed his cut."

"Whoa! Back up and tell me slowly!!"

Ariane told her the whole story including the parts about David healing animals and saying that Peter was like Buster.

Jo just sat there flabbergasted. Boy, she had a lot of catching up to do with everyone it seemed. She looked at the clock; it was 1:40 a.m.

"Ariane, let's try to go back to sleep. It's really late."

"Mom, can you sleep with me?"

"Yes, but I'd like you to do me a favor before you go to sleep every night. I'll write this down for you, but I'd like you to say this out loud,"

'In dreams, I must not be allowed to get lost again for the health of my body and ask that when I dream, my physical body, my dream body and my astral body be kept safe from harm. I ask that a cord be established to lead me back to my dream and physical body if I travel astrally.'

"Say it three times each night before you go to sleep. Three times. Do you understand me Ariane? Will you trust me and do as I ask, without fail? I need you to promise to do this until we figure out what's going on, ok?"

Jo was looking at Ariane very seriously. "Because Ariane, I have to tell you this. What you are doing is called astral projection, and if it isn't done safely, you might not get back to your body in time."

Ariane looked scared. "…In time?"

"Yes, it is very dangerous…very dangerous. It's not a game, and it's not just a dream. I think you know that." Jo held Ariane's face and looked deeply into her eyes. "What if I had not been here tonight with you?"

"The last time I was **going** to go down the side ways, and not go straight, you know, Miss Phit jumped on me and woke me up suddenly. Do you think cats can see your dreams too, Mom?"

"I wouldn't be a bit surprised. Let's go to sleep now. It's past two."

Chapter Four
Sunday

✶

Vanderlin/Selph Family and Spero Zezas

Jo woke up at 6 a.m. Ariane was sleeping soundly. Jo left a note for Ariane to wake up David and meet Spero and her in the restaurant downstairs. She also reminded Ariane to take the spare room key with her. Jo got dressed quietly and slipped out the room. She knocked softly on Spero's and David's door. Spero answered. He was fully dressed. Jo motioned him out of the room and whispered, "I need to talk to you."

They both went quietly down the hall and entered the restaurant of the hotel. It was almost deserted. They sat across from each other and ordered breakfast and sat with their coffee looking at each other. Spero didn't talk.

Jo looked deeply into his eyes and said quietly but very coldly and seriously, "Do you want to let me know why I had to go rescue my astrally projecting daughter in a crystal cave last night? Rescue a child that didn't know what the rules were and was comatose in her sleep? Do you want to let me in on what is going on with that crystal? Why did you ask me to show it to my children when it was going to put them in harm's way?"

Spero looked devastated, "I didn't know for sure that David or Ariane would be the able to relate that deeply to the Record Keeper so soon, and I didn't know that it had gone so far with Ariane."

Jo was quick on the uptake. "But you suspected it would, right?"

"Yes. I was hoping it would. But I was also hoping that I would be able to connect with them in time to keep this kind of thing from happening."

"Would you like to tell me what's going on?" Jo asked.

"I'd love to, and I'll tell you what I can," Spero replied.

"What does that mean?" Jo snapped.

"It means… that you didn't react to the crystal and both of your children did. They both received the implanting, and Ariane has received the pre-dreams, and remembers them, and can relate them. That makes her the person I've been looking for…all over this globe… for over twenty years."

"And why were you looking for her?" Jo asked. She was beginning to be very uncomfortable.

"Because she may be my last hope, and it is up to me to keep her and the crystal safe."

"To keep them safe?"

"Yes, and to help her understand the gift she has been given and how to work with it without getting into the kind of trouble she got into last night. It's a good thing her mom is so smart."

"Yes, I'm so smart that I know you're not telling me the full story. I know you're not telling me the whole truth, and I want to hear the whole truth so that I, as her mother, can protect her, even from you if I have to."

Spero looked at her for a long time and didn't respond.

He finally said. "I never expected that the human Record Keeper would be a child, and I honestly don't know what to do except take the crystal and disappear in order to protect all of you. At least for a time, but time is critical, and Ariane has been chosen to help something bigger than you, and bigger than me. I honestly don't think we can stop her from trying to fulfill her destiny, especially when her brother may share her problem."

"David? What does David have to do with it?" Jo asked loudly.

"He has great gifts. Didn't you know?" Spero asked.

Jo responded first by throwing up her hands, and her voice got loud. "I don't know my children at all, apparently. I only know that I won't allow them to be some kind of guinea pigs in something way over their heads… way over MY head."

Spero reached across the table and held both of her hands. He looked deeply in her eyes and said very quietly, "Jo, do you trust me?"

She pulled her hands away and looked at him wearily and didn't respond.

He reached over and grabbed her hands again. "Jo, do you trust me?" He looked very sad.

She looked deeply into his eyes and said, "Yes, with all my heart. But I don't have to tell you that I'm really afraid for my kids. You have to promise me that they won't come to any harm with this stuff."

"Well, there are two ways to handle this then; I have to move in with you so I'm with them constantly until we all figure out what needs to be done, or I can take the crystal and leave for awhile until we all figure out what needs to be done. But there is an element here I haven't told you that I must."

He explained as much as he could to her about Tazman Khan. "I stole the crystal from Tazman to protect it and the light world. I am very aware of the light world at the end of the tunnel that Ariane sees, and I have been trying to find the human Record Keeper to help them. Tazman Khan's family may have had the Record Keeper since Genghis Khan's time, but it doesn't belong to him or anyone. It is a tool to be used by the human Record Keeper, and that person is Ariane and possibly David, too."

"Spero, can't you tell me what you're so carefully not telling me? Don't you think I have a right to know?"

They were so intent on their conversation they didn't notice that David and Ariane had been standing there for a short time.

Ariane spoke up, "But Mom, didn't you know? Spero is from the light world."

Jo looked at Spero. He looked sheepish and shrugged his shoulders. Then he showed her his pointed ears. "Sorry."

Jo just about fainted and looked around to the three of them who were looking at her matter of factly.

"Well, guys. Guess Spero is moving in with us for awhile."

☆

Jo and her new roommate, and David and Ariane finished breakfast. They all made a pact just to enjoy each other and the day. They drove the short distance to the dirt road turn-off to the fair grounds. They followed the signs leading deeper into the forest and the mountains. After what seemed like a good long time on bumpy forest roads, they turned a corner, and thought they were seeing an illusion! A colorful and magical kingdom surfaced into reality.

After they paid for their tickets and were inside the fair grounds, their senses were overwhelmed with a million things to see and do. There were jesters hamming it up, and jugglers juggling, and various people entertaining different groups. There were booths with colorful and wonderful things for sale, food everywhere, and crowds and crowds of people. Jo gave both David and Ariane extra spending money, and everyone decided to go their own way to explore. They all agreed to meet at the Central eating area at 12:00 noon.

Ariane was in seventh heaven, not only was there a Fairy booth, but many of the people were dressed in period clothing, and some chose to dress in the fantasy garb of Fairies, trolls, and witches. She purchased some purple and turquoise Fairy wings made from real feathers that strapped to her back and a small Fairy figurine. Ariane even got to ride an elephant and swing in a giant swing that made her feel like she was flying to the sky!

David went his own way and ran into some friends from school. He was particularly happy to see Sonya Wallace. She was one of the brightest students in school. She had long blonde hair and had her own quirky way of dressing. He admired her for her brains, of course, but also her individuality and smile. He could hardly breathe when she smiled. He had a crush on her from the moment he saw her, but in school, he couldn't get up the courage to really talk to her. Everything around them at the fair felt free and happy and that helped to loosen things up. They walked side by side and seemed to have a lot in common. She was really easy to talk to and seemed interested in everything. The group went to see a rather risqué slap stick comedy act. They all laughed and laughed.

Spero seemed more interested in eating everything in sight and watching the jousting displays. He had the best time winning prizes for insulting "The Insulter."

Jo was fascinated with the clothing and jewelry stalls and couldn't resist purchasing a few items. When she found the booth for the hammocks and low gravity chairs, she didn't get much further than that.

They had all arranged to meet at noon at the central eating area for lunch. After eating turkey legs, meat pies, whole artichokes and orange sherbet for dessert, everyone was in danger of sinking into a stupor.

Jo asked them to take time out to do a family portrait, with Spero in it too, in period clothing. It was so much fun trying on the myriad of costumes until they all found their special look. Jo dressed up like a queen. Ariane put on a little white toga, a flower wreath for her hair, and of course her new wings. David dressed like a jester. And Spero, well, he was keeping them waiting. They waited and waited and finally he came out of the dressing room. He was dressed up as a wood Elf with a green and brown tunic and pointed leather moccasins. He even let his ears show. The lady taking the pictures remarked how realistic his ears were. His eyes twinkled, and he laughed. He really had fun blowing their minds.

The pictures were funny and priceless. The photographer agreed to send them four copies in the mail, one for each of them. It was pretty hot out, and they all decided to leave after the pictures. David's friends had left, so he was ready to go.

As they were driving home, there was such a sense of happy relaxation that none of them really talked about much that was serious. It seemed to be an unspoken agreement not to break the spell of the day.

When they stopped in Ft. Collins for gas, Jo called home to get her messages. There was a message from one of their neighbors to invite them to a neighborhood impromptu gathering at Bette Postelwaites' place. There was something about bringing a live tree to help them start a Christmas Tree Farm and to bring in a carry in dish and plan to stay late. The lady inviting them gave the address and directions to the property. Jo realized that the Postelwaites were their nearest neighbor, so she decided to see if everyone would like to try to make the party.

"Wasn't Peter's last name Postelwaite?" Jo asked.

David answered, "Yes, that's him. This party doesn't make sense, Mom. Something had to have happened. Peter's father must be out of the picture or something, or nobody would be going over there. Nobody. He has a reputation for being a really nasty character and really abusive. The guys I hang with said he really hurt Peter. Word was Peter was out of school for six months. Ariane had never met him before, had you?

Ariane's eyes got big and she nodded "no."

David continued, "His four brothers go to school with me. They are all really a rough lot and bully everyone. I honestly can't imagine the whole neighborhood coming to their house unless something drastic happened. I'm not too interested in going but you all can go if you want to."

"David, if something *did* happen like that and Wyoming neighbors call for you to gather together like this, especially on short notice, it's a sign of solidarity for the family. It's hard to explain, but when really awful things happen here, a pioneering spirit prevails and your neighbors come to you and pitch in and show how much they care. We are really obligated to go. Their father may have died."

Ariane chimed in, "No, I don't think so, because Peter just said he had to get home before his dad got up and that was just the other day. But Mom, we need to go for another reason too. I might see the other people in the cave circle there."

Spero clapped his hands, "Well, I guess that settles it. We need to go. If you don't mind me tagging along, I'll join you."

"Where are we going to get a live tree?" Jo asked.

Spero said, "Be right back."

The convenience store had a sandwich shop. Jo bought a "Giant Party Sandwich" for the carry-in item and paid for the drinks and "puke food" the kids couldn't resist having. When they got back to the car, Spero was loading a small live tree in the trunk with the roots protected by earth and a burlap covering.

"How on Earth?" Jo fumbled with what was in her hands and just about dropped her pop.

Ariane's eyes about popped out of her head! "Spero! You're magic."

"Yes, I am," said Spero with a wink. David was totally cracking up.

☆

The Christmas Tree Farm Party

When the Cresenzos drove into the Postelwaite's gate, they caravanned in with their car and several other cars containing the rest of their big family. They were closely followed by an additional three pickups full of tables and chairs and equipment and half of their ranch hands. The rest of the ranch hands piled on a truck with a flatbed carrying a tractor with a post hole digger.

Bette Postelwaite came out of her back porch door and stood there with her hands over her mouth. The boys came out and stood around her.

Martin Cresenzo got out of the car and went over to Bette and put his arms around her. "Heard there was a party going on here!"

"Marty, what have you done?" Bette said in his ear as she was hugging him.

"We're all going to help take care of my first Bits girl and hers." We're having a Christmas Tree Farm party."

The boys looked from one to the other and at Mr. Cresenzo. Martin noticed that Jerry was sporting a really bad black eye. Jerry shook his hand enthusiastically, "Wow, Mr. Cresenzo....Just wow!"

"Ladies, please excuse the guys for awhile. Bette, do you want to show Lynne where we should set up the tables? I'm going to go with the boys and make sure we choose the right spot for the trees." He left with all five boys and most of the men.

"Whoa, guys. I need about six of you to help set up," said Lynne. Some of the ranch hands peeled off from the large guy group and came and stood beside her. Bette walked over to a group of Aspens that had a nice flat space. "How about here?" she asked shyly.

Lynne gave her a hug and whispered, "You go get beautiful, and we'll take care of it from here. The rest of the party should be her in about an hour."

"The rest?" Bette's eyes got big.

"The whole dang Fire District will be here!" Lynne spread her arms wide.

Bette's eyes filled with tears, and she took the opportunity to hide by heading toward the house. "Well, I better go get beautiful then!"

By the time everyone started showing up with their trees and food carry-ins, Martin and the men had strung string in about a five acre area showing the lines where the trees would be planted. They decided to place the trees 8 feet apart, and they had already started digging holes.

"I've got a drip line system that we'll help you set up to water the trees after we get them all planted that will attach to that outdoor spigot," said Martin pointing.

"How can we ever repay you for this, Mr. Cresenzo?" Ernie asked.

"Well, the tree farm is a long-term work in progress. Those smaller trees will take a few years to be the right size, so it will go slow at first, but in a couple of years, it should be a real cash crop for you. I'm sure people will come to you, so you won't be cutting trees that don't sell. I'd suggest at first that you put as much as you can into replacing what you sell with bigger trees."

Mr. Cresenzo was on a roll. "It would be smart to build a green-house to have a lot of saplings in containers in one small area and then put those in the ground when they get to be a couple of feet tall.

A solar greenhouse won't be as expensive as you think. I can help you with that. I'd probably invest in some kind of low voltage electric fencing to keep the deer and antelope out. I'd put in planking, probably, down the road a ways, so customers can walk from aisle to aisle and stay out of the muck and also so they don't damage the smaller trees. You got a good area here for parking and people can see this part from the road, so I think it's a good location. Oh yeah, and a great big sign." Martin spread his hands way apart.

"We would have never thought of this, not in a million years. Maybe we can put up a nice stand around this area too for mom's jams and jellies...or I dunno, maybe we can sell mulled cider, Christmas wreathes, and decorations, too," Blake said.

"That's the spirit, boy!!" Keep thinking of different ways to make money." Martin patted him on the back.

Jeff looked around him and shyly asked, "What do you want us to do now, Mr. Cresenzo?"

"Start planting, boy!!" He pointed to the gate, and the nursery truck was pulling up with three dozen trees.

The men separated the trees by size and everyone decided to divide the lots into fourths with the largest ones closest to the road and the smaller ones in the furthest square.

People started showing up and just started rolling up their sleeves to plant trees. The Postelwaite boys were totally overwhelmed with the number of people bringing in more and more trees of all sizes. There was a lot of laughing and good humored digging, not all of it with dirt, going around. It made the Postelwaite boys humble to see girls and guys they usually hassled at school, right in there helping along with everyone else. The brothers all made an effort to apologize for how they treated each one and to shake their hands and thank them.

Those who weren't planting trees were helping to set up tables and food. More and more people kept pouring in.

Jo and her family arrived about 5:00 p.m. as the group was getting ready to eat. David took their tree down to the lot to plant it. Jerry came over to lend him a hand.

Jerry said shyly, "David, thanks for coming. I wouldn't have come if I were you. Sorry for last year. Hope you'll accept my hand," and he offered his hand. David shook it and smiled. The other Postelwaite boys came over and shook hands and apologized too.

David shook each of their hands. "Just let me know if you need some help putting in more trees or laying the drip line." David had noticed the hoses and parts. "My dad and I put in a system at our house in Washington."

Jeff was surprising everyone by talking so much today. He said, "Can you come over tomorrow, then? Happy to have your help."

"Sure, I'll be happy too!"

Peter came over shyly. "Sorry about coming onto your property the other day. Your house was empty for a long time, and I found that place…uh…where I saw you, and that I used to like to visit."

David put his hand on his shoulder and said, "That's Ariane's favorite place too. Funny you both have the same favorite place, huh?"

Peter smiled shyly. "So, I better make sure it's ok with Ariane to visit there again, huh?"

Ariane had just joined the group and heard Peter's last comment. "We'll have to see about that."

Peter introduced her to his brothers. She shook their hands shyly and said, "Hello, nice to meet you." They all finished helping David and then spread out elsewhere.

She was acting really strangely though, and David took her aside. "What's the matter, munchkin?"

"All of those boys are in the circle," Ariane said simply.

"Well, good thing we came then so you could meet them. Don't say anything about it now; we'll figure all of that out later. Keep your eyes out for anybody else in the circle though, ok? Try to have some fun though. This has been a great day, so far, hasn't it?" David asked.

"One of the best days I can ever remember," Ariane said. "Just wish Dad was here."

"Yeah, me too."

David finished packing the earth around their tree, and he and Ariane dumped two buckets of water into the well around the tree to finish. They started walking back to the food area with everyone else when Peter dodged between everyone and came up to David and Ariane with another boy that Ariane remembered vaguely from another class at her school.

"Guys, I'd like you to meet my best friend, Demy Cresenzo. Demy this is my new friend, David Selph and his sister, Ariane."

Demy nodded to David and shook his hand. Then he glanced sideways at Ariane, and there was uncomfortable silence. He was speechless and really acting dumb. Finally, he raised his eyebrows and said to Ariane, "Uh…I saw you at school, in Miss Titchner's class, right?"

"Yes, I saw you too. Nice to meet you," Ariane said and looked at David and nodded "yes."

David patted Demy's shoulder. "Why do I get the feeling I'll be seeing a lot of you guys?"

Ariane said simply, "Because you will."

Both boys looked at each other and grinned but didn't have a clue what to say to that.

They all joined the line winding around the buffet table and found places to sit. Jo was sitting at a table that was full, so Ariane and David sought out Spero and sat by him. He had his plate piled high and was thoroughly enjoying everything. He had a blissful, contented look and actually hummed when he ate.

David looked at his plate and teased him, "Spero, think you could get any more on that plate?"

"I don't know, but I'll try!" Spero stood up suddenly and went back to the food line, and then he came back to the table. "I *decided* that the pie would clash with the baked beans, so I made a **decision** not to pile more on one plate, but it was physically possible, I assure you!"

"Spero, I have to tell you something important. I found five other people that are supposed to be in the cave circle," Ariane said as she pointed them out. "All of Peter's brothers and his friend Demy, so with you, and David, and Peter, and me, that makes nine."

"We're getting closer to being able to help our mutual friends, then, aren't we? He put a big bite of pie in his mouth and said, well maybe said, "I'm really glad," only it sounded like "Grilm rrhhyry cld-ddd."

The five Postelwaite brothers and Demy walked shyly over to their table. "Mind if we join you?"

Spero looked up and said, "Hfrryy to haff shewww."

David laughed and said, "Everyone, this is Spero. He's a friend of the family. He's staying with us for awhile. He talks 'Foodspeak.' Don't worry, you'll catch on." Everyone laughed and sat down.

Jeff, who wore his white/blond hair long, sat next to Ariane. He looked over at her and nodded a greeting. She smiled, and when he smiled back, for some reason, she felt "tingly." She blushed. She had never seen such incredible clear blue eyes. She was pretty sure he understood everything…about everything and everybody…probably even about her. She blushed again and hastily looked away.

The boys ate and ate like they've never seen food before and had each other cracking up speaking "Foodspeak."

By the end of the meal, they had all decided to meet the next day at 9:00 am at the Postelwaites. Spero and Ariane were invited to come back too and help.

Someone started playing a fiddle and then someone joined in with a guitar and others joined in with whatever they could play or bang on. Pretty soon people were getting up and dancing. It was the perfect end to a perfect day.

✧

Vanderlin/Selph Family and Spero

Jo gathered up her family and Spero about ten o'clock and headed for the van. The party was still going strong, but it had been a long day. Spero got in the passenger seat in the front, and David and Ariane hopped in back.

"Spero, are you going to need to go back to your apartment tonight for clothes and things? "

"I've got some extra clean clothes for tonight. Everyone is tired, let's just settle in tonight at your house. Tomorrow, can I borrow the car? If it's ok, can I go into town with you to get a bag and a few things. I'd like to load up my bike if that's ok? I need to give them notice at work and then would you mind if I drove back so David and I can help the Postelwaites like we promised tomorrow? We can come and get you after work and I'll buy dinner in town."

"Spero? You're going to quit your job?" Jo asked.

"Jo, I need to be with David and Ariane while you're at work." He looked at her, and she nodded.

"I don't mean to be too personal, but can you afford to do that? Isn't that going to cause you problems?"

"No, if all goes well, I'll be going home soon, for the first time in… well a very, very long time. David, Ariane, and I have our work cut out for us and I need to get the confidence of the circle group. We all have a lot to learn together. Things are worse for the light beings than I told you; we don't have much time."

"Mom, I found five more people who are supposed to be in the circle. That makes nine, and we have to find the other three still. If David and Spero go to the Postelwaites tomorrow, can I come with you to the store so I can see if I meet any more?"

"Spero? Does that sound like a plan?" Jo asked.

"I think that would be fine. Before you turn in, can you spare a few minutes to talk, Jo?" Spero asked.

Ariane popped her head between Jo's and Spero's seat. "I don't think it's fair for you two to have secrets. We all have to all know what's going on. I'm really tired of people not trusting us." She flopped back in her seat and crossed her arms.

Spero pulled down the cosmetic mirror on his visor and looked at her in the back seat pouting. "I'll promise you this, there will not be any secrets between you and me, but what I need to talk to your mother about is private between us, and when it is time for me to tell you, I will tell you too, fair? We have to trust each other, Ariane."

"I just don't want it to go back to the way it was. I don't want adults talking things over because you'll probably include David and everyone will leave me out. I'm very, very tired of being left out with nobody talking to me!!"

David said, "But, Ariane. You are the human Record Keeper. Don't you know that? You will be the one in the end telling us all what we need to do to help YOU. You are the one the Rainbow World chose to be its voice and to help save it."

"I need to know what everyone else is saying to each other and doing from now on. I just do." Ariane was really being stubborn.

"Ariane, I think what Spero wants to talk to me about has to do with possibly a bad man who wants the crystal. He wants it very badly for lots of wrong reasons." Jo explained

"Who is he? Is he from where you're from too, Spero?" Ariane asked.

"His name is Tazman Khan and his ancestor, Genghis Khan was an Elf so he is part Elf. He is a very tall, dark eyed, handsome man with long brown hair. He is in town, and he knows your mom and I are friends. That's all he knows for sure, but he suspects more, and he does know a lot about magic. Genghis Khan stole the Record Keeper to come to Earth. He knew that the crystal was important, but he didn't know HOW important. It is the Record Keeper of the Rainbow World, and that's a secret he didn't know and Tazman doesn't know either.

Spero continued. "When his ancestor stole the crystal, it was up to me to recover it. I was forced to leave the Rainbow World when it became evident that things were starting to go badly. When I recovered the crystal, it was up to me to search for the person or persons who could understand enough about what was needed to help save our world. I happen to think that you and David both are meant to help.

Remember I said I got a phone call from home? The outer space screaming was an evacuation alarm. Hawk Point must be a natural vortex, and you two had the Rainbow World crystal with you, huh? Basically, if I were not already here, I would have had to leave my world now because it is being destroyed, and everyone who can leave has left. Other Walkers have left with the other crystals of other worlds and dimensions to protect the information in the crystals. But there are a lot of my friends who may not leave. If the light world is destroyed, they may be destroyed, and this world will follow in a very short time."

He had everyone's attention now. "We are guardians for the Earth. It is our responsibility to help keep Earth healthy and safe. If we are gone, pollution will destroy your ozone layer more quickly than man can imagine, because we will not be there to help you."

"I need to tell you all this. Jo or I need to be with one or both of you most of the time unless you're with a group of people. I don't know what Tazman is capable of, and he feels the crystal belongs to him. I have the skills to keep you safe. Part of my training is as a warrior and shaman and I'm really good at it. I was a teacher. But there are times when you will not be with me, and you will be with your mom. I have to train her how to contact me, as I will train you, but I have to train her first, ok?"

"Sorry, Spero." Ariane realized she was being selfish.

"You never have to be sorry with me. You are always to be honest with me, promise?" Spero asked.

"Yes, I can do that," Ariane said sadly. "I just hope I don't disappoint you. What if I'm not the one? Or if I'm not, what if David isn't?

David was looking to Spero for the answer to that question too.

"Then we will all do what we can do to help, and we'll all pray for extra guidance and help. Because at the end of the day, we pray to the same Spirit, no matter what name or what form, it is the same Great Spirit over us all, protecting us all. I believe, no, I KNOW that. Hope you do too!"

Jo had pulled into the drive way. "We're all really tired, and we're not going to save any worlds tonight, so let's call it a night, please. I'm beat."

They all got their bags from the weekend and trudged in. "Ariane, please remember the mantra I gave you. Say it three times before you sleep."

Ariane yawned and stretched, "I promise, Mom. Do you think it would be too selfish to ask if I could just sleep tonight? It feels like I haven't slept for a long time."

"I think that's an excellent idea. Just add it to your mantra that you would like to have a dream free night to rest," Jo answered.

She unlocked the door and the group trouped in. She kissed David and Ariane goodnight and motioned to Spero. She walked upstairs and he followed her into the fourth bedroom, which was actually a guest suite with its own bathroom.

"Here's home for as long as you want. You're welcome and because you might be leaving us soon, I want to tell you that I'm really glad you're staying with us so we can keep you as long as we can... well, it's all relative, isn't it? But I think you know what I mean. Hey, I just thought of something. Do you know how to drive a car, and do you have a driver's license?"

"Yes, I can drive, and no, I don't have a license. I'm an illegal alien," he laughed.

"I think, then, if it's ok, I'll ask David to drive you in early in his car and then he can chauffer you around. Would that work too?" Jo asked.

"Sure, we'll just get up early. I'll just write a letter to the Cheyenne Family YMCA and drop it off so we can meet our commitment with the Postelwaites on time."

"Jo, I just need to give you this." He handed her a crystal. "If you see Tazman, if he comes anywhere near you, I want you to whistle your natural whistle into the crystal, and I'll hear you and come. I've got one for David and Ariane too."

Then he looked at her and smiled and said, "Let me hear your whistle."

Jo whistled a long high note and Spero touched his crystal to hers. On impulse, Spero gave her a goodnight peck on her whistle. Jo laughed, "So that was a trick for a goodnight kiss, too?"

"Worked, didn't it?" He pulled a crystal out of a hidden breast pocket. "No, I needed to hear the tone you use, so I can tell my whistles apart. My master crystal needed to hear it so it will recognize you and let me hear the whistle."

"So, if I pucker up and whistle, you'll...let me see... you'll beam over?"

"Yep! Quick as a wink. Just to be clear though, it isn't something I do on a constant basis. It's a little wearing. Only whistle if you're in trouble, ok?"

"Someday will you tell me a little more about you?"

"I promise. Sweet dreams, my friend."

"And to you."

Jo went downstairs to let David know he'd have to drive Spero in to town tomorrow. When she got to his door, it was slightly ajar, and he was crashed out and sound asleep. She decided just to wake him early in the morning. She checked in on Ariane, who was wide awake laying in the dark.

"Mom?"

"Yes, my darling?"

"When I go to bed and you are here, can you come kiss me good-night and tuck me in like Daddy used to do?"

Jo couldn't stop a tear from falling. "There is nothing in this world I would rather do." She leaned over and kissed her beautiful daughter and smoothed her hair and tucked the covers around her.

Jo smiled and said softly, "You know, those Fairies left that beautiful baby for me too! I love you, Ari."

When Jo left the room, Ariane looked out the window. "Thank you," she whispered.

Chapter Five
Monday

✲

Jo Vanderlin

Jo got up about 6:00 and went in to wake David.

"David, I'm sorry to wake you darling, but Spero needs a ride into town to get his things. I'm going to take Ariane with me so you two can go work over at the Postelwaites afterwards, ok?" Honey, are you awake enough to hear what I'm saying?"

"Ok, Mom. I'll get up in just a minute," David said sleepily.

"I'll give you the time it takes to get Ariane up and going, and then you need to get moving." Jo's voice was louder this time.

Jo knew that he would go back to sleep. They went through this every morning when school started. She smiled seeing that he always had one sock on and one sock off.

She went into Ariane's room, and she was sleeping soundly too.

"Ariane, it's a new day!" Jo started singing her wake up song, "Wake up and sing, tra, la, la, la la, start the day right, start the day, right." Jo was one of those annoying morning people.

"OK, OK! I'm up! STOP SINGING!" Ariane covered her head with the pillow.

"Did you sleep the whole night without dreaming about the cave?" her mother asked.

"Yes! It was great! I really slept hard."

Ariane could be trusted to get up, make her bed, and get moving. Jo went back down the hall to David's room. She pushed open the door, and to her surprise, he was out of bed and judging from the closed bathroom door, he was taking a shower. "Well, will wonders never cease?" Jo said to herself.

She went into the kitchen to make coffee and Spero was already sitting there drinking coffee.

"Helped myself to breakfast. Is that ok?" he asked.

Jo laughed when she saw that he had leftover spaghetti and meatballs. "What kind of a breakfast is that?" she teased.

"The best possible kind! You could sell this at Prism. Put the sauce in jars and make a million dollars. This is the best spaghetti and meatballs I've ever eaten!"

"My mom's recipe…well close to anyway. HERS was the very, very best."

"Do you miss them?"

"Every day," Jo said sadly. "Spero, I never asked if you have a family?"

"I have all of you guys!"

"Spero, how old are you, dare I ask?" Jo queried.

"I'm very, very, very old." I'm the oldest Elf in Rainbow World."

"How old are you in Earth years?"

"Time isn't linear like people think. In the time I've been on Earth, I could have theoretically gone back and forth to the Rainbow World and met younger and possibly older versions of myself."

"You are not answering my question, Oh Wise One," smiled Jo.

"I have been on Earth off and on since the year 1200 and even before that. I came back semi-permanently thirty years ago, and I was old when I got here."

"So, HOW old are you in Earth years?" Jo asked, raising her eyebrows.

"You wouldn't believe me if I told you. Actually how old I really am doesn't compute here. To your concept of time I'm thousands of

Earth years old at the very minimum. But in the Rainbow World, I'm just a spring chicken," Spero snickered, and then he went back to eating spaghetti.

Jo just stood there with her mouth open.

David came into the kitchen, "Ready to go?" He grabbed a couple of granola bars and a pop.

"We'll see you later." David kissed her on her cheek, and he and Spero went out the door to the garage. They opened the garage door, and David did his usual "peel out."

Jo was still standing there with her mouth open.

Ariane came into the kitchen. "Mom, ready to go?" Jo looked at her dazedly. "MOM, I said are you ready to go?"

"Sure. Sure."

Ariane grabbed an apple and a glass of milk. "Let's go then, ok? You all right?"

Jo pointed down the drive way and pointed to the kitchen chair, "Umm…" she looked at Ariane like she was confused and said, "Sure, why shouldn't I be? I always serve spaghetti for breakfast to… say, three thousand year old men! No, *excuse me*, to three thousand year old Elves."

"Cool."

Ariane went out of the door and got into the van. She rolled down the window and yelled, "MOM! You'll be late."

"I'm coming." Jo got a "go" cup and poured coffee in it until it overflowed.

She said aloud to herself as she was cleaning up the overspill, "I'm ok, I'm ok, I'm ok."

✡

David Selph

David and Spero got into Cheyenne by 7:00 a.m., so there was plenty of time to get Spero's stuff. David waited in the car at Spero's house per Spero's request. Spero apologized, but said his housekeeping left a lot to be desired. David was trying to load Spero's bike in when a man came up alongside.

"Need a hand?" the man asked.

"Yes, please. Do think you could help me get this seat down? I know it drops somehow."

The man got in on the other side of the car and felt around the head area of the back seat, "The catch is usually somewhere around here; some of them need a key. Nope, not this one." He showed David where the catch was and then he moved out so that David could maneuver and was able to drop the seat.

"Thanks!" David looked up and the man was gone. He didn't even see him down the street. He looked back the other way, and there was no sign of him.

Spero showed up with a duffle bag and a basketball. "Ok David, all loaded up? This is the rest."

"Is that all?" David asked. "That's not very much stuff."

"I travel light. I've moved around a lot," Spero answered.

"Spero, this probably isn't important, but a man stopped to help me put the seat down. I was busy so I didn't look at him very closely at all, and then he seemed to disappear. I went to thank him, and he was simply gone."

"Think, David. You didn't see his face at all?"

"No."

"How about his clothes?" Spero asked.

"Brownish? I'm a blank on that. Wait, I did notice a ring on his hand. It had a Boy Scout emblem, I think?" David said.

"Boy Scout emblem? What does it look like?"

"Oh, yeah, it's a French symbol too?"

"A *fleur d'leis*?" Spero showed David his hand, "kind of like this one?"

"Yeah, that's it," David said and looked quizzically at Spero. Spero's ring was gold and had gems and diamonds on it, whereas the ring the man had on was silver and a plain pattern.

"Well, you met Tazman Khan then; he wears Genghis' Initiate Walker ring. I assume he figured out where I live, and now he's met you and knows what you look like. Now he knows, too, that I'm moving. He must have been watching my house over the weekend."

"What do we do now?" David asked looking around.

"We go about our day and don't worry about it," Spero said matter of factly.

"What if he follows us?" David wondered.

"I would expect him to. I imagine he's been researching your mom's address and already knows where you live. He was just playing games, letting me know he knows," Spero explained.

Spero put his duffle bag and basketball in the back seat and climbed in the passenger side. "Would you stop at the Cheyenne Family YMCA so I can drop off this letter? I need to give them enough time to find someone for tomorrow."

David drove Spero over to the Cheyenne Family YMCA and waited for him in the car. He was gone for about fifteen minutes. When he came back to the car, he had tears in his eyes.

"I really hate goodbyes; I avoid them where possible. Lots of wonderful people there," Spero explained.

"I'm sorry. You've had to say a lot of goodbyes, huh?" David put his hand on his shoulder.

"More than I can count. Let's head down the road to the Postelwaites. Ready?"

"Need some comfort food?" David asked.

"Boy after my own heart. Fast and greasy?"

"You choose."

Spero chose a nearby popular fast food restaurant, and David drove through the drive up. Spero ordered almost everything on the menu. David just ordered another soda and breakfast sandwich. Spero seemed to get back to his happy self the more food he consumed. David was sure he would be ok when he heard him humming as he was eating.

☆

Monday is a Busy Day

They reached the Postelwaites about 8:30, and Demy and some of the hands from Cresenzo's ranch were already there.

David parked the car, and the Postelwaite brothers waived from the tree lot.

Spero looked around and asked David, "Where's Peter?"

David looked at him in a confused way, "He's the one with the aluminum hat."

"What aluminum hat?" Spero asked.

David laughed; he figured Spero was pulling one over on him. "Very funny, Spero."

David walked over to Peter with Spero and said, "Peter, Spero didn't recognize you with your hat on."

Peter took off his hat and wiped his brow, and extended his hand to Spero. "Thanks for coming, Mr. Spero."

Spero had been kind of looking in his general direction and over his head, but when Peter removed his hat, he looked directly at him and said, "Oh, there you are. Hello, Peter."

Peter's brothers were cracking up.

Blake said, "Good one, Mr. Spero. He wears the hat, so that he's invisible in the Fairy world."

"Works!" Spero exclaimed.

Peter smiled at him. He was getting used to his brothers giving him a hard time about his hat, and Spero's reaction was appreciated. Demy smiled at Spero and winked.

They all laughed and started working. They still had a number of trees to plant so they did that first.

When they were ready to work on the drip line, David was really a lot of help getting the drip line established. As soon as they got the general idea of how it worked and how to set the drip buttons in, it went very quickly. The ranch hands gathered up their things and left. Demy was able to stay behind because he was going to spend the night at the Postelwaites.

It was about 4:30 p.m. when Spero asked, "You guys interested in some dinner? Meet us at David's about 6:00 p.m. Your mom is welcome to come too."

"Just a minute. Let me ask our ma." Peter ran into the house and was soon back. "She said one of her friends from a long time ago is coming over this evening to help her make curtains. She said we could all go, but could she get a rain check?"

"So are you guys all game then?" Spero asked.

"Sure, sounds great," Jerry said. The other Postelwaites and Demy nodded enthusiastically in agreement.

David and Spero got into the car and David turned to Spero and asked, "Got a game plan?"

"How are you at burning steaks?" Spero asked.

"Fair, but we don't have any. I've got charcoal and a grill and that's about it," David said.

"Have you got baked beans, tomatoes, corn on the cob, and salad?" Spero asked.

"I'm fresh out. How about peanut butter and jelly sandwiches?" David asked.

They pulled into the Vanderlin-Selph turnoff, and David got out to open the gate. Spero got out with him and headed into the woods. He waived and said, "Be right back. Call your mom and Ariane and tell them we're making dinner and to be home at 6:00."

David saw a light flash in the woods and smiled and shook his head. He drove down the driveway and opened the garage. He walked in and called his mom's cell and left a message for her to be home by 6:00 because Spero was getting dinner for them. He was cracking up at the end of it so his mother would probably wonder what was going on.

He went out to the garage to get the grill and move it to the outdoor fire pit area. When he returned, Spero was standing in the driveway with a paper bag full of groceries.

David laughed, "Boy that teleporting stuff comes in handy, doesn't it?"

Spero laughed and said, "Yes, it does."

David set up the grill and got the charcoal going while Spero took the groceries into the kitchen and banged around looking for the stuff he needed to prepare the food. He had bought steaks, corn on the cob, baked beans, fresh lettuce, and lots and lots of tomatoes.

David came in and said, "The grill is heating up. What do you want me to do?"

"Can you shuck that corn, and wash and tear up the lettuce for salad, and I'll prepare the meat with my secret Elfin ingredients, put the beans in the oven and cut up tomatoes."

"Have you got enough tomatoes?" David asked seeing probably a dozen tomatoes there.

"That's the best part of having steaks! Don't you eat tomatoes with your steak?" Spero asked.

"No, can't say as I do," smiled David.

"Then you haven't lived, boy! You haven't truly lived." Spero was apparently a whiz in the kitchen. He was humming and moving around like a chef. He cut up the tomatoes in microseconds and layered them in a casserole dish like a deck of cards and cut up green onions and put them on top.

"Now for the secret Elfin ingredient," he said in a whisper. "You are bound to silence forever. NEVER tell the secret of great tomatoes," he warned and proceeded to get soy sauce and sprinkle it over the layers.

He kissed his fingers and said, "Wha- la! It is z secret sauce."

David was totally cracking up.

"Now, for z secret of z meat marinade." He pulled down the coarse ground pepper, garlic, and about every herb in the kitchen and sprinkled it on the meat. And then got Worcestershire sauce and the famous secret soy sauce and sprinkled that over the meat and said, "Wha-la! The secret Elfin marinade." David was watching in fascination.

Spero then got a fork and poked the meat enthusiastically all over. He bent down and examined it and poked it once or twice and said in a deadpan voice, "I think it is quite dead now."

David was laughing so hard, he was about in tears.

Just then the four Postelwaite brothers and Demy and showed up. They had cut through the woods and walked over.

"Hello the house!" Ernie said happily.

"Welcome!" Spero flourished his fork. "Come in. We're creating z masterpieces!"

The boys all gathered in the kitchen, and David served them sodas. They hung around watching Spero cook. Spero got out two of Jo's deepest big pots and put about two inches of water in them and added cream and butter, then put the corn in the pots to steam. The boys were actually silent; they were fascinated with his strange ingredients.

Jeff quietly asked, "Cream?"

Spero affected a French chef's accent. "Trust the master chef! It makes z corn so very happy." The boys all laughed.

The salad was already made and everything ready except the corn and steaks, so the boys moved out of the kitchen to the firepit area which was semi-circular and had benches with tables between the seats. The charcoal had a few minutes yet to be ready to cook the steaks.

Peter had set his hat on the porch, but now put it on. He had always put the hat on away from them and hidden the aluminum foil in the crown of the hat to avoid who knew what reaction, but he decided to be himself. He had taken to wearing it around his brothers.

Peter even had told Jeff the truth about why he wore it when he walked in the woods by saying, "Well, think about it, the inexperienced and out of state hunters are much less likely to shoot me for a cow, but they might think I'm an alien, so maybe they'll get scared and go home. Besides, it hides me from the Fairies."

Jeff had related the Fairy part to his other brothers, and Peter's brothers had yet to let up on the ribbing. Things were different now, though, it was good natured ribbing, not shoving, hitting, and terrorizing. Peter was thinking to himself that Ma's speech and their father's violence had really hit it home to all of them to try to live another way. None of them wanted to hurt their ma ever again. None of them wanted to see her cry. They had watched a transformation in their ma.

With their father around, she seemed really old. She was stiff and held her arms across her chest most of the time and had a scowl on her face. Now she was smiling and even laughing out loud. She stood up straight and was actually younger looking and beautiful. She moved with an easy grace they had never seen before.

Spero joined the group. They were busy teasing Peter about his hat again.

"Where is Peter?" Spero asked.

"Spero, it was only funny the first time," David teased.

"No, I'm serious, where's Peter?" Spero didn't smile. Demy looked at Peter and kind of crooked his head.

Peter took his hat off and looked at Spero; then, like before, Spero tracked.

Peter said shyly, "I know it's a silly thing. It's hard to explain, it just makes me feel safe and protected. I do realize it's not entirely normal, but it makes me feel better."

Blake was sitting on one side of Peter jabbing him in the ribs and laughing. Peter was giggling and said, "Honest, I SWEAR to all of you, I'm serious."

Jeff kept tickling him from his other side.

Peter was trying to get away from both of them and was laughing. "I DO see Fairies, and they don't see me."

Spero asked, "Where do you see them?"

Peter hesitated. The newfound trust in his brothers was still too new to jeopardize the tree circle and the magic Fairy tree. He fell back to his standard line, "I'd tell you mate, but then I'd have to kill ya and eat ya."

Spero turned and faced the group and said, "Tell me what you think, guys. Is a belief in fantasy, Fairies, Elves, etc. contrary to a Christian life?"

They all had a lot to say about that, and there was some disagreement in the group for awhile that it was contrary to their Christian beliefs.

"Where in the Bible does it say anything about whether Elves and Brownies and Fairies are real or not real or whether they are good or not good?" Peter asked.

"Yeah, there's even a part in the Bible that says giants came to Earth from heaven and mated with the women and produced great men…something like that!" Jeff said.

"That's not true." Jerry, who had been strictly against believing in such things said, "But it does say not to suffer a witch to live, doesn't it?"

"Where does it say that? It doesn't say that," Ernie argued.

The other's argued that, "Yes, it does say that, somewhere in the Old Testament."

But the argument decided that evil witches were only people doing evil witchy things, which was different than natures' creatures, which were more ancient and still connected in mythology to the Earth. Jerry finally conceded that point.

"That whole witch thing caused lots of innocent women who were healers and understood how to treat people with herbs and things to be killed!" Jeff was getting excited.

David was being silent and watching the discussion. He was amazed how Spero got them all to open up.

Spero stood up and started to move off but left them with a question. "What if the existence of a Fairy world could be proved, and what if they were helper to your natural world and to mankind in general, and what if they were in trouble? Could you step over your prejudices and belief systems enough to keep an open mind and try to help them? Talk that over and I'll be right back. I need to go get the steaks and check on the beans and corn."

This opened up a lively discussion. It was getting pretty animated when Jo and Ariane drove up.

Jo and Ariane joined the group. Spero was carrying out the steaks to cook. David got up to help, and Spero waived him away.

"Mom, to fill you guys in. Spero posed a question to us," David said and related the question.

Jo and Ariane looked at Spero. He winked and put his finger to his lips so they understood to be quiet.

Jo asked the group, "Have you come to any consensus?"

Jerry said, "These guys have all agreed that belief in Fairies is a separate thing from faith, but I'm not sure I agree." They all started to shout him down again. "No listen, what if something is really power-ful, almost as powerful perhaps as Angels? What if that something is bad? What if these things came from hell and not heaven? Maybe that's why they aren't here anymore."

Ariane couldn't be silent a minute longer. "But they are good, and they **do** help, and the Fairies are here, and they believe in God too. They told me, and I've seen them too." She looked at Spero.

Jeff asked her quietly, "Where have you seen them, Ariane?"

"In my secret place. Peter knows about it too."

Spero asked gently, "After we all eat, will you show all of us the secret place?" He looked at her, and his eyes said "trust me."

Ariane looked at Peter. He didn't look convinced and looked up-set. "I want to talk with Peter first. It was his place first."

"Steaks are ready," Spero said. "I've set the food out buffet style in the kitchen. Let's all get our plates and meet back here while these two talk."

The group walked back to the house. They were still pretty ani-mated, but the prospect of eating was now foremost in their minds. Demy didn't quite know what to do. He kind of held back.

"Ariane, can Demy stay?"

"If you want."

Demy and Peter and Ariane walked a little way into the woods.

"Ariane, did you mean it when you said you had seen the Fairies?" Peter asked gently.

"For reals, guys, you've both actually seen Fairies?" Demy asked.

Ariane answered, "Yes, I have, but I wouldn't have shown anyone the secret tree before because I was afraid that the Fairies would leave and never come back."

Demy asked Peter, "No bull man, you've seen them too?"

Peter looked him in the eye. "Yes, I have, and I agree with Ariane. If we bring a bunch of people there, they'll never come back."

Ariane said simply, "Well, what I said was, '*before*.'"

"And things have changed somehow now?"

"Yes."

"How have they changed?"

"Because now, their world is dying, and there are more on Earth than ever before because this is their home too and besides…" She hesitated and looked gravely at both boys.

"Besides?" Demy prompted.

Ariane took a big breath and was trying to decide how much to say. She decided to be truthful because time was running out. Peter and Demy were looking at her waiting for her to answer.

"Besides…Spero is from there, and he has been looking for humans to help them save their world. If we don't help them, our world will soon be destroyed, too. We'll all die."

The other boys were coming to the firepit with their plates and Demy and Peter looked at each other and were silent, not knowing what to say or do or think.

Demy finally said, "Let's go get our plates."

The three of them filed toward the house silently.

Peter said, "So, I guess we're going to take them to the magic circle?"

"Yes, but just let Spero talk and handle it, ok? I think he can talk to them all so nobody will misunderstand or be afraid."

The group ate everything in sight and everyone agreed that the tomatoes added just that certain something to the thick steaks. David was honestly impressed with the meal. The steaks, having been killed so voraciously, were melt-in-the- mouth tender, and the flavor was out of this world.

Jeff ate about three ears of corn and just kept saying, "I can't believe how good this is." Butter was dripping off his chin.

Jerry handed him a napkin, "Apparently not."

Spero lit a fire, and they were all sitting around the fire after they ate. The boys offered to do dishes, but Jo told them the dishes could wait until later and to just enjoy the evening.

After everyone had gathered around, Ariane surprised them all by standing up suddenly.

"Before Peter and I agree to show you the magic circle and the Fairies and their magic tree, we need to know if you all had agreed that you would help them if they needed it?"

Jerry said, "I can speak for the group and say, they have beaten my logic down. I concede that if creatures that once lived on Earth or live on it now, asked for our help, we would help."

"Good," Ariane smiled. "Ready?"

Ernie looked around, "Ready for what?" Everybody laughed in a nervous or excited way.

"Are you ready to meet the Fairies?" Peter said smiling at them all.

Jo stated, "Before we go traipsing off into the dark woods, we need to bank this fire. And do you guys need to get back home at any special time? Do you need to call your mom?"

Jeff answered, "Let me just call her and tell her we're having a good time, and we'll be home late, ok?"

They all waited for Jeff to call. He told his ma, "We're off to visit Peter's Fairy tree. That is a pretty trusting thing that he wanted to show us, so we'd like to go, if that's all right. We'll be home a little late."

She said she was glad, and she'd see them when she saw them. Jeff told her that Mr. Spero and Jo were coming too.

"That's even better," Bette giggled. "Have a good time. Tell the Fairies hello for me." Jeff was a little surprised at that last comment.

Jeff came back to the group. "Ma says to tell the Fairies hello for her."

Peter and Ariane led the way. It wasn't far from the house. There was a sense of expectation and adventure. It was a full Moon, so it was easy to see where they were going.

Spero stopped dead still…They all stopped and listened and were silent. Spero said softly. "Thought I heard something." He listened for a long time and then he said, "Let's continue on. It was probably a squirrel or something."

Ariane and the group got to the tree circle. The Moon seemed to be shining more brightly there. It was lighter than all the trees around, and the tree in the center of the circle seemed bathed in luminous moonlight.

Peter said, "It's here. Inside those trees."

The group started to move through the pine circle but Spero stopped them. "Before we go in, I wonder if you will do me a favor?"

They all agreed. Spero pulled the Record Keeper out of his vest pocket. He explained what a Record Keeper was.

"One, by one, I would like you to hold this crystal and when it is time, and you'll know when it is time, pass the crystal back to me to pass to the next person."

The Postelwaite boys all figured he was just getting into the spirit of the fantasy adventure so they agreed. Ariane was holding hands with her mom on the way to the circle, and her mom put her arm around her. David came and put his arm around his mom.

Peter asked, "Can I be first?"

Spero said, "You be the man." Spero whispered in Peter's ear, "Don't tell anyone what you see or feel, ok? Let's see how each one reacts."

Peter took the crystal from Spero and held it looking down at the ground for a few minutes. He tried not to respond, but brusquely wiped away a tear, and then handed it back to Spero. Demy saw Spero do something strange, but was pretty sure the rest of the group didn't catch that he had picked up dirt before he took the crystal.

Demy couldn't stand it. "Please let me be next!" Spero whispered the same thing in his ear, and then handed him the crystal. Demy's eyes got really big and he seemed to look off in the distance for a time and then he handed it to Spero.

This was repeated for each of the four brothers. Each time, Spero bathed the crystal in dirt before handing it to another person.

After all of them had held the crystal, Spero asked what they had experienced.

Each one of them said they had felt energy in the crystal and had seen a flash of images that they weren't sure what was, but it was bright and felt good, except that the images in the bright light seemed to be in trouble.

The group was really silent now. They were beginning to understand that this was not a joke.

Spero asked, "Did all of you feel the energy in the crystal and see the images?" They all nodded "yes."

Jo said, "Spero had us all try before and, no, I'm very sorry to say, I did not. I wish I had."

Spero looked at her with sympathy. "Well, I've got you covered though; you hold this." He handed her his Walker Bearer ring.

Spero motioned to Ariane and Peter who was still wearing his aluminum hat, "Lead on!"

The group went through the pines and there in the center of the circle stood a tree bathed in gold shimmery leaves, surrounded by a light much brighter than the Moon.

Spero said, "Hello, my friends. I've bought people to help us. Will you greet them?"

Suddenly, the leaves on the tree came alive. Hundreds of tiny light forms surrounded the group, flitting in and out among them. The group was mesmerized and they stood very still. They didn't feel afraid, they just felt very privileged to be able to see the Fairies. They were about the size of a small baby dragonfly. Their four tiny wings fluttered like dragonflies' wings, and their bodies were various shades of sand and brown earth coloring. They had two arms and two legs.

Fairies' clothing was very colorful and seemed draped in a way that was common to all of them to accommodate their wings, but some had added their own style. The males were draped differently than the females and actually seemed slightly smaller than the females, but their little bodies appeared to be muscular. Their hair looked very fine and delicate, like transparent multi-colored prism cellophane. It seemed to be styled in many ways according to individual styling and some of the styles were rather outrageous. It was apparent that they took pride in their uniqueness. Their eyes were like Spero's. They were deep hues of sea blue, turquoise, green, or brown, but slanted.

They had very long eye lashes, and their eyelashes matched their hair. Their eyebrows went up, like Spero's too. Their noses were almost nonexistent, just tiny protrusions with slits for nostrils, but their mouths were full, and they did seem to have slightly sharp teeth. They seemed very happy to see them all.

Jo was overwhelmed at what she was seeing and was crying. The Fairies grouped around her, obviously trying to comfort her. "Feels like Fairy kisses!" she said quietly.

"That's just what it is," smiled Spero.

Peter, on the other hand, had no Fairies around him. Every once in awhile, one would kind of bump into him and veer off. "Spero, don't they like me?"

Spero laughed, "No, that's not the case. Take off your hat! Remember? They can't see you!"

Peter took off his hat, and the Fairies all flocked to him. They seemed really excited.

"You have performed magic to the magical. You're their star!" Spero laughed. The whole group joined in and the Fairies were laughing too.

There were other things in the circle. It took them awhile to see them because they looked like dust in the air at first. There were tiny pink floating spheres with even smaller light specs that flitted in and out of the pink spheres. The spheres were often grouped in strands that were held together with light filaments.

Jeff noticed them first, "Spero! There is something else here. They have transparent pink around them and light in the middle? I've seen those outside of here! I see them all the time! I always thought it was just dust in my eye because it tracks with the movement of your eyes. It seems like it's there, but not there, transparent but still light within? Kinda with a pink outer ring?"

Spero had tied back his hair and the boys noticed his ears for the first time. They didn't really seem all that surprised. By now they had guessed he wasn't from here.

Spero addressed the group, "Ladies and gentlemen, I'd like to introduce the Lemp, the historians of our world and your world and many worlds. They are around you all of the time, documenting each of your lives, and all of your deeds, and keeping your history, and the history of all the sentient creatures, of all the worlds and dimensions for posterity."

As soon as he said that, they grouped in one big ball so they could be seen better. The closer you looked at the ball, the more you could see that the filaments attached to the next ball forming a three dimensional web or mandala. It was beautiful and very elusive.

"In our world, the Rainbow World, the Lemp may come out of their pink light transports and then they are the same size as us. It is my hope that someday you may see them there because words can't describe how beautiful they are. But here, they may only come out to move from one transport to another quickly. The transports are really like individual cities. They attach to hair follicles and live on each human. There are countless numbers of Lemp, and they are all historians. They communicate psychically in your world, but in our world, they can sing/talk to you and you can hear them. Here on Earth, if you are very open, you can hear them and talk to them, too."

The other Postelwaite boys were silent. Everyone sat down in a circle and the Fairies and Lemp settled down on them and around them.

Ariane said to Peter, "I've only ever seen a few Fairies. I've never seen this many." Peter agreed.

Ariane stood up in the group, and she addressed the Fairies and the Lemp, "Thank you all for trusting us and visiting us. Spero has told us about your world, and we are so sorry. You are welcome here, and we'll do everything in our power to help you all. Won't we?"

She turned to the group and they all agreed unanimously. Then the Fairies grouped in a circle around them, holding tiny hands and they bowed and went back to their tree.

Jo stood up. "By the way, I'd like to introduce you to Spero Zezas, Elf Walker Bearer, shaman, and warrior from the Rainbow World."

Spero stood up and bowed. The group cheered and whistled.

Jo said, "I am blessed to call Spero my best friend. Spero is here for our help. He needs our help to save both of our worlds. Time is running out for them and running out for us. We have to work together. It will take every one of us here and three more people that we must find. I've asked myself why I'm here. I think that I must have been chosen, somehow, to help and support all of you. I've been training for this job all of my life."

Jo looked at her children and smiled. "Ariane and David have been able to remember a lot of the programming you have just received.

They are my children, and I'm only just discovering how gifted they are. Spero is going to help you all tap into your gifts too."

Jo continued. "The Fairies and Lemp and other beings have been with us on Earth, helping us, sacrificing themselves for us, and still people don't see and appreciate them. They are a part of us and have been caretakers of Earth longer than we have been here polluting it."

Jo went on to say, "Do I have to say to keep this confidential among us? Much of the world mocks things they don't see or understand and makes us doubt ourselves, but it is too important that we stay strong and trust." Jo sat down.

Spero stood up and addressed the group."Now, our Ariane has a dream to tell you all about. This dream takes place in a cave. I would like her to relate it to you because it involves all of you." Spero sat and waived over at Ariane.

Ariane had been quietly visiting with her two Fairy friends who were staying close to her. She looked up at Spero, then shyly stood up and told them her dream.

When she was finished, they all looked at each other. Ernie was the first to say, "We go out of our bodies? How do we do that?"

Spero said, "Jo will be able to teach you that. She is better qualified than I to do that."

Demy said, "You said, the cave you see in your dreams has pictures on the walls? What kind of pictures?"

"Stick figures, and hands, and buffalo, and hunters hunting buffalo and deer," Ariane answered.

"There's a cave like that on our property," Demy said. "I can show it to you all tomorrow, if you like. It will still be a full Moon, but it is as dark in there in the day as the night, so it doesn't matter when we go. If you all want to meet at my house in the day or early evening tomorrow? I'm sure it would be ok."

Demy looked at all of the Postelwaites, "My dad and your mom know about it. They spent lots of time in there all the time exploring it when they were kids."

Jo said, "Please talk it over with your parents. Ask if it's ok as long as you have Spero and I as chaperones. I would love to see the cave for history sake if for no other reason, so it's a good excuse. How about at 3:00 tomorrow?"

David looked at her funny, "Don't you have to work, Mom?" Ariane giggled.

"Nope, I have a new lady coming in who started today and will close tomorrow." Jo smiled.

Blake pointed out what everyone else was thinking. "What if we can't find the last three people to complete the circle?"

Spero said, "I have faith in our Miss Ariane. She hasn't missed finding one yet! We'll continue with the training, and Jo and I will fill in the other three when they are found. By the way, who did you hire, Jo?"

Jo looked impish. "Someone I think you all know…." She was being mysterious for drama's sake. "I hired…Sonya Wallace."

David about choked. Ernie was pounding him on the back, and the Fairies all raced excitedly to both of them thinking David was in trouble.

"I'm ok, um thanks, Ernie. Thanks, everyone," David addressed the Fairies.

Spero said, "I know this has been a long and eventful night, but there is one thing that Jo needs to tell you." Jo looked at him quizzically.

"Mantra?" Spero reminded her.

Jo proceeded to explain that the crystal seemed to bring on dreams of the cave in Ariane and that Ariane had gotten lost. She explained how to "cord" from the dream to the astral body in case they happened to have the cave dream. She explained that the energy leaving the body was called "astral projection," and when it is practiced, there is a danger of the body temperature and metabolism dropping. It is important not to travel astrally for too long. Cording serves the purpose of helping the astral body, which travels dimensionally to other places, to find the physical body again.

She said, "A mantra is like a prayer. You could even call it a prayer. It needs to be repeated three times. Once to set the intent, once to send it, and the third time to seal the intent. If you'd rather, instead of repeating it three times, it is acceptable to say, "I repeat this saying the perfect number of times in the perfect way." She repeated the mantra she had given Ariane to them three times and asked them to repeat it back.

Spero asked if they were comfortable doing this, and all of them said that they were. They all practiced the mantra she gave them aloud. When she was comfortable they had it down, she asked them each to promise that they would repeat it every night, without fail, before they went to bed.

Jerry said, "I'll add it to my nightly prayers. Nothing that you told us to say is anything I can find any reason to object to." He looked at his watch and it was 10:00. "Guys, we better head home."

David piped up, "I'll drive you, ok?"

Jeff answered, "Sure, we'd appreciate it." He just wanted to get home as soon as he could and find some private space to think about all of this. It was a lot to digest. Part of it was, too, he had hoped his whole life that what he saw when he was a little kid had really been real, now he knew it was.

Jo gave David her car keys, "David, take the van so there is room for everyone."

Everyone said goodbye to the Fairies and Lemp who were settling down for the night and seemed to be sleepy too.

When the group left the "magic circle," the trees appeared to be normal trees and nothing around them gave away what was within the circle.

Jerry asked, "Spero, if we had not reacted to the crystal, and we walked to the center of that grouping, would we have seen anything?"

"No, probably not, unless you had the absolute faith of a child."

Jo handed Spero back his ring, "Thank you for letting me see." She hugged him. The group walked toward Jo's house and went in under the broken fence.

The boys dispersed into the van, and Spero went to make sure the firepit was cool. Jo and Ariane waved goodbye and went into the house. Spero followed shortly after. Everyone promised to see each other tomorrow at Demy's at 3:00. Demy was to call if that wasn't convenient.

Moments went by, the night grew very quiet and only the crickets could be heard. A shadow crossed by the fence and a man came out slowly from behind a tree.

It was Tazman Khan.

✡

David drove the brothers and Demy back to the Postelwaite place. On the way over, they were all talking at once, in high spirits and enthusiastic about what they had seen. They had a million questions for David. Everybody kept doing reality checks with each other. Yes, they really did see Fairies and Lemp. David explained that the Fairy's world was one-half a dimension off from ours and how some of the Rainbow World's inhabitants had always shown up in the sky. He promised to point them out now that they were open to seeing with "Fairy Sight."

David dropped them off and headed home.

Jeff asked everyone to stay outside for a minute to talk. They all headed for their "talking place" by the coup.

"We need to decide what we're going to tell Ma," Jeff said quietly.

Blake said, "We're not going to tell her anything."

Jeff pointed out, "But she said, 'Tell the Fairies hello for me.'"

"That's just because she was giving lip service to it. I don't think she really believes in Fairies, that just doesn't sound like her," said Jerry.

Ernie pointed out, "We don't really know Ma, not really. We don't know anything about her childhood or what she's like inside, well, other than being Ma, religious and stuff."

"She sounded to me like she did believe in them," Jeff said.

"But what if we all tell her what happened, and she tells us we can't help them? What if she thinks they're evil or bad or something?" Peter was talking softly, but he felt like screaming at them, "As far as I'm concerned, we have to keep it a secret from EVERYBODY! That's what we all agreed to do, isn't it?"

Jeff was usually the go along get along guy. He was so quiet; they really didn't think about him caring about anything one way or another. He had never really expressed an opinion very different than his siblings, so they were very surprised to hear him say, "I think we have to talk to Ma, because I have a feeling she's supposed to be with us. I just have a feeling, the way she said to say hello to the Fairies, that she's met them before."

Peter was adamant. "This is too important, Jeff. We can't be in a position of disobeying her if she tells us to stay away from this. We may be in a position to save Earth! Have any of you thought about that?"

Jerry had been really quiet for a long time. "If Ma understood it was that important, do you honestly think she would tell us not to try to help? Remember, I was the guy you guys had to convince. I didn't believe in Fairies and this stuff AT ALL, and you guys convinced me, and I saw them with my own eyes. I agree with Jeff. We need to be honest with Ma. We owe it to her, don't we?"

"And if she forbids us to do this, we do it anyway?" Peter asked.

The rest of them looked at each other and agreed it was an individual's choice.

"But we can't go thinking that way, what if one, or two of us decide not to do this? Their **world** ends. Our **world** ends!" Peter was almost crying.

"We're not that important," said Ernie.

"We are! We all are! Don't you understand? Weren't you listening? Ariane dreamed us. We are already there doing it." Peter was really getting upset.

Demy was shaking his head "yes."

Ma surprised them all by walking around the chicken coup where they were all talking.

"I'm sorry to have been eavesdropping, boys. I came out to meet you and just kind of got caught here. Let's go inside, I have a very long story to tell you."

She sat them all at the kitchen table. They were all really surprised to see the transformation in the kitchen. Ma had made bright yellow curtains, and there was a green and brown stencil border around the top of the walls that looked magical and woodsy. She had painted the front of the kitchen cabinets yellow with white trim.

"Wow, Ma! This is beautiful!" Jeff exclaimed. The rest of the boys were all ooohing and ahhing too.

"I have to admit that is why I came out. I wanted to catch you before you came in so I could get you all to close your eyes and open them when I said to, so I could enjoy your reaction," Ma said with a smile. "Will you all sit at the kitchen table? Demy this includes you too."

Bette turned out the lights. She had made little shelves for candles and lit the candles for them. There was a lot more oohing and ahhhing going on.

"Now it looks like a magical kingdom, Ma!" Jeff exclaimed.

"Nice intro to the story I want to tell you. It's been a long time since I told you all bedtime stories, huh?" She smiled at them all.

"This is a true story, but I'm going to start it off as all good stories start...."

All of the boys said, "Once upon a time...."

Bette smiled,

"Once upon a time.... there was a lonely twelve-year-old girl named Bette who lived on a cattle ranch. Her family called her 'Bits.' She didn't have any brothers or sisters. She had to be home a lot because her mother was going to have a sister or a brother, but there were serious medical problems, so her mother had to stay in bed in the last few months of her pregnancy. It just so happened that the last few months fell around the time when it was summer vacation, so Bette was stuck at home almost all of the time until Pa could come in from the ranch duties.

She only had one friend, a boy named Marty who had been her very best friend since kindergarten. He used to ride his horse all the way to her house to play with her in her yard where she could keep an ear out for her Ma in case she called. This was the first year they were able to ride their horses wherever they wanted, as long as it was on either one of their families' properties, and as long as Marty took his rifle in case they ran up against a bear...or a troll."

Bette smiled mischievously and the boys all looked at each other in surprise.

"Most of the time they explored Marty's ranch… It was a little bigger than Bette's." All the boys chuckled.

"When Bette's Pa could take over, she and Marty were free to ride their horses and search for the fantasy land they had been looking for since they were itty bitty. They named it 'Prismland.' When they were smaller, and their parents would bring them to each other's house, they were only able to look in their yards, so lots was left to explore. You see, they believed in Fairies and magical kingdoms with beasts that tracked you, and Trolls that guarded the gateways to other Universes, and ugly witches who would eat cha if you weren't careful. They believed in Prismland so strongly that they were convinced that some day they would find it.

One morning, very early, an old man knocked on Bette's door. He asked if there was any work he could do for food. Bette's pa was always kind to strangers and he offered to share his breakfast. All of a sudden, Bette's ma cried out and Bette's pa raced upstairs. She had started hemorrhaging. The doctor warned that if that happened, she needed to get to a hospital fast. The old man helped Pa carry Ma out to the car, and Pa asked if he would watch over his wife while he drove. Pa got in the driver's seat, and I got in the front seat beside him. Pa was driving faster than I ever saw him drive.

The stranger put his hand on my ma's head and closed his eyes and kind of hummed. My pa didn't notice. My ma seemed to quiet down some, and it didn't look like she was hurting as bad. I kept watching them. Ma kept looking at him with tears in her eyes, almost like she knew him and trusted him…like he was an old friend.

He whispered to her, 'Don't worry, you and the baby will be fine.'

She whispered, 'We will now, thank you.'

You see, Ma and Pa had been honest with me saying that I was to check my ma very often to make sure, even if she was asleep, that she wasn't bleeding 'down there.' They told me if she started bleeding that she and the baby could die. We had all worked hard to do everything the doctor told us to do, but there was always this risk.

When Pa got to the hospital, they sent my ma immediately to the emergency room. The old man sat with me while my pa went with her.

There was a grassy area with trees just outside the waiting room door, and the old man asked me if I would like to take a walk, assuring me that we would be able to see my pa through the window if he came back. We went and sat together under a tree. I can remember being so frightened, I could hardly breathe.

The old man said to me, 'Bits, your mom and the baby will be ok.' The way he said it, made me feel like it could really be true.

'How did you know my name was Bits?' I asked him.

'Well, the Fairies told me,' he said.

'My Fairies?'

'Your precise Fairies. They told me about your mom, and I came to see if I could help her. Didn't you ask the Fairies to help you find some way to make your mom ok?'

'Yes, I did…. Did they really ask you to come?'

'Yes, they did. They said that you were very afraid and that your mom and the little baby inside her were in trouble. Fairies know these things you know.'

I looked straight at the old man for a long time. The man had long white hair and the greenest eyes and the longest, blackest eyelashes I ever saw. His eyebrows were also black and went up at the ends."

The boys smiled knowingly at each other. This sounded familiar.

"The more I looked at him, the more I saw that he wasn't really so old, he just had very white hair. His hands were slender, and he wore a very strange ring. It was a gold ring with a iris flower with diamonds and sapphires"

The boys couldn't resist looking at each other and shaking their heads "yes" and smiling.

'Are you an angel, because you don't look like an angel?' I asked.

'No,' he said, 'I'm an Elf. See?' And he showed me his ears. They were pointed."

Peter and Demy put their hands over their mouths. They were trying not to make the guy error of giggling like girls. Jerry shushed them.

'Did you help my mom in the back seat then? I thought I saw you help her,' I asked.

'Yes, I did, and guess what? I'm here to help you too,' he said.

'Help me?'

'Yes, I'm here to give you something to help you find your magical kingdom.'

And he handed me this crystal."

Ma took a bag out of her pocket and inside there was a crystal clear crystal.

"He told me if Ma and the baby ever got into trouble again or if I ever needed him, to just whistle into the crystal, and he would come.

He pulled out a crystal like mine and told me to show him how I whistle, and I whistled for him. He said now his crystal knew my whistle, and he would know to come to me wherever I was, anytime. He told me to only whistle if it were a life or death situation.

I looked up to thank him and he was just gone!"

Bette's eyes were big. She was being so cute, Jeff and Blake were about in tears.

"I went back into the waiting room, and pretty soon Pa came to talk to me. He said Ma and the baby were fine, and the doctors said the bleeding stopped in time, and Ma should be able to come home tomorrow. Pa asked where the old man was, and I told him the story he told me and showed him the crystal.

Pa said something that surprised me. He said that miracles could come in many ways, and he wasn't one to question how they came; he would just always be grateful they did come."

The boys clapped and talked all at once, but Ma shushed them and demanded the floor still.

"Wait boys. Wait for it. This isn't the end of the story, I told you it was a long one." They sat back down and were silent.

"My ma didn't have to be in bed anymore. The doctors said her case was a textbook miracle. So I didn't have to stay home. All that summer Marty and I were able to explore our days away. Marty's dad told us about a cave he had found on their property when he was a boy. He wouldn't tell us where it was, just the general area. We searched and searched and then we finally found it!"

"Demy, do you know the one I'm talking about?" Demy nodded "yes."

"And for sure, it was the entryway to Prismland! We just knew it! We found crystals and tunnels that lead to underground springs and lakes. We spent the whole summer exploring, then something really awful happened."

"Do you know this story, Demy?" she asked. Demy shook his head "no."

"Marty and I went deeper into the cave than we had ever gone. And guess how we didn't get lost? We tied the end of a ball of string to a log in the central cave and let the string play out off the ball as we walked, so we could always follow the string back. We had a whole backpack full of string! We were in an area that had a drop off and the rock was wet and slimy. Marty slipped and fell a long ways down. It was totally dark down there, and I couldn't see him. He didn't answer when I called.

Guess what I did? I got out my crystal and **whistled,** *and then you'll never guess what happened! The Elf appeared beside me in the cave! I hugged him and told him what had happened. I watched him. He was there one minute, and in a flash of light, he was gone the next.*

I heard my Elf friend call me, 'Bits! Go to the main cavern and get the rope that's on the ledge above the six hands and toss it down here.' I followed my string back as fast as I could, gathering it up as I went. I got the rope and realized I didn't know how to get back to where they were! I had gathered up the path back to them! I was frantic and closed my eyes and concentrated as hard as I could, but I couldn't figure out how to get back! I yelled and yelled; they were too far to hear me.

Then I saw a light come into the main cavern. I watched the light come closer and closer. When the light was in the room, I realized, it was Fairy light. My Fairies had come and brought hundreds of their friends with them! One of them, who had the deepest sea blue eyes and always wore turquoise and purple, was the one I had seen off and on my whole life. I was so glad to see them!

I was crying, and they all fluttered around me, kissing me, patting me and consoling me. Then my special friend motioned for me to follow them. They led me back to the Elf and Marty. I started to drop the rope down, but my other friend, who had green, green eyes and liked to dress in yellows and oranges and tied small leaves in her hair, shook her head 'no' and the Fairies flew the rope down gently.

I watched as they carried one end back up to the cave and fastened it to a large rock outcroppin' by working together. The Elf had secured Marty to the rope. He popped up beside me, and the Fairies went down. He pulled Marty up on the rope. The Fairies had surrounded Marty and were protecting him from getting hung up or bumped. Marty was still unconscious but nothing was visibly broken. He was covered in blood. It was shocking how much blood.

I started crying and asked fearfully, 'Is he dead?'

My Elf friend said, 'No, just unconscious. He has a really nasty cut and bump on his head, and he'll have a doozy of a headache, but he'll be fine.'

He carried Marty to the main cave and laid him in the center of a circle the Fairies made that had strange symbols inside. The Fairies gathered inside the circle, and the Elf sat beside Marty. 'Bits, you're going to need to go get help. Marty is likely to be out a while.'

I got on my horse and rode as fast as I dared back to Marty's house. His pa and some ranch hands drove back around the county road to get *him. When they got there, his cut on his head was closed and practically healed. He had a great big bump like an egg. Never saw anything like it! His pa told me later that he was sitting up holding his head talking pretty goofy, something about an old man helping and Fairies kissing him."*

  "THE END"

Ma smiled. She sat back and looked at her boys and Demy, and they were positively speechless.

She giggled at their reaction, and then said, "Guess you figured it out too, huh? It occurs to me that I've met your Mr. Spero before. I kept looking at him and looking at him the other day at the party and couldn't place him."

"Shall we see?" She took out her crystal and whistled.

There was a bright flash of light, and Spero was standing in the kitchen. "Who died?" he said.

He looked around and saw all the boys and Bette. She was smiling from ear to ear.

Spero looked kind of sheepish. "Hello, Bits. I wondered if you'd recognize me."

The boys were going nuts. They were all laughing and pounding Spero on the back. Bette walked over and gave him a big hug. "I never got to thank you…for everything. Sorry to break the rules, but it had to be done," and she hugged him again.

Spero looked at her and looked around at the boys and said, "Well, I'll bet you a dollar to donuts we've found our tenth person." He was smiling from ear to ear. He suddenly looked hopeful, "Do you have any donuts by the way?"

"Would banana bread do instead?" She had just made three loafs. Bette went over and got a huge piece for him and a glass of milk. "You boys are welcome to some if you like!" She didn't have to say that twice. Blake got out glasses and poured the milk. Jeff got out plates and forks. Jerry cut the slices and served them all. They decided to be civilized and sat down with Spero. He was working on his second piece, chewing slowly with his eyes closed, and he was humming.

☆

Tazman Khan

When David got home he parked his mom's van in the garage and went through the mud room. He was really tired and went straight to bed.

Tazman had waited until everyone was fully settled. He heard everything that had been said in the tree grove, and he "ticked" off mentally what he learned. It was as he expected. Spero was a Walker. He learned a few other helpful things too. Spero's ring seemed to give Jo the ability to experience what the others had experienced. This was news. He learned that the cave Ariane dreamed about must be the portal to the place he wanted most to go, Rainbow World. He learned that Ariane dreamed of twelve people astrally projecting themselves through the portal. He learned that they only had nine, so he needed to bide his time until they found a full group and actually attempted the crossover.

He hadn't thought of astral projection as a means to enter the portal. That wouldn't work for him; he needed to be able to take his body for an extended stay. He learned that Rainbow World was indeed in trouble and that many more Fairies and Lemp were visiting Earth than usual. He learned that Spero couldn't see Peter in his aluminum hat. He snickered at this, wondering how he could use this to his advantage.

He had parked his rental car just off a dirt road nearby. He had used some of Genghis' magic incantations to conceal it. The magic was old Druid hocus pocus, a deflection charm. Anyone who neared the car suddenly got an urge to go another way. It came in handy.

The group had all made a date for 3:00 at the Cresenzo Ranch. He decided to go back to the hotel and study the county map he had purchased to familiarize himself with the layout of the ranch and see where the access roads were. He would at least try to place himself in a position to see which direction they all headed. He would check out the local library for known cave locations. It might be just that easy. Probably not.

He decided that he needed a horse. Now where does one get a horse? He had the whole day tomorrow to arrange something. He couldn't think of any better way to access someone else's property on the sly and get away with it. For all he knew, the cave may only be accessible by horseback. He was frustrated with this plan. None of this was really feasible.

Maybe he just needed to use a direct approach.

Tazman went back to his car and traveled back to his hotel, looked around on the Internet for awhile on his laptop and went straight to bed.

He had a plan.

✫

Very Late, Busy Monday, Spero's Lesson

After Spero had eaten almost a whole loaf of banana bread by himself, he told Bette about the properties of the Record Keeper. He pulled it out of his pocket and handed it to her. Just as he had predicted, she reacted to the energy and saw what everyone else had seen, but also saw something they did not.

"What is the dark presence?" she asked. "Just off to the right of the group?"

Spero and the boys all looked at each other. "Did any of you notice such a thing?" asked Spero.

All of the boys indicated that they didn't.

"Well, it is really getting late tonight, and there is a possibility that more of you will come up with more details as we go along. I've been in the cave many times, and Bits spent a fair amount of time there too. Did you ever feel that something was bad there or wrong when you were a child?" Spero asked.

"Quite the contrary, it was always full of light and goodness. It felt almost churchlike to me," Bette said.

Spero shook his head, "I don't know. I'll talk it over with Ariane, Jo, and David tomorrow and ask them to try to figure it out too. Will one of you boys fill your mom in on the mantra and what you learned tonight at the Fairy tree? I'm sure she'd love to hear you tell her about it. I need to get some rest, even us old Elves need our beauty sleep."

Spero stopped himself as he was about to walk out of the door. "Oh, before I go, I have a gift for all of you." Spero reached out and twisted his hand and pulled a velvet bag out of the air. Everybody clapped and he waived his hand in a flourish and did a deep theater bow. He looked over at Bits as he was putting his hand into the bag and said gently to her, "Did you say your old family's name was 'Whistler?'"

She smiled and put her hand over her heart and mouthed, "Thank you."

Spero took out one crystal. "Will one of you get me a pan full of clean dirt?" Jeff raced out and was back in a jiffy. "It's not from the chicken coup, is it?" Spero joked.

Jeff smiled and said, "It's from where we are planting the trees."

"That's a most excellent place to get dirt!" Spero exclaimed. "Bette, may I have a small glass bowl for salt, a clear glass bowl full of water and one of your candles? Let's put these things in the middle of the table."

Spero explained, "The crystals I have in the bag are straight from the earth. They've never been living with anyone, so they need to know what we expect from them. The bowl of salt is the first thing we will use to roll them around in. This washes any residual negativity or the energy from another person if it had been touched before, or if the bag containing it had been touched by another. The crystals in the salt act as energy cleaners and magnifiers for white light, so you're bathing it in white light first.

Every stone is alive and has its own life. They'll need to be treated with respect and cleansed regularly. It's like giving them food to allow them to sit in the Sun and the Moon and to be among the elements that it is made of. Crystals are white light beings, and that means that they need all four elements to stay in good strong working order. Sun which is fire, or the energy from fire, earth, air, and water. Now some colored stones have only one elemental affiliation, some two or three. You'll have to find out what they are, by either asking it and listening for the answer, or by working with a pendulum over it. We'll talk more on that later. But, whatever elements they name are what they need, see?"

Spero continued, "All stone people expend energy every time they do something for you, and it is important to allow them to recuperate their energy before too much more is demanded of them. We all worked with the Record Keeper pretty hard tonight, and believe me, I've thanked it hardily." Every one chuckled. "But I wonder if any of you noticed me doing something before I handed it to someone else tonight?"

Demy popped up, "You picked up dirt each time and kind of washed it."

"Right! Proud of you boy," Spero beamed. "You paid attention! I bathed it in the element of earth to help give back some of the energy it was expending."

"I did something else mentally that you didn't see. I visualized my hand turning as bright as the Sun to give some of my energy to the crystal to help it. On Earth, what is visualized is done. Humans are very powerful beings in this Universe, blessed of God or Spirit whatever name you have for your higher power to have physicality. Because of that, and some other things we'll talk about later, you can extend your power just as easily to a large Universe as to a small rock. You are more powerful than you can possibly imagine. Have you heard the saying, 'What you can imagine you can do?' Well, it's true. Absolutely true. And, you're so blessed to be on Earth! You are so lucky to be able to touch, smell, see, and … EAT!" Spero said as a side comment, "I just LOVE eating!" Everyone cracked up.

Spero got serious again, "OK, to continue, I then asked the crystal, in my head, if it was ok to go on to the next person…and then I listened for its answer. If you do something like this," he rolled his eyes and was silly, "talk to rocks, that is…then trust the answer you hear in your head. If at any point I would have heard a 'no,' we would have needed to stop and test the rest of you later when the stone had recovered, ok?"

"Remember, you are a partner of something so much more ancient than you; it is always to be treated with the utmost respect, got it?" Everyone nodded "yes."

"Everybody with me so far? Are all of you ok with this?" Spero said, "See you need to check things out with people too." Everybody said they were fine.

"I know we're all tired. Ok if they sleep in tomorrow, Bette?"

"I plan to! They can too!" Bette said smiling.

"Do you have two white clean towels, Bette?"

She went and got her special ones from a drawer. "I just re-washed all of these," she assured him.

"Boys, I need you all to wash and dry your hands, please." said Spero. They all crowded around the sink, and there was some silliness associated with trying to wash each other's hands instead.

Spero took around two dozen crystal shards out of his bag. He spread all of them out on one of the towels.

"Each one of these has six sides on at least one end; that's the type of crystal we need for what we're going to do. Those are called 'communicator crystals.' I'd like all of you to just look at the crystals without touching them and decide which crystal feels like it belongs to you. Don't worry if someone else chooses the same one you do, you'll see why."

"Bits, I know you already have one to contact me, but I would like you to choose one so you can tie in with your family and Demy, ok?" Spero said.

Everyone grouped around the crystals and looked them over. "Have you chosen your crystal?" They all nodded "yes."

"Reach for your crystal." Each of the boys chose their own, and no one chose one that someone else did. They all looked surprised!

"I just love it when that happens, and it seems to always happen!" Spero said smiling. "Now go around the table, and rub it around in the salt first. Then rub earth on the crystal, wash the earth off with water, and sort of wave it through the fire. Don't ever put or hold a stone directly in fire. That may harm it. Now, hold the crystal and pretend that you can turn your hand as bright white as the Sun. Do that now." Everyone seemed to be concentrating hard.

"Now, we need to let the crystal know that we would like it to work with us as a communicator. Stones work with us, not for us, remember. Frame this question in your mind and ask the crystal."

Spero interrupted himself, "Bits, you need to ask your crystal if it can be a master crystal for your family."

He continued, "All of you listen for its answer, and if the answer is 'no' don't take it personally; it probably has good reasons. If the answer is 'no,' put the crystal down. Go wash your hands again and choose another crystal." They were all silent for a time, and nobody put their crystal down.

"Good. Good sign. Can you all whistle? They all nodded yes. If you'd rather, you can hum. Just practice the whistle or the hum so you hear it in your head. Do the sound that naturally comes out." Everybody practiced. Jerry did a loud "Whee o wheet." Spero put his fingers in his ears and said loudly, "Whatever's natural." Everybody laughed.

"Now, in turn, whistle into your crystal one at a time, and afterwards touch the six-sided face to your mom's six-sided face. The six-sided face should be on top when you whistle," Spero said.

The boys all whistled or hummed into their crystal and touched Bette's crystal.

"Bette, if they call, you're going to probably feel an energy surge in your crystal, or it might get warm or cold, and then you'll hear a tone either from the crystal itself, or in your head. Trust either one. Close your eyes, and you can visualize which one called. You guys can practice later with your mom so she can learn your signature vibration, but don't overdo it too much. Keep checking for the health of the crystals. This type of communication takes a lot of energy, so cleanse it regularly."

"Oh, and if someone else touches your crystal, bathe it in sea salt or salt water to cleanse the foreign energy from it. Communicator crystals are unique only to one person, and only one person should touch them."

Now, if it's a matter of life and death, Bette has your whistles and hums, but as she can't disassemble and reassemble, she'll need to whistle for me on her communicator, and I'll come.

"Remember to take care of your crystals." He picked up the rest and put them in his bag. "See you around 2:30 tomorrow here?"

He opened the screen door and walked out the door and started walking home.

Ernie opened the back screen door and yelled, "Hey Spero, aren't you going to give us a great exit?"

"OK!" He wiggled his bottom at them and did a little happy dance and kept walking home.

"I'm really getting too old for these late nights," Spero thought and wondered if the Fairies would like company for the night in the tree house under the stars.

Chapter Six
Tuesday

☆

Tazman Khan

Tazman got up early and carefully dressed in college professor type clothes. He laughed at himself, realizing this was actually his normal attire. He stopped at a "Mart" on Dell Range, purchased a weak pair of reading glasses, aluminum foil, a cowboy hat, two flashlights, two cameras and film, and an artist drawing pad. Then he got into his rental and drove straight up to the Cresenzo property. With every confidence, he drove into the complex and parked. He walked up to the main house and knocked on the door.

Martin Cresenzo answered. "Can I help you?"

"I hope so. My name is Professor Mamut Sinkh. I'm working on my doctorate thesis on the cultural development of written language, and I'm studying the Plains Indians. I'm very interested in gathering data on any written hieroglyphics they may have left. I realize there is not a lot of evidence around this area. I've seen what the museum has to offer. Quite frankly, I'm having trouble substantiating my theories but I have heard there is a cave on your property that may shed some light for my research? Is there such a cave?"

Martin knew that quite a few people knew about it, but he really wasn't interested in it becoming common knowledge. "The cave is on my family's land. It isn't public domain."

"I can understand that you don't want it to be violated by those who don't understand the treasure you have in the historical informa- tion it may contain. I assure you, if you could allow me to just pho- tograph the hieroglyphics, I can keep the location very general and not disclose the location in my book. I would be very willing to sign something to that effect. If you don't want it to be photographed, I would certainly be willing to pay you just to have the privilege of **see- ing** it and making some drawings."

"What kind of payment are you thinking about?" Marty always got more interested when someone talked dollars.

"Would $1000.00 for the photo rights be acceptable? I can call my attorney, and he can draw up the agreement. I can leave the film cartridges until the agreement is all signed and sealed, if you like."

Marty looked at him. He really didn't know what to think, but part of him felt guilty. He had always felt that history belonged to eve- ryone, but he just didn't want to deal with everyone. "I'll have **my** attorney draw up the agreement. When did you want to see it? It's accessible by horseback. Can you ride?"

"Yes, I was raised around horses too. I wonder if it would be too much of an imposition to see the property today? I flew in for just a few days, and I have to fly back out this evening," Tazman lied.

"I think that can be arranged," Marty said. "Did you come pre- pared to pay today?"

"Yes, of course." Tazman pulled out a slender brown wallet and gave him ten $100 bills. "Here is the address to mail the contract. I'll mail it back, and you can send my film on. Would that be agreeable?" Tazman gave him a bogus address to a copy store that he had looked up on the Internet last night.

Martin stuck the bills and address in his pocket. "Give me a mo- ment to get my boots on."

Tazman waited patiently. In a few minutes, Martin joined him.

They walked to the barn, and Martin excused himself for a few minutes and left "Mamut" outside the barn. Martin privately took one of his ranch hands aside and said softly, "Jock, this dandy wants to take some pictures in the cave. Why don't you take him and let him take whatever shots he wants in the main cavern. Tell him we've explored the cave, and there are no other drawings anywhere else. Don't let him go much further than ten yards in any direction down the side passages. I can't have him falling down breaking his danged neck or getting lost in there. You stick with him."

Jock started to walk off, and Marty stopped him. "Oh, I've arranged to keep his film until he signs an agreement to keep the location hush-hush, so make sure you get his film straight out of the camera as soon as he's done shooting. Watch him remove it, I mean it." Martin looked Jock in the eye, and Jock could tell he meant business. "Saddle up Rae for him, please."

He walked back to the Professor. "Jock here will take you out there. Rae's a good horse, she probably won't buck you off. " It took a few minutes to saddle up, and then the two were ready to go.

Tazman was being escorted to the cave, slick as you please. It was well worth $1000.00.

Jock took the lead, "If you'll keep to my tail here, I'll take you the easiest way I know. Some rocky patches here and there, but besides that it will be easy going."

Tazman kept up an easy conversation. "Does Mr. Cresenzo own all this land around here?"

"Most of what you see in every direction. Forestry has some access roads that butt up against the north end where we're going, but to get into the area round the cave, it's best to ride in," Jock explained.

They rode around in silence for awhile before Tazman spoke again. "Do you guys get a lot of looky-loos around here?"

"No, the dude ranch up by Granite leads a trail not far from here, but nowhere near the cave. It's pretty quiet out here. We're not running the cattle in this area now, so we don't get much company." Jock looked back over his shoulder and smiled.

After about thirty minutes, they reached a wooded area, and Jock pulled up. "We're here."

Tazman could not see the cave entrance. "Where?"

"You'll appreciate what I'm about to show you. I'm pretty sure if Martin's dad hadn't found it when he was a kid that nobody would have ever guessed it was here to this day."

Jock dismounted and attached the reins to a nearby aspen and Tazman did the same. He would have **never** found it if he had not been shown the way. The entrance was hidden by a slab of granite that blended in perfectly with the walls around. You had to walk behind the granite slab at an angle to get to the entrance. It looked like a solid wall from visible directions.

Jock lit a torch that was wedged in the wall. "The old way is still the best way."

"Can I get a picture of that?" Tazman asked. Jock held the torch out, and Tazman shot a few pictures. "What is it made of?"

"Mullein stalks and natural fiber strips soaked in tallow. There's a real art to making them. Martin's dad, George Cresenzo, used to be a real nut for researching this stuff too. He played around with these torches using an old one they found in the cave until he figured out how they did it."

"Did he write anything for any journals on this kind of research. It's really important!" Tazman tried to sound as nerdy as he could.

"Doubt that," Jock smiled.

They walked around a few turns here and there, and there were passages leading off in several directions. "Where do these go?" Tazman asked.

"This cave system is really vast, but most of the side passages don't go far. They were probably used for storage. You get to the main cavern where them paintings are this way."

Whenever there was a choice for a turn, Tazman noted that he followed the largest passage. They traveled on a very well worn path for a hundred yards, he guessed.

Jock stopped once and lit up another torch and handed it to Tazman. "Here, it's easier to see with one of these, and this one's about out."

They made a right hand turn. Tazman was not prepared for what he saw. The vastness of the main cave literally took Tazman's breath away.

"I never, in a million years, supposed there was something like this here. I can't tell you how exciting this is." Tazman was genuinely very impressed. He took two rolls of shots. Jock wouldn't let him shoot any with him in it.

Tazman asked if he could look down one of the side passages to the main cavern.

Jock apologized, "No sir, I'm right sorry. These all go deeper down, and there's some treacherous drops. Martin told me not to let you get into danger. This big cavern is the only one we've found with pictures in it, anyway."

"Understandable. Wouldn't ask you to disobey the boss. I have more information than I ever hoped to get. I'll have you to thank for helping me prove my theories for my doctorate thesis." Tazman smiled as he was taking out the roll of film and handed both rolls he had shot to Jock. Jock put them in his shirt pocket.

Jock headed back toward the horses, and they mounted up for the ride back.

"Would you mind taking me a different route home? I'm a pretty good rider, and I'd sure like to see some different views of this beautiful country," Tazman asked.

"I noticed you sat a horse pretty well. There's a trail that cuts a way into public land up here and then pops back along the ridge there," he pointed. "It's actually shorter going back, just a little more climbin'. I think you can handle it."

"Lead on, my man! What a wonderful adventure!" Tazman smiled widely.

In a very short period of time, Tazman saw the county road he was hoping to find. Bingo. He had it made. He could drive in to that point and walk in from there. So horseback wasn't the only way to get there. Old man Cresenzo was pretty sharp. He wouldn't appreciate Jock showing him this.

Tazman and Jock got back to the barn, and Tazman dismounted. "Thanks for your time. Can I pay you for it?"

"No, that's fine. I enjoyed seeing the cave again too." Jock tipped his hat, "You have a nice day. I'll give the film to Mr. Cresenzo. Did you leave an address or phone number with him?"

Tazman said, "He has a copy."

☆

Bette Postelwaite

The Postelwaite household plus one slept in. Bette was the first to wake up about 11:00. She started a pot of coffee and opened the kitchen door. She sat at the kitchen table and just admired her handiwork. She had kept herself so busy that she really didn't have time to think of much. Her marriage had ended abruptly, but she was beginning to realize that any tender feelings she had for Nels had died many years ago. She felt like she was coming out of a black cloud into the light. She was remembering herself. The self she was before she was Mrs. Nels Postelwaite. She was bits of "Bits" and enjoyed the reacquaintance. Eavesdropping on her boys, she saw herself in their eyes. Ernie had said it best; they really didn't know her at all. She didn't know herself, but she was starting to find herself again. This would be a long process.

She worried that Nels might get out of jail and do something drastic. She had requested and been granted a restraining order, but that wouldn't stop Nels. She would have to figure out what to do to protect her property and family.

She called the attorney that Martin had referred her to and set up an appointment to talk to him about filing for divorce. She needed to find out if the pre-nuptial property agreement would stand up in court. The Sheriff had called and told her that Nels had accepted the money for the truck and flatbed and had signed off on the titles. That was good news. The Sheriff also told her that Nels would be held without bond until his trial due to his recent threats to one of the deputies and the fact he had been overheard threatening his family's lives. Maybe the time in jail would help to calm his temper, she told herself, but she doubted it. Knowing Nels, he would have to have payback somehow.

She was so totally tired of being afraid. She wasn't even with Nels, and she had to be afraid of him. Even the prospect of surviving on the income the boys could generate wasn't as intimidating as having to ever see or deal with Nels again. She was sure they would make it somehow. She'd get her thinking cap on. Nels had really not contributed much in their marriage. She'd always scrimped by somehow. It had always been a struggle.

Spero must have picked up how frightened she was for her family. She appreciated more than he could possibly know that she had some means to watch out for them. Just knowing she would have Spero's help if something went wrong made her feel easier. Well, what could be better than the help of an Elf?

She realized it was getting late, and Demy hadn't asked if they could all visit the cave. She was torn in what she should say to Martin about the work they would be doing with Spero. It felt to her like he should be a part of it somehow.

She picked up the phone and dialed the Cresenzos.

Marty's wife, Lynne, answered, "Lynne here. Spit it out!"

"Lynne. Hi. This is Bette. The boys are still sleeping, but I wondered if it would be possible to show them the cave and spend some time there. Jo Vanderlin and her kids and her friend Spero have asked to join in. Demy is anxious to show them."

"I'm sure that would be fine, what time?" Lynne asked.

"How about 3:00?" Bette asked.

"That's fine. How are you going to go in? Do you need mounts?" Lynne wondered.

"I think we'll just take the county road and walk in, if that's ok? Then it won't be such a hassle for you guys."

"I'm happy to see you getting out and having fun. I don't have to tell you to keep them from breaking their heads up there, do I?" Lynne teased.

"Only one hard head ever got broke that I know of. What is the hard head up to?" Bette laughed.

"He got up really early before I did; I'm not sure what he's up to." Lynne said.

"Lynne, I'm not sure how long we'll be, but Demy is in good hands. I would like to talk to both of you, though, when you get a chance. Maybe sometime this weekend?" Bette said.

"Anytime. Have I told you lately how glad we are to have you back in our lives? Now, how many wives could say that when their husbands refer to another woman as their first best girl?" Lynne teased.

"He usually says it, his first "Bits" girl. Didn't you ever notith the listhp?" Bette laughed.

"There's that laugh, I remember. Welcome back, my friend," Lynne said affectionately.

"I can't begin to tell you how happy I am to be back. Feels like I just came out of a coma. I keep waiting for it to be a dream!" Bette confided.

"It's going to take time and then one day you'll look in the mirror and see a whole different girl," Lynne said.

"I'm starting to see parts of her every day. You'll have to come over and see what I've done to the kitchen! It's a radical change! We'll drive Demy back home this evening, I would guess by 9:00 at the latest. Talk to you later, ok?"

"Sure thing." Lynn hung up.

Bette started cooking bacon. That would get the boys up.

✲

Marty Cresenzo

Marty Cresenzo was no fool. Something about that professor guy just didn't gel. He just had an uneasy gut feeling. He decided to use his cell to call Jim Riggs at the Sheriff's department

"Jim, Martin Cresenzo here. I wonder if you can do me a favor? I just had a guy snooping the cave. I've got a real bad feeling about him. He gave me a $1000.00 just to take pictures of the drawings up there. When he pulled out his wallet, there was no identification, no credit cards, pictures, nothing. I have an address for him, can you run it and see if he's legit?"

"Sure, but all I can tell you is whether or not his name is attached to the address. What's his name?

Marty started to tell him Mamut Sinkh, but when he looked at the piece of paper it said, Memnon Singh. "I just realized, looking at the piece of paper he gave me, that he gave me two different names." He gave both names to the sheriff and the address.

"It'll just take me a minute. Hang on." Jim said.

While Marty was waiting, he was processing. What on earth did the guy want? It isn't like he could steal the paintings off the wall. He had gone to a lot of trouble just to see the cave.

"I'm back, Marty. No, that address is a business address. Nothing comes up under either one of those names. Do you need me to come out?"

"No, he just left. He left two rolls of film here. This just doesn't make sense. Thanks, Jim. I owe ya." Martin hung up the phone.

He went out to the barn. "Jock, can I talk to you a minute?"

"Sure boss."

What did you think of that guy?"

"Nice enough guy, rides a horse like he was born on one. That seemed a little strange for a nerdy professor, I thought," replied Jock.

"What did you guys talk about?"

"He didn't talk much. He asked if there were many looky-loos around and asked me if he could look around some of the side passages, but I didn't let him, boss, don't worry!"

Jock added, "Oh, and he asked if I could take him back a different route so he could see some more scenery."

"So you showed him the shortcut?"

"Yeah, did I do wrong, boss?" Jock looked a little worried.

"Well, just for future reference, if we ever take strangers to the cave again, I don't want them knowing they can access it from the forestry road on foot. They might go back and vandalize it or hide drugs in it or something," Marty explained.

"Man, I'm sorry. I never even thought about someone doing something like that. Is that all you needed, boss?"

"Yes, Jock. Thanks. You can go back to doing what you were doing."

Marty had decided that the whole thing was trumped up to figure out how to access the cave from a road. "Wonder what the guy is up to?" he said aloud.

It was about 2:00. Marty decided to see if the guy drove back around and went back in. He saddled up his horse, Ornery, and took the shortcut back. He didn't see any cars around, but decided to wait. He didn't have to wait long. Mamut or Memnon or whatever his name was, just drove up. He took time to park so that the car was not readily visible from the road. Then he took some weird stuff out of his car, a roll of aluminum foil, a cowboy hat, and two flash lights.

"What on Earth?" Martin said to himself.

The guy didn't waste two seconds; he went straight to the cave and went in. "Dang," he said aloud. He should have brought a flashlight himself, but he knew that cave like the back of his hand. If the dang fool was going to go get himself dropped off a slimy ledge in there, he'd have to rot.

Marty placed himself out of view of the road and the cave. He dismounted and tethered his horse to a nearby rock. He went into the dark cave trusting that he would be able to keep hidden by the darkness. The guy went straight into the large cavern and a little ways into the smaller passages to the right. Marty knew that those didn't go anywhere. The guy briefly looked around the other legs leading out of the large cavern and apparently opted for a small niche to the right of the main room that was a little hard to get in and out of.

The guy sat on the floor and covered his hat with aluminum foil, just like Peter does.

"What the hell?" Marty whispered under his breath. The guy then proceeded to wrap aluminum foil around some of the out juts of rocks inside the small enclosure. While he was busy doing that, Marty took the opportunity to position himself where he could watch the guy better. He went up a side leg to the left of the cavern that he knew took him up to a small area that was probably used by the medicine men as a voice amplifier. Whenever you spoke in there, it echoed through the whole cavern like a sound system. The room had a small opening that served like a viewing window where he could see, but not be seen.

The guy positioned himself in his small area and didn't come out from there. Martin sat and waited too.

They didn't have long to wait. He heard a lot of voices of adults and kids making oohhhing and ahhhing noises.

"Oh no!" he thought. He stood up, ready to move fast in case the guy meant harm. He immediately recognized the group. It was Demy and the Postelwaite clan and that gal and her family who lived next door to the Postelwaites. He didn't remember her name. There was also a gentleman who looked vaguely familiar. The old guy that the gal had bought to the Christmas Tree Party. He had meant to get over there at the party and talk to them all but didn't quite make it. The teenage boys seemed to be enjoying the old guy's company, so he decided just to let them have their fun.

The old guy looked straight up where he was standing, just like he was looking him in the eye. "Who is that guy? I know I know him," Marty thought to himself. He backed a little further into his small area.

Bette was with them. She was looking better. She spoke, "Demy, your dad and I spent lots of wonderful days in here."

She addressed the rest of the group. "If you're all curious where all these legs out of here go, most of them don't go very far back before they end in a wall of some sort. But these two here, go deep into the system. You all have to promise me not to explore down there without Marty, Demy, or me, to help guide you."

She addressed Demy again. "When I think of some of the things your dad and I did, it's pretty scary. We used to tie an end of a ball of string to that old log and trust we could find our way back by following the string back."

"Hey mom, that's like 'cording' only with real string," Blake said. Everybody laughed.

"Cording? What on Earth are they talking about?" thought Marty.

Spero spoke. "We're not alone." Everyone looked around.

Spero raised his voice, "Would you like to come out?"

The game was up, Marty thought, and started to move down to the group. Suddenly the man in the aluminum hat stepped out of his enclosure.

Everyone gasped when they saw the man holding an aluminum covered hat. Jo recognized him immediately, and David and Ariane guessed who he was too.

"I thought you couldn't see with aluminum, Spero," Tazman said.

Spero was genuinely shocked to see Tazman. He looked up towards Marty and said clearly, "Anybody else want to come out?"

Marty said, "No, not really." The sound echoed throughout the cave and everyone jumped. He came down the ledge and joined the group.

"Does someone want to tell me what the Sam Hill is going on around here?" Mary exclaimed.

Spero looked at Tazman and spoke first. "Everyone, I would like to introduce you to Tazman Khan. Descendant of Genghis Khan and Sherlock Holmes, apparently."

Tazman didn't look the slightest bit embarrassed at being found out.

"Are we having a party?" he asked.

Marty's patience was wearing thin. "You all know this guy?"

Spero looked deeply at Marty for the first time. "Oh yes, he and I go way back, and so do you and I. Remember?"

Marty looked at Bette, and she nodded "yes."

"Well, I'll be." Marty smiled widely and crossed over to shake Spero's hand. "Never got a chance to thank you for saving my life."

✫

The Twelve

Ariane had been trying for some time to get Jo's attention by tugging on her arm. "What *is* it, Ariane?" Her mom sounded a little annoyed.

Ariane spoke up. "Excuse me, everybody, can I talk?"

She pointed to Tazman and Martin. "Both of these men belong in the circle. That's our twelve."

This time Spero looked shocked. "Ariane, are you sure?"

"Yes."

Spero scratched his head and spoke, "I admit, I'm flummoxed. I'm speechless. I don't know where to go from here."

"Well, I guess we better declare a truce and pow-wow," said Bette.

Tazman seemed reticent so did Spero. They both rather squared off and stood there glaring at each other.

"I knew what you were doing all along, *ELF*. You are an Elf, I know that now." Tazman fairly spat out these words.

"Well, so are you, partially, aren't you?" said David directing his question to Tazman.

"Mr. Khan?" Ariane asked quietly, "Do you really want to die?"

"Excuse me, young lady?" Tazman turned and faced her. "What are you talking about?"

"The only way for you to get back home is with us. If you steal back the crystal and try to go anywhere with it like Spero does, you'll just die. The crystal can't go back. The Rainbow World is in danger, and it is meant to survive the danger. The crystals to the other worlds and dimensions have gone back to their home planet or dimension, didn't you know that?"

He was taken aback by what she said. He turned to Spero, "Who is this kid?" asked Tazman.

Spero came and put his arm around her. "Her name is Ariane Selph, and she is one of the human Record Keepers for the Rainbow World. She is one of the rightful heirs to the Record Keeper, not you or me."

Tazman just looked darkly at everyone. "What is it you think YOU PEOPLE are going to accomplish here?"

"Why, Mr. Khan, that should be evident," said Spero. " We're here to save you from yourself, and if we can save a couple of worlds while we're at it, we're going to try to do that. Are you in?"

He looked around at them for a long time before he answered. "Better in than out," he said. At least if he went along, he could assess things for himself.

"Shake," said Ariane, and held out her hand to Tazman.

When Tazman took her hand he felt a jolt of energy even stronger than he felt the first time he held the crystal. He saw, again, the circle of people…these people, astrally projecting. He saw the rush of images of the light beings he saw as a child. But this time he saw something else, too. He saw his ancestor Genghis Khan in among the flash of images. He held onto his head like it was going to explode and heard clearly, in his head, a voice that said, "Take me home." He dropped to the ground in pain and rocked. Ariane patted him and said, "See, you belong with us."

He still had his head in his hands and said in a muffled voice, "I'm in."

Spero offered the crystal to Marty, "Let's get you up to speed." Marty took the crystal from him and looked far away.

"Prismland!" he whispered and looked at Bette with tears in his eyes.

As soon as the images stopped, he walked over to Bette and hugged her and whispered, "It took us a lifetime, Bits, but we're going to get to see it, aren't we?"

She whispered back, "Did you ever doubt it for one minute?"

Demy was visibly moved with his father's tears. He came over to his dad and put his arms around him too. "I'm really glad the crystal chose you too, Dad!"

Spero and the group had given them all a few minutes of privacy. They got busy bringing in the wood Jo had in the back of her van to start a fire. They chose the exact center of the main cave where there was an ancient fire pit for the fire. But, before the fire was laid, Spero stood in the middle of the fire pit. He took a string from his pocket and stood at the center of the fire pit holding one end and handed the other end and a piece of chalk to David.

"David, go out to the end of the string and walk in a circle around me." The radius was about 8 feet. "Mark a cross with the chalk every so often to put the rocks around. We want twelve rocks around, so every few steps make a mark. We'll position them finally after we get the initial circle marked."

Spero had them gather twenty-four large stones about hand size and put them off to the side. Spero was a little surprised to see Tazman joining in the stone gathering.

Spero said, "Now, let's get a fire going here where I was standing. It'll be nice to be able to see, and it will certainly warm this place up a bit."

Blake and Ernie Postelwaite took over the fire task, and in short order they had a good size fire going. The cave was so vast, the light generated only lit up part of it. It felt like they were enclosed in a bubble of light in a vast black space.

Spero walked around the inside of the circle and had David place marks here and there. From experience, David knew that he was structuring a Star of David inside the circle.

Ariane was watching and once in a while she would say, "No, Spero, move the line just slightly that way." Spero would always just smile and do exactly what she said.

The rock gathering was complete, and they were ready to build the circle. "Ariane, do you have an idea how exactly you want the circle to be built?" Spero asked.

Ariane said, "I only know what feels right; I'm not absolutely sure."

Spero said, "Are we so far going in the right direction with what we've done?"

"Yes," she replied.

"Then if it's ok, I'll build it the way we were taught and you can fine tune the design, ok?" Spero asked.

"That sounds fine," Ariane replied.

Spero explained, "This is how we build the structure that Walker's work in for healing and for divination. The stones are always placed clockwise on the outer ring, first with the north stone, then east, then south, then west. Then the ordinate points in between each of the four starting with the Northeast. That puts twelve stones in the outer circle."

Ariane couldn't help but to think of the little numerologist always saying, "3, 4, 6, 8, 9 12= 1 +2 = 3." Maybe she should have listened more.

The Star of David had been chalked in by David and Spero.

"At the points where the lines intersect, we place the other six stones." Everyone looked at the design. In places where people would be sitting there were either 4 stones or 3 stones surrounding them. Everyone noticed there were stones left over.

Spero said, "When I was visiting the Postelwaites the other night," everyone chuckled, "I told them that stone people have to be willing to do the job that is requested of them. Because we need to be able to talk to them all and hear them all; I'm going to ask the Record Keeper to help."

Tazman drew in his breath when he saw the Record Keeper after all the years he had been searching for it.

Spero took out a string and tied it to the Record Keeper snuggly. He said, "I'm going to say aloud what I usually just think, so we can all track. Please move in a direction that means 'yes.'" The Record Keeper went back and forth. "Please move in a direction that means 'no.'" The Record Keeper twisted slightly. "Please move in a direction that means 'I don't know or I can't answer.'" It just held still. Ariane caught David's eyes, and they smiled at each other.

"Would each of the twelve of you place yourselves where you think you should go? If two people think they should go in the same place, just stand there together and the crystal will advise." The group that had been at the Postelwaites caught each other's eyes and smiled. Everyone walked to their own place and nobody doubled up. Jo stood back and watched.

Spero walked around the circle working with the crystal as a pendulum over the stones, and the crystal and stones communicated. Some of the stones did not want to participate, and they were replaced by stones that the crystal said "yes" over for each spot. Some wanted to participate, but wanted to be turned slightly, some wanted to be placed in another part of the circle. Everyone watched as Spero explained exactly what was going on.

Spero asked, "Ariane are we good?"

She answered, "We'll find out for sure when you step into the star."

Spero handed Ariane the crystal and took his place. As soon as the star was complete, the group felt the structure come alive. It was a veritable birth of energy that flowed over everyone. Ariane smiled and said, "I guess we got it right!" Everyone laughed.

"Hope nobody has to go to the bathroom for awhile," Spero joked. It lightened the mood.

"What do we do now?" Martin asked.

"We need to set some ground rules," Spero answered. "Nobody can leave the circle while we're working, especially if we are in astral travel, agreed? Jo, you are our facilitator, and if someone violates this you must step in and fill the void, understood?"

She answered, "Yes."

"Jo will you go over the safety rules for astral travel?" Spero asked.

"Happy to. I told some of the group part of this already, so please bear with me." She explained to the whole group what she had already told the Fairy circle group.

Then she went on to elaborate, "I've done some additional research, and it is found that you can only be safely out of your body one-half hour at a time before you must return for the health of your body. That doesn't seem like a lot of time, but Spero tells me that time is not linear, so time may flow differently where you're going. Spero says that every crystal except the Rainbow World Record Keeper crystal may cross over with you, so he has devised this crystal for me to use as a Master crystal to yours so that I can notify you when to come back. If you get into trouble, whistle, and mine will react. I will do what I can do to help."

She interrupted herself, "Marty and Tazman don't have crystals, Spero." Spero did his twisted hand bit and pulled the communicators from the air. Everyone clapped again. Marty's and Tazman's eyes about popped out of their heads seeing something like that for the first time.

Marty was on one side of Spero and Tazman on the other. Spero chuckled that these things seem to happen in the universe. Spero laid out six crystals on either side of him. "Please just look at them, and then choose one." Tazman and Marty scooted over and chose.

He explained what they needed to do as he had explained to the Postelwaite's late night party. Jeff had a bottle of water, so it was passed clock wise until it reached both Marty and Tazman. After he explained that they needed to get the crystals' permission and the crystals agreed, Spero put the rest back.

Spero asked the two of them to practice the whistle or hum they would use. In this case, Jo walked over with hers, and they touched communicators together. Spero explained that everyone else would need to do their whistle or hum and do the same. Jo walked around the circle and touched everyone's communicator to hers. Bette's master communicator would still respond to her children and Demy, so that had not changed, it just happened that now, Bette's whistle would react also on Jo's master crystal.

"I'm sorry to ask for this extra time, but I need to make sure I have everyone and can pick each of you up. I'm going in the other room. Would each of you do your thing, and I'll yell if I can feel it and guess who it is? Yell at me if I get it wrong and tell me who you are, ok? I bet I'll know which one is Jerry!" Everyone laughed.

Martin suggested that she go in the amplifier room so she would be safe, and they could all hear her.

"Good suggestion! Thanks!" Jo got a flashlight and headed in that direction.

Spero whispered, "I'll start and point, then after you whistle, point to someone else so there's no pattern, ok?"

The group did as he asked, and there was a lot of silliness going on. Jo got most of them right. "One more time, please," she asked. "This is important." Her voice sounded like it was in their chests, it was so loud.

They repeated the maneuver, and this time she got them all right. "I think I've got it!" Her loud enthusiasm just about blew their eardrums out.

Everyone covered their ears and Spero yelled, "Come back down!" When Jo rejoined the group, Spero suggested if she was ever up there again, she should talk in a conversational voice, instead of yell. Everyone laughed at her embarrassment.

Jeff asked, "How did you hear us, how did it work?"

She said, as she was rubbing her crystal in some earth, "In stereo. I heard you with my ears, and it was like the crystal was a little transistor radio playing the tone softly. It got warm first, and then I heard you."

Jeff asked, "How will we hear you?"

Spero said, "Let's experiment. Jo, go somewhere else." Everybody chuckled. "Go where we can't hear you in stereo and whistle into yours."

He addressed the group, "Your crystals all are unique and may not react like hers did so be aware of warmth, coldness, vibration or tones. Maybe they'll blow raspberries, I don't know!" Everyone laughed, and even Tazman almost smiled. Everyone scattered to a more private place.

Jo walked the hundred yards outside of the cave and whistled into her crystal.

Everyone reunited.

As Spero said, everyone's crystal reacted a little differently, but they could either feel it vibrate, emit energy, get hot in their hands, and/or they heard the tone. Some heard it plainly in their head, and others heard it in their crystals. They were all animated, telling each other what they felt and telling each other they didn't hear one raspberry. Darn.

Jo walked back in, "Were we successful?" Everyone indicated "yes."

Jo said, "Well are we ready to try to practice astral projection together? Ariane are you ready?"

Ariane was looking at the Record Keeper. "I'm not sure where this should be; it can't pass over to the Rainbow World, but it needs to be here to help. Any ideas?"

Tazman spoke up, "I could hold it for you." They all cracked up and this time he did smile.

Jo caught the smile and could feel her face flushing. She said under her breath, "Oh boy, that is a beautiful man."

David spoke softly, "Spero, do you think Ariane could carry the crystal up to the door to the Rainbow World, and then could she drop it or take it off before we actually go through astrally?"

Spero pondered that. "How could that be set up?"

"Well, I have an idea. We're just practicing today, right? Not going all the way there?"

Spero answered, "Right."

"By the next time we meet, I'll have my idea ready to show you."

Spero said, "For now, Ariane, just place it in the dirt before you."

Jo said, "We need to keep your physical bodies as comfortable and warm as possible. Next time we'll bring blankets to wrap up in. Here are some logs to build up the fire so it stays warm. Spero, does anything entering the circle need to come to your position first?" He nodded, "yes." She handed the logs to Spero at the North, and he sent them around clockwise. People shifted to the fire pit to place the logs where they were needed.

Spero instructed. "Please resume your places and sit as you all saw yourself sit in the images you saw." They all sat with their legs crossed in front of them. "Is everybody ready?"

They all replied, "Yes."

Jo did a visualization to put them in a relaxed, meditative state. When they were all relaxed, they all dropped their heads as instructed. She had them visualize a light cord running from their belly button, and then had them visualize the light body they had seen in the images they saw above them. She asked them to attach the light cord from their body to their astral body. She instructed them to move energy from the physical body through the light umbilical cord into the light body until they were floating above themselves, looking down. She asked David separately that when he established his astral body, to have it whistle into his crystal to make sure she could hear him. After a time, she heard his whistle, and his body had not moved.

She spoke aloud to the whole group, "Good, good. I could hear David's whistle. I'll give you all five minutes. Stay in the group together, and do not stray further than the group. In five minutes, I'll whistle into my master crystal. When I whistle, move the energy from the astral body down the cord toward your body. The cord will become shorter and shorter until your astral body merges into your physical body. 1, 2, 3. The five minutes has begun." She walked around the circle making sure nobody's breathing was impaired or no visible struggling was going on, and she watched her stop watch.

After five minutes, she whistled. In a few minutes more, everyone started waking up and moving around within their area. Some moved a few inches closer to the fire and just warmed their hands. "Everyone ok? Was everyone able to move into their astral body?" They all indicated "yes" and began to get animated again.

They soon realized, though, that something was horribly wrong. Spero had not moved. His head was still dropped, and he was visibly struggling. His solid body seemed to be fading.

"Mom! Mom! Help Spero!" Ariane cried. The group started shifting toward him.

"EVERYONE, STAY IN YOUR PLACE!" Jo yelled.

"Did any of you notice anything when you were up there?" Jo asked.

Bette had been hugging herself and rocking.

Marty said, "Bits! Snap out of it, what's wrong?"

Bette whispered, "The darkness got him. I saw it. It was like a black hole, and it just swallowed him."

Jo paced for a moment, "Think, think!" she said to herself. She wasn't coming up with anything.

David said, "Mom, I've dreamed this. I should have warned him. I have to go get him."

Tazman said, "I'll go with you."

The group still didn't trust him. Jo asked, "What will you two do?"

Tazman said, "I have Elf blood, and I have had at my fingertips my whole life, many men's lifetimes of shamanistic and magical knowledge from all over the world. I am very practiced in astral travel. Can any of you say the same?"

None of them could.

"How can we help down here?" Ariane asked.

"Visualize the darkness as a black tornado with Spero in the middle. Put all the white light you possibly can into that vortex, and visualize the boy and me being successful getting Spero out. When you can replace the blackness with white light, we will be able to retrieve him, I think. Then visualize all of us coming back into our bodies," Tazman said.

"What if you don't, and we have three of you gone?" asked Martin.

"What you can visualize, you can do. We are infinitely powerful in this universe," quoted Jeff. "We can do it, just put your minds to it, and together, I bet we can do anything!"

"Good, good," Jo said. "He's been out for fifteen minutes now. Good luck."

Everyone was silent concentrating on putting white light in the vortex. Spero's sitting form was very translucent now.

David's and Tazman's heads soon dropped, and the group kept working. Energy was building in the circle rolling around and around. Blake complained he was feeling really "light headed" and kind of nauseated. Martin's eyes were scrunched tight, and his head was actually sweating he was working so hard.

Jo regained her composure and started leading the visualization again. "You are building energy, and now it needs to be sent where it needs to go. Everyone should feel the pressure that is building up release when you do."

Everyone relaxed, and it was apparent that worked much better. Jo thought that the energy in the circle must be really heavy and ready now. She asked Ariane to focus the energy in the circle and direct it towards the vortex like a laser. Ariane sat holding the Record Keeper. She moved her mouth asking permission to have it help her, and she received her first "hearing." It said, "Not alone."

Ariane said to the group. "The crystal talked to me. It needs all of the stones in the circle and our crystals to help. Everyone please direct your energy through your crystal where it will be amplified into the sky into one point over the fire pit and then visualize a strong beam directed at the black tornado. Ready? 1, 2, 3 go!"

Everyone directed their crystals at a point above the fire pit and actually heard a cracking slightly sonic sound as it moved away.

Ariane asked the crystal aloud, "Did it work?"

The crystals were silent, but the energy in the circle was gone. Everyone looked around them and waited.

"It's thirty-five minutes," Jo said.

Pretty soon, David's eyes fluttered, and Tazman's eyes fluttered. Jo started crying. Spero's body started taking on more solid form. He looked up and said weakly, "Well, that was interesting."

Everyone started laughing and a few were crying. It was really an intense experience.

Bette said softly, "Can we move out of the circle now? I have to go to the bathroom!"

Everyone laughed and started moving out of the circle.

Jo and Ariane went over to Spero and helped support him as he stood up. He was pretty shaky. Spero walked slowly over to Tazman and shook his hand. "You saved my life. I owe you a life."

Tazman returned his handshake and said, "Well, you probably saved mine by stealing the crystal, so we're even."

Spero walked over to David and hugged him hard. He touched his forehead to David's, which is an Elf's blessing, and said, "I told you, didn't I? You are gifted, and I owe you more than I can say."

"Just don't get eaten by any scary black things again or let us get eaten and that will be payment enough. Deal?"

"Deal. Anybody else hungry?!!!" Everyone laughed.

Those who couldn't "hold it" any longer went outside to find bushes for the problem Bette mentioned. Girls right. Boys left.

The stones had exerted great effort, and even the Record Keeper's energy could barely be felt.

When the group rejoined, Spero held the Record Keeper for a moment and said, "The stones in the circle and the crystals that helped you are really drained. They're going to need to be outside in the Sun and elements for a few days to recuperate. Be sure to take care of them; they sure helped take care of us!"

Everyone left the chalk Star of David and circle intact but moved the stones that had worked with them in the circle outside to the sunshine and elements. They would have to re-set the stones in the star each time they worked. The business of asking the stones permission to participate and set the exact placement would have to be repeated each time.

Generally, when Spero worked in a circle, he brushed away the markings; to keep it intact makes it continue to work. As they would be working with it in the near future, they decided to leave it as it was structured.

"What was the darkness, Spero? Are we going to run into that again?" asked Jerry. The rest of the group stopped to listen.

"I got **myself** in that situation by being curious what the darkness was and investigating away from the astral group. We won't see that in the cave anymore, no. I'll go back in to double check and ask the Fairies to check around too, so that we're absolutely sure."

"Tazman guessed right what had happened. Thank goodness he knew what to do." He bowed to Tazman and said, "Thank you, again." Tazman bowed back.

Spero continued, "The Earth has layers of energy called an aura, and little swirling points where one energy meets another called vortex or chakras, just like the human body has. Energy moves throughout the Earth through lines called meridians, branching out like a tunnel, well, really more like a spider web.

The meeting places where the meridians of energy intersect are chakras. They look and act like tornados. Earth's energy moves within the Earth using this spider web system, but Earth sends energy mainly through the poles, or the center of the web, to other planets and through other dimensions. Then conversely, receives energy back from them and through them, again, mainly through the poles. This energy exchange is visible in the Aurora Borealis. This constant exchange of energy keeps the planets in their orbit and in their proper place in relation to one another and in the solar system and the universe."

"The darkness was a compromised chakra in the Earth's vortex system. When the energy can't move or be redirected, it backs up on itself. If it stays in that unhealthy position too long, the energy becomes corrupted, and light becomes dark, and the chakra's energy distorts and becomes compromised. If you don't take care of it, the chakra can become something akin to a black hole, or it will begin to die and the area around it starts to disassemble.

This creates dis-ease, so Earth can be ill too. Just like our bodies. When disease hits our body, it does the same thing. If one clears the aura and the chakras, then the body can, most of the time, repair itself unless it has gone unchecked for too long and destroyed too much, or it may just your time to go."

Spero sat down suddenly and held his head, "Sorry, I'm really tired." He continued, "It's that kind of thing that the Rainbow World helps Earth with. I wasn't thinking and didn't realize what it might have been. I **should** have realized what it was when Bette said there was a dark presence, but I just didn't think."

"If you are in your Earth body, your heavy body, and you cross an area with a compromised chakra like that, it won't affect you. It just feels heavy there, and people register a creepy feeling. Most people pick up on that and just avoid those areas.

In your heavy body, you can do what you did when you find those though, visualize white light and put it down the chakra. Pour white light into it to turn black or muddy colors to white light and heal it, so keep that in mind to help the Earth in the future.

BUT if you are a light body or in our case an astral body, you need to steer very far from it or it sucks you right in like a tornado. Once you are in there, the chakra has to be released of the dark energy and flow again, or you'll be killed, consumed, disassembled. I don't have to tell you, I was in big trouble. But I'm *so* thankful it was me instead of one of you guys because I can reassemble. You can't."

Tazman excused himself from the group and moved to leave. He did look tired. "Well, I've had more fun than I can stand for one day." He moved about ten yards from the group.

Jo rushed over and stopped him. "Wait! I have to know how to get ahold of you…um, for the next time we meet…I mean, so we can… um, make arrangements for when we *all* meet in the circle…again."

He tilted his head and looked deeply into her eyes. He smiled in one corner of his mouth. "This is my cell number, but I'm staying at the Nagle Warren Mansion Bed and Breakfast if you can't reach me for some reason…or if you want to reach me for another." His eyes flashed with amusement, and Jo blushed.

"Just contact me at Prism if you can't get my cell." She abruptly reached into her jean pocket and handed him a business card. "Both numbers are there. Just call if you need…to…ah get ahold of Spero, or anything."

Everyone had come together and piled into the van except Marty and Demy, who were going to ride back on ol' Ornery together.

Marty used his cell phone to call Lynne to let her know that he had been at the cave with Demy and group, and they were on their way home.

"I have to figure out what to tell your mom," Martin said. "I don't know what she'll think of all this, so just let me handle that part. Ok, son?"

"That was magic, what we did, wasn't it, Dad? Really magic. I want to keep helping and do what I can Dad, but I'm so glad you're there too. I feel better that you're there," Demy confided.

"I'm so glad I'm there too. You didn't know you're old dad believed in Fairies, did you?" Marty teased.

"Why don't you ever want to play Fantasy Kingdom, then?" Demy asked.

"Why play with the fantasy things when there are real things?"

"I guess because playing with those makes me really tired," Demy yawned.

"Are you going to be all right doing this Demy?" Martin was concerned.

"We have to Dad. If their world dies, our world dies. Guess you weren't there for that part huh?" Demy asked.

Martin hugged Demy close as they were riding. "Well, we can't have that then, can we?" Martin said. "Who would have thought that ten humans, one Elf and one part Elf would save the world together, huh? And we won't even be able to tell anyone. That's kind of the pits, isn't it?" Marty said roughing up Demy's hair.

"I'm just proud that I was chosen to help. It feels like we're all special, doesn't it?" Demy asked.

"You just said a mouthful, kid."

☆
Friends and Dinner

The Postelwaites and Jo's group decided to go to the Bunkhouse Bar for dinner. It was halfway to Cheyenne and was known for its steaks. There was a restaurant part so the under-aged of the group could go in there.

Spero was ravenous. They didn't see how he could eat one more bite, but he surprised them by ordering another steak. "Have you got some sliced tomatoes?"

The waitress smiled and looked at him, "There's ketchup if you want."

Spero raised both eyebrows and said very coldly, "Tomatoes, please."

The waitress left, and everyone could hear Spero mumbling under his breath, "KETCHUP!! rar rar rhizlefrazen ketchup rar rar rar".

They all started laughing and it took on a life of its own. The more they laughed, the more they laughed, and pretty soon Jo started snorting and snorting. The more she snorted, the more she snorted. The boys were falling off their chairs, and the whole restaurant smiled and laughed too.

"Well, so much for living here; I have to move now," Jo said loudly. And everyone laughed some more.

Spero put his arm around her and moved so that he was talking softly in her ear. "Look around you, kiddo. There's not one person in here who isn't smiling. Not one person in here who didn't laugh with you, not **at** you, **with** you. What a blessing you are!"

Jo patted him on his cheek and kissed it. "Thank you for you," she smiled gently.

Everyone finished their meal and Spero said, "I've got the tab."

Jo kind of looked at him sideways, and whispered, "I can buy, you're not working, remember?"

Spero whispered to Jo, "It's not a problem. I didn't work at the Cheyenne Family YMCA for money. I volunteered so I could play basketball and swim free. I saved enough through the years that I don't really have to work."

Bette and the boys thanked Spero for his generosity. A meal out for them was a rare treat. They were so genuinely thankful.

Spero said, "You are most welcome, but I'd do almost anything for more banana bread?" He looked at Bette and batted his eyes.

Bette smiled, "There's one more loaf left, and it's yours!"

Everyone got into the van. Jo was driving, and Spero was sitting behind her leaning over her shoulder. "Can't you drive any faster? Are you even going the speed limit?" He was almost drooling.

Jo pulled into the Postelwaite's place, and Spero was poised ready to get out to get his banana bread.

Spero caught up with the group after they unloaded and said, "Oh, I forgot to tell you all something. As of right now, as long as we're working together, no pig meat of any kind. Will you call and let the Cresenzos know?"

"Why?" whined Blake, whose favorite meal was bacon and more bacon.

"There are enzymes in the meat that interfere with creating white light, and I think we're going to need to help generate a boatload of it to save Rainbow World. Oh, and please remember to give your crystals water if it doesn't rain, ok?"

Peter said, "I'll go get your banana bread!" He was the first in the house, and he came out with aluminum foil covered bread.

Spero looked at him wearily and said rather petulantly, "Well, where is it?"

Peter put it in his hands. Spero smiled from pointed ear to pointed ear. "Oh, there it is."

✪

Martin and Demy Cresenzo

Martin and Demy were silent for the rest of the ride home. Martin had taken the longer way because he had Demy, and the short cut would have been too steep for them. Besides that they were both tired and the short cut took energy.

When they got to the barn, Jock was there to take the grumpy horse and take care of him. "Bet he's hungry and thirsty," Martin said. "Thanks Jock, appreciate your help. Mama's waiting."

As they were walking back to the house, Demy asked. "What did you decide to tell Mom?"

"The truth. Watch and learn, my man. Watch and learn," Martin smiled.

Lynne was in the kitchen finishing dinner. Martin and Demy came in the back door, and Martin immediately went over and gave her a hug and kiss. He got a glass of water for them both, and they drank the water greedily.

"Long day, guys!" Lynne came over and hugged her son. "What were you guys doing up there?"

Martin went over and hugged Demy too and replied, "Well, first we had to hold the magic crystal and see who could pass the test and sit in the circle. THEN, the guide woman...what was her name, Demy?"

Demy replied, "Jo Vanderlin."

Martin continued, "Right, then Jo told us what to do, and we traveled outside our bodies. Then Spero, the older guy, who is the Elf, right?" Demy nodded. Marty finished his water and then continued, "Ya, he got lost."

Demy said, "Right."

"Because HE was swallowed by... what was it Demy?"

"A black tornado thing," Demy replied.

Lynne was smiling and listening and working at the same time. "Scary, what happened next?"

Martin got serious and said matter of factly. "He was almost killed!" He looked again at Demy who was shaking his head and trying not to laugh.

Demy added, "THEN two guys had to go rescue him. One of them was only half Elf, and he might be the bad one, we're not sure yet."

Then Martin remembered a step they missed. "Oh! I forgot, before they could save the Elf, we had to turn the tornado white, right?"

Martin was grinning and so was Demy.

"Right, Dad."

Martin looked at Lynne and smiled, "And then we all saved the Elf and came home, so you could feed us dinner. Smells great!"

Demy added, "And Dad and I are going to go back, maybe a few more times so we can save the Magic Kingdom and Earth. OK, Mom?"

Lynne looked up from shredding the lettuce for the salad. "Sure, honey. I can't believe you finally got your dad to play with you! See, honey? Pitiful, relentless begging sometimes pays off. "

Martin said, "It wasn't like that. This was real!" He looked very serious.

Lynne smiled, "That's cool, honey. Wash up for dinner. It's ready."

Martin and Demy headed for the sink. "Demy did an "OK!" sign under the water and Martin did one back, and they started cracking up!

✰

Bette Postelwaite

Bette Postelwaite had a call on the machine when she got into the house from Jim Riggs, from the Sheriff's department. She took the phone upstairs and shut the door to her bedroom and called him back.

"Jim, Bette Postelwaite here, returning your call."

"Bette, I called to let you know that Nels' attorney got a release after the hearing. He will have worked off his time in lieu of fine by tomorrow morning. His attorney argued that a black eye didn't warrant them holding him any longer. Technically we couldn't hold him more than seventy-two hours without charging him with a crime. I'll be honest with you. We could have charged him with felony child abuse if you had ever admitted last time that he had hurt your little one but everybody insisted it was an accident, remember? We all knew Nels, and figured out it wasn't an accident. Some of us grew up with the guy. But not filing against him then didn't help you this time."

"I see," Bette said simply.

"Bette. We've got the restraining orders signed by the Judge. He's not supposed to come within four hundred yards of the house."

"You and I both know that won't stop him," Bette said sadly.

"You call us if you see him anywhere near you or your boys, and we'll be out there pronto. I'm sorry. I can't be more help than that."

Bette hung up the phone and just sat there. She didn't have a clue what to say to the boys or what to do. Nels would be back, probably tomorrow.

She picked up the phone and dialed Marty.

✫

Marty Cresenzo

"Martin Cresenzo here."

"Marty. Nels is being released tomorrow."

"WHAT! How is that possible?" Marty yelled.

"It's my fault. We hid that he beat Peter and said he had fallen off the roof. Nels convinced me that filing charges against him, with attorney fees and court costs and all, would cost me the house and land if I told the truth. So this time when he hit Jerry, they didn't have anything to charge him with except a black eye and empty threats. He served an extra few days to work off his fine, but that's all that they can hold him for."

"Did you get that restraining order filed?"

"Yes, it's on file. He's not supposed to come within four hundred yards of us, but that won't stop him. You know that, and I know that."

"Have you got a gun, Bette?" Marty asked.

"No, that's not the answer; he'll be more likely to take it from us and use it on us," Bette said. "I had the boys take them out of the house."

"Where are Nels' guns?"

"In the garage with the rest of his stuff."

"Let's move those out and at least not make it convenient for him to get a hold of one in the near future. I'll come get them right now."

Lynne had been standing there listening to the conversation. Marty hugged her and told her he'd be right back.

Marty hated feeling this helpless. Nels would be back for sure. Bette knew it, and he knew it. He wouldn't put it passed Nels to do serious damage or harm for pay back. He drove out of the yard toward the Postelwaites and saw Spero riding his bicycle on the right of way. He pulled over to talk to him.

"Spero, have you got a minute?" Marty asked.

"Sure." Spero stopped and took the chance to take his water bottle out for a long drink. "What's up?"

"Bette just called, and Nels is being released tomorrow. I'm on the way to her house now to get the guns out of the house so he can't get a hold of them. You're closer to her than I am. Can you keep an eye out for her?" Marty asked. The concern in his face was obvious.

"Bette has the means to call me on a communicator crystal, and I can be there immediately. Also, just so you know, Demy has one too and can call her, and then she can call me, if you two need me quick. Life or death quick that is. I have another idea though."

"What's that?" asked Marty.

"I think I'll pull a disappearing and reappearing act and pay Mr. Postelwaite a little visit. Did I tell you I was a 'warrior class' Shaman Walker, by the way?"

"So, what will you do?"

"Well, what I'd like to do to the coward and what I will do are two different things. But I can sure scare him away. Tell Bette not to worry. You and I have it handled," Spero said.

"You don't know Nels. He doesn't scare easily, and attempts to keep him from getting his revenge just make him more determined to have more revenge," Marty said.

"I've met his type time and time again. If worse comes to worse, I can make him think I'll plant him in Antarctica." Spero looked determined.

"I can see that it is very helpful to have an Elf as a friend," Marty said. "I'll tell Bette you have it covered. Thank you. Hope it works!" Martin smiled. "Can you come see me, no matter how late, and let me know what happens?"

"Shall I pop over?" Spero asked with a grin.

"Yes, please do," Martin replied. "I'll be sleeping on the couch waiting."

✦

Spero Zezas

Spero looked at his watch; it was starting to get dark. He headed back to the house. He told Jo and her family that he decided to get some shut-eye and turn in early.

He set the alarm for 2:00 a.m. and quickly went off to sleep.

When the vibrator alarm went off at 2:00, he got up and dressed. He meditated on Bette and linked into her memories of Nels. He became more and more angry to see the horrible treatment that the whole family had lived with. The man was purely sadistic and cruel.

He visualized Nels in his prison cell and disassembled.

There was a bright flash, and Spero reassembled into his cell. The cell was dark and the flash of light woke Nels up.

"What the…" Nels jumped out of his bed when he saw Spero squatting there staring at him.

Spero's green eyes looked black. He stood up slowly, never taking his eyes off Nels. "I understand you'll be getting out of jail tomorrow. Are you planning on visiting your lovely family any time soon, you coward?"

"Who the hell are you, and how did you get here? GUARD!" Nels started to yell.

Spero walked over and grabbed his trachea and his hand flashed blue with St. Michael's Fire. Nels started to gag and choke and couldn't talk at all. He struggled for his breath. He fell back on the bed.

Spero went back and leaned against the wall. "There. That's better. You'd be surprised what you can learn in several thousand years of being a warrior. How to paralyze muscles and explode organs, for example. How to kill someone in interesting ways. I once saw one of my companions turn a fiend inside out just to see if he could. The fiend who got that punishment didn't do anything compared to you."

Spero was deadly silent for a moment. "You're a real piece of work." Spero was getting too angry, and that wasn't helpful.

Spero crooked his head to one side and kept looking Nels straight in the eyes. "Here's the thing. Your wife has been a friend of mine since she was tiny, and I really won't let her or those wonderful boys you have be hurt by you, so I'm going to help you not to hurt anyone ever again. I thought you might like to see what some of my large friends and I could do to you if you come anywhere near them, EVER!"

With that Spero moved so fast at Nels he didn't have time to back away or do anything. Spero put his hand over the top of Nels' head and sent telepathic images of some of the more graphic battles he had witnessed and participated in. Images across time and dimensions of Dragons battling alongside the Elves, Minervans, Jupiterians, and other Rainbow World creatures against demons and fiends and cruel, horrible beings of a black heart during Earth's and Rainbow World's Armageddon. The horrific images during the battles fought against "hell," or the lower dimension, when it existed, were violent beyond any human's capacity to understand violence. They were more gory than a Hollywood film could ever depict. Spero bought up images of himself doing things he wished he could forget, but they served good purpose here in remembering. The battles were fought and won and over and the cost to all of their lives was astronomical.

By the time Spero released his head, Nels was stoic, but his eyes were still full of hatred. He was, apparently, not impressed.

Spero took note of that and simply said, "You will not regain your voice. Maybe that will qualify you to receive benefits, I don't know. You'll want to write lots of notes checking into that. I don't care, but what you will not do is ever say another mean thing to another living thing as long as you live. I have also put in place a means to make you keep your hatred and violence to yourself. Any attempt to do violence, in any form, to another living being, will result in harm to yourself."

Nels was looking daggers at Spero, looking like he would kill him if he had a chance.

"Go ahead, hit me," Spero taunted. "Big, big man capable of putting an eleven-year-old in the hospital for a week. You would have just kept kicking and hitting Peter until you killed him, wouldn't you? You would have kept hitting him until he was a bloody puddle if your family wouldn't have stopped you."

Spero kept goading him and goading him and getting in his face. "What did he do? Look you in the eyes and see you for the coward you are? Go ahead and see if you can turn me to a bloody puddle. See if you're man enough to hit another man. I'm an old man in your eyes, that ought to be enough advantage for you. Why, that should be almost like hitting your kids, or your wife. I'll even let you have the first shot." Spero jutted out his jaw.

Nels jumped off the bed and tried to strangle him. His hands had no strength around Spero's neck. The more violently he tried to strangle, the less strength he had. He tried instead to hit or punch; the punches landed weakly. He was enraged and doubled his efforts which doubled the weakness in his body. He was totally ineffectual in connecting his punches. He was so weak he couldn't stand, but his eyes told Spero that hatred was all he had.

Nels gave up and sat down. He was winded and weak.

Spero said calmly. "You can lead a normal life. You will regain strength in working with your hands in service to others, or you can continue to weaken yourself to the point of death by persisting in your violent tendencies. That's as fair as I'm going to be with you."

There was a flash of light and Spero disassembled out of the cell.

He reassembled in Martin's living room.

Marty was up and waiting. "What happened?"

"He is physically incapable now of hurting anyone without hurting himself. He won't be able to talk about it because he will not have the ability to say one more hateful word. I tapped into Bette's memories. I'm frankly appalled she didn't call me to help her a few times. I would say a few of those times could be classified as 'life and death' situations."

Marty looked like he was in pain. "Or call *me*. Why didn't she call me? I'm ashamed I didn't help her. I knew the guy was bad news, but I had no idea how bad until Peter's hospitalization. I wish she would have trusted me enough to tell me what was going on."

"Wish she would have trusted us both. I could live thousands more Earth years and still not understand the dynamic of taking abuse like that or allowing it to be done against others, especially children. I'm sure the whole family is going to take a long time to heal, but I think they're on the way." Spero was always hopeful.

Marty sighed, "I do understand, somewhat. Bette is a very gentle and religious soul. She threw love and understanding at that man in equal measure to his hatred for years, trying to change him. It took Peter's incident to open her eyes, I think. It's my guess she took the abuse more times than not to keep it from the boys."

Spero looked at Marty. "I wish I could say we'll never see him again, but I think he will still try something. He's been neutralized, but I've seen his kind of hatred before. They're still not safe."

Marty was adamant. "Then I'll have men there night and day for as long as we have to. I'll build her a fifteen foot fence and get her vicious pit bulls. Whatever it takes."

"Do you honestly think Bette will let you do that?" Spero asked.

"Not for herself, no, but she better let us do something for those kids. Nels will be out for blood. I know him."

"She must have lived in terror of that very thing. I bet that is what kept her from ever exposing him before."

"We could pay him off? Would that work? Would he leave?" Marty asked.

"No, he would just be back for more, and she'd still be living in fear waiting around for him to come back around anytime, year after year. There would be no end to it."

"What else can be done?" Marty was back to feeling helpless.

"We wait and see what he does and try to do the damage control we can. If he acts greatly upon his violence, he will probably not survive. I've seen to that," Spero said.

"I appreciate what you did, but I have to admit I'm confused about you," Marty said. "You can do something like this being from your world with your philosophies and beliefs?"

Spero looked at Marty for a moment. His eyes looked weary. He quietly replied, "We are the caretakers of Earth. We are the caretakers of those who Angels guard on Earth and those innocents who are oppressed and suffer at the hands of hate and violence. We can't always save their bodies. We help to move their light bodies into various levels of transformational states."

He explained further. "We have fought a war across our two worlds, across the galaxy and into other galaxies against gross imbalance and evil that would destroy good. We all destroyed that evil forever. We are the survivors of the Creator's judgment on all living things."

Spero sat down and put his head in his hands. "What part of being the Creator's warrior does not involve fighting evil for the sake of another or sacrificing yourself for your fellow man as my fellows sacrifice themselves everyday for you and yours. For Earth's health and continued survival, I am a warrior. I'm trying to save both of our worlds. My world is dying to save yours."

Marty sat there stunned. He didn't say a word.

Spero leaned over and looked into Marty's eyes. "I would like to be able to save one beautiful soul and her family from one of the most evil beings I have ever met. I'm going to try to do that."

"Me too. Sorry, Spero. I will do everything in my power to do that and to help you in any possible way I can save our worlds. Demy told me today that we don't have a choice. To use his words, he said, 'We HAVE to, Dad. 'Not only do we have to, we want to. Just tell me what to do and I'll do it."

"Let's put a guard around her house, so we can at least get a possible forewarning. I have a feeling he'll act soon because he's getting weaker by the moment. He will realize that he must act soon before he dies of his hatred," Spero said.

"Done." I'm going to get them out there first thing in the morning," Marty said. "Well, it's almost morning now."

"Could you give me a ride home? I'm pretty tired. It's been a hard day and night," Spero asked.

"I'll take him, Marty," Lynne said. "You get some rest. This is the Elf you were talking about, I presume?"

Marty's surprise was evident. His head whipped around, and he blushed seeing Lynne standing in the living room. "Where did you come from?" he asked.

"I can't sleep without you, you know that. I've been listening to the whole thing. She's my friend too." Lynne's look at Marty was a little dangerous. "So, your story this afternoon was true, huh? I think you're in trouble for the WAY you told me the absolute truth," Lynne admonished.

"I know, Babe. I didn't want to lie, but I didn't see any way to tell you the truth either and have you believe me. You've never believed what I told you happened when I was a kid and always blew off what I saw to a concussion. I'd like you to meet the man, well, the Elf, who helped saved my life, Spero Zezas. Spero, my wife, Lynne."

"Pleasure, Lynne. You and I can talk more on the way home, ok? I'm really tired. 'Night, Marty."

Lynne was dressed in pj's and just slipped a coat over and slipped on her sandals. "This way to conventional travel," she said.

"I like her already," smiled Spero looking back at Marty. Marty was standing there like a little boy in trouble.

Spero and Lynne went through the kitchen to the garage, and Lynne opened the garage door. She backed out the car and stopped the vehicle.

"If what they were telling me today was the absolute truth, people I love and my entire family are in some jeopardy doing whatever you're doing. I want you to promise me that you will not let any of these people come to harm." Lynne's look was deadly serious.

"I will give my life, if necessary, to keep that from happening. The work they will do will keep their physical body on Earth. Their astral body will travel across a dimensional door to visit my world and assess the damage only. Then we will work together in our physical bodies to do what we can to help. Humans are more powerful than any of you know. What you can visualize, you can accomplish. I'm very confident everyone will be able to work together to save both of our worlds."

Lynne's eyes seemed to burn into Spero's. "And I have to be left out? I can't help too? I can't be there to help my family?"

"No, you are most certainly welcome to be there if you can believe in what we're doing. But you may not touch them or interfere with what we are doing, even if it appears they are in trouble to you. You would have to trust them, and me, that they will be safe. Any positive energy you can lend to us is welcome. More than welcome. Jo can help guide you in what you can do to help."

Lynne just looked at him for a long time. "I have never believed one iota of this stuff. I'd have to change my personality and total philosophy to even BEGIN to accept what my son, and his father, apparently, have inherent belief and faith in. Whether or not I believe you, I do believe in them, and I will do what I can to help them. I have to be there for my own sanity and to make sure my family is safe."

Spero leaned forward and spoke softly, "There's the rub. You don't know what is safe and not safe. For instance, if you pull your son out of that circle when he is in astral travel with us, you will endanger not only him, but us all. Depending on what we are doing, you could endanger both worlds."

"Then my husband and son may not be in that position. That's just what I'm talking about."

"Lynne." Spero looked deep in her blazing eyes, "Was there ever a point in your life that you believed in something larger than yourself? That you knew something was out there bigger than you?"

"Like God? No. I've tried my whole life to believe that. I just don't," Lynne answered.

"Then it makes it almost impossible for you to help them or help us. The energy you will expend in judging our actions and doubting us will be detrimental to what we are doing and to everyone's safety." He looked at her mischievously, "So, I guess you will have to be convinced, huh?"

"I guess so."

"Did you know you are pregnant, by the way?" Spero asked.

Lynne kind of twitched. "That may or may not be true."

"How would you like to meet some Fairies?" Spero asked.

"Sure. Why not," Lynne responded. She tore out of the driveway. As she drove, her cold silence made it apparent she wasn't buying any of this. Spero was always amazed at how hard some people held on to their disbelief, even in the face of proof to the contrary. She was going to be a tough nut to crack.

She pulled into the Vanderlin/Selph driveway. It was about 3:30 a.m.

"Park just here so we don't wake everyone in the house up. They don't know I'm gone," Spero said.

"OK," Lynne said in a deadpan voice.

"Follow me please." Spero led the way through the hole in the fence through the woods to the magical circle. "Please give me just a moment to explain what we're doing to the Fairies. They're a little shy to show themselves to unbelievers."

Sure. Take your time." Lynne said under her breath, "Whatever."

Spero was gone for about five minutes. She was getting cold, and she was getting mad. "What on Earth am I doing out here at 4 am in my pajamas?" she mumbled to herself. "Enough!" She started to turn around to go home when he came out of the closely packed trees.

"The show is ready to begin. Here. You'll have to hold this ring to see them." Spero dropped his Walker Bearer ring in her hand.

She looked down and was very amazed at the workmanship. She knew a thing or two about jewelry, and this piece was exquisite.

"This must have set you back a pretty penny."

"No, it was given to me by a Sentinel being, Dragon to you, when I became a Walker Bearer on my world several thousand Earth years ago."

"Whatever," Lynne said out loud in reply. She had definitely lost her sense of humor.

Spero walked into the Fairy tree area. Lynne noticed some brightness that seemed to get brighter as they stood there. "This is it? This is your proof?" she said sarcastically.

"No, this is." He stepped sideways, faded and stepped back dressed in a shiny, pink satin "Big Top" Master of Ceremonies garb complete with a top hat and cane. The Fairies, who had been damping their light for dramatic effect, gave her Fairy light full blast and all lined up in a chorus line and did the can-can. They could only hold on to such a ridiculous display for so long until they could be heard twittering and laughing. They flew in twenty-seven directions in a whirlwind display around her. They rarely touched her but hovered close so that they could look her in the eyes and wag their fingers at her to indicate their displeasure in her disbelief.

Spero said, "Thank you, my lady and Fairies. The show is over for the evening." He thought he'd better get Lynne out before they started biting. Fairies do bite if they're mad or upset.

He literally pushed Lynne out of the circle. She glared at him and, practically threw his ring at him. She walked off without saying a word.

"Wonder where this will end up?" Spero thought. He took one last admiring glance at his spiffy pink satin sleeve, stepped sideways again and reappeared wearing pajamas. He went back into the house quietly and got into bed.

Chapter Seven
Wednesday

☆

Spero Zezas

It seemed like Spero had just put his head to the pillow when Jo was shaking him awake.

"Spero, wake up! There's smoke at the Postelwaite house!"

He jumped out of bed, grabbed a robe, and hastily put it on.

"Meet me there." There was a flash, and he was gone.

When he got there, he saw Nels Postelwaite lying in the yard with a gasoline can beside him and matches in his hand. He was dead.

The kitchen and living room were burning and both exits were blocked by fire. Nels wanted to make sure his family couldn't get out alive. The upper stories were filled with smoke. The cracking of the fire in the early morning silence seemed deafening.

Spero disassembled and popped himself into the upper stories and reassembled. He held his pajama top collar over his face against the thick smoke. "Bette! Boys! Are you here? Is anybody here?"

He searched for their energy link and didn't feel any of them there. To make sure that they weren't just unconscious, he went through the whole house and didn't find anybody.

He disassembled again and sent himself out to the yard and reassembled. He grabbed a hose from the front yard and started applying water where he could reach. He heard a fire truck in the distance and help was soon there. The fire district "hurry come" call system was extremely effective.

They moved fast for humans. But even using big hoses, it soon became apparent that they wouldn't be able to restrict the fire to the first floor. It consumed the entire house. The fire fighters doused the surrounding trees and ground with water. They were diligent to make sure it didn't spread from the house to anything else.

Jo drove in and talked to Spero through the car window. She said, "I called the ranger station where the district keeps the fire truck, and nobody answered. They must have already been on their way here."

Lynne and Marty drove up with the Postelwaite family in tow. One of the firemen had covered Nels' body and corded off the area around him.

The boys and Bette all gathered outside the taped area near their father's body. Spero heard Bette say softly, "Didn't have to be like this Nels." The boys were all hugging her. Spero and Jo and Lynne went and stood beside them.

The Sheriff drove up and talked to Martin. Martin came over and said, "They moved him to infirmary because he lost his voice. He apparently couldn't wait for this afternoon to be released. He snuck out and stole a vehicle from the lot about 5:30 this morning.".

Spero was struck with how the Universe played these things out. Spero's interference had created the situation that led to Nels' escape. If he had not done what he did, Nels would be in prison still, at least until the afternoon. Some of what he was thinking must have shown on his face.

Martin walked over and looked at him. "Spero, I know what you're thinking. If Nels didn't do that, he would have just found a way to hurt them some other way, probably this afternoon instead of this morning. Thank goodness Lynne kicked them all out of bed at 5:00 to come home with her."

Spero looked at Lynne, and she smiled and said, "Women are sometimes just logical. He can't hurt what he can't find."

☆

Why?

Martin went over to Bette and was holding her, and Lynne went over and put her arms around both of them. Bette kissed Lynne on the cheek and thanked her. Bette had a glazed look, and the women met eyes, "Lynne. If we had been in there….if we had been in there…"

Lynne said, "I know. It's over now. He can't hurt anybody anymore."

Spero was standing with the boys. Peter went over to him and buried his head in his chest and held on tight. "I should be sorry, shouldn't I? I should be sorry to see my father dead." His brothers came over and patted him and stood close.

They were mesmerized by watching the flaming house. They had to stand back further due to the intense heat. Jerry observed, "He would have killed us all. He would have trapped us in our burning home to burn alive."

"How does someone have that much hate?" Ernie said. "Why? What did we do that was so horrible? What did any of us do that was so horrible?"

Blake shook his head, "Was it because we wanted to do the hard business instead of him having to do it? Did he hate us that much just for wanting to buy his truck and trying to take over the lumbering business, which he couldn't do anymore? We always gave him and Ma most of what we made, and we would have been more than fair to keep the family going."

Jeff said, "No, it was because we were traitors because we wouldn't take our beatings for our own good anymore. We were too old to mind him, and we fought back by tying him up and humiliating him. He no longer had absolute control and could no longer rule us with fear."

Peter asked everyone, "I don't remember something. What did I do to make him beat me so hard?"

Jeff said, "You told him if he ever hit Ma again you would kill him, so he was going to kill you. He was going to kill us all for the same reason."

Lynne walked over. "Boys. Let's go away from here now. We'll come back later, and we'll all help you rebuild your new life. This is the ugly old one. You don't need to be here."

Jerry looked at her sadly. He said respectfully, "Yes, we do. This *is* our life. The ugly parts, and just recently the good parts. Thanks for looking out for us though. We all appreciate it."

"Mrs. Cresenzo?" Peter said, "I would appreciate it if you would take me back to your house with you. I think Ma might like to leave too. I'm worried she's too tired. I know this was our ugly life, but I've seen enough of it, and I think Ma has too. She doesn't have her kitchen to sit in."

Bette walked over to the group. "Let's all go, please. We're going to have to stay somewhere else and come back over to work on the house. The Cresenzos have offered us the old hunting cabin for a time. I want us all to go. Please. Now."

Marty and Lynne asked the Sheriff if they could take the Postelwaites to their house and get them settled. The Sheriff said he'd get their statements later.

Nobody noticed right away, but Spero had disappeared.

✷

Jo Vanderlin

Jo went back home when everyone dispersed. She whispered aloud to herself, "My goodness, what a monster that man must have been." Who knows what kind of nightmare those kids and Bette lived.

It was 7:15 a.m., and a little later than the time she usually started getting up. She decided to let the kids sleep in like usual and let Spero tell them what had happened.

Where did he disappear to? For a guy who only disassembled from place to place in case of life and death, he'd been popping around like popcorn in the last week. Hope he was ok. He was sure acting strange. Wonder what he and Marty were talking about?

She decided to get dressed and go into work. There wasn't a whole lot they could do today.

☆

Spero Zezas

Meanwhile, Spero was on a mission. He was in Cheyenne waiting at Sharis on Dell Range, his favorite breakfast restaurant. He needed to unwind and think. He had opened up a safety deposit box at a nearby bank to keep his accumulated wealth and important documents in. He had everything sent to him from trusted sources a week ago. He used the identification that the real Spero Zezas had given him when he went through his transformation and shifted into the Rainbow World.

Spero human had been a great philanthropist and had spent his life and his fortune trying to help organizations that were trying to take care of the Earth. He had recently been involved with Citizens for the Earth. Spero human gave the majority of his wealth and investments to that organization before he disappeared to the world. He had no relatives. He instructed his attorneys to give Elf Spero all of his personal papers and photographs so that he could assume his identity. He gave his estate to the people who had taken care of him all his years. He made them wealthy too, and then he disappeared. They didn't know if he was alive or dead.

Elf Spero was grateful that the real Spero had offered him the documents sufficient to function on Earth. Elf Spero moved far away and took over the paper life of Spero Zezas. He looked enough like him that he probably could have used the identification to get a driver's license and have a job that paid money, but he didn't want or need that. He only needed one id, a rent receipt, and utility bill, showing a current name and address to get a safety deposit box, and that was all he needed. The rest he handled in cash.

He had been named Spero for so long, he even thought of himself as that name. He would probably keep it from now on. He had outgrown his first name, which must always be a secret, for there was nobody in Rainbow World old enough to know the truth of his existence…well, save one. Spero was better known by his title, "Walker Bearer Prime." Somehow, Prime didn't fit his Earthly ego. Prime is what he was called in the Rainbow World.

In spite of everything, he allowed himself to just enjoy a quiet breakfast. He always got a kick out of bantering with all the crew at Sharis. They all made a point of stopping by his table to greet him. He couldn't help processing that he would soon be going home and no longer be able to enjoy the heavy body physicality and the joys of touch, smell, taste, and everything that went with it. There was so much he would miss about Earth.

He would *really* miss eating. There was no reason to eat in Rainbow World. He thought, though, that he would always be hungry for cinnamon rolls, fast food hamburgers, french fries, and soft drinks. If he became desperate, he told himself, he *could* sneak down and go somewhere and eat. Just come back to Earth and savor a good steak, or popcorn, or tomatoes. He was getting hungry just thinking about not eating anymore. He knew deep down that when he went home this time, he would probably not come back again.

He thought of his idea for the Wordsmith's writing club and was really sad he'd never do that. He really wanted to do that. And he'd miss Jo, David, Ariane, the Postelwaites, the Cresenzos, and all the wonderful people he had met here. Having a heavy body was a wonderful experience. He would never forget having the privilege of living on Earth as a human. They were a wonderful lot. Most people were good, they really were.

It was 8:00 a.m., and the bank was opening. He went in and checked out his safe deposit box and cleared it out. He stuffed the contents into his backpack. He cancelled the contract and asked to see the Bank Manager.

He put his backpack on the Bank Manager's desk. Grant Morrison looked at it and then looked back at him and said with one eyebrow raised, "What can I do for you?"

"I just closed out my safety deposit box, and these are the documents to that effect. Here is my identification. With what is in the back pack, I would like to put part of it in a cashier's check, distribute some of the bearer bonds, set up trust accounts for a number of people, and one long-term trust with two names with the rest of the bearer bonds."

Spero said arrogantly, "Are you able to handle that, or should I take what's in this bag and go see an attorney?"

"I manage a complete trust department here. We can certainly accommodate any program you have in mind." He kept looking at the backpack. "What do you have in mind?"

Spero spent the next couple of hours working with Grant Morrison to distribute the wealth he had accumulated in some two thousand Earth years to the people he cared about most. He had given a lot of thought about where it needed to go to be used as he needed it to be used. There was a lot of paperwork to get it finally accomplished.

Grant Morrison shook his hand and said, "It's a pleasure doing business with you, Mr. Zezas."

✡

Marty Cresenzo

Marty called a contractor friend to go over to the Postelwaites and give him an estimate on the house. Pat Griffin crawled around through the black soup and made notes here and notes there. When he came back a couple of hours later to the Rocking C Ranch, he was black from head to foot.

"What's the damage, Pat?" Marty asked.

"Do you want the quick and dirty bottom line? Quite frankly, if it were mine, I would bulldoze what's left and move to a new location starting over, foundation and all. The house had real structural problems before the fire, and it hasn't had the maintenance it should have had through the years. I'm sorry. I'm just being honest."

"Can you give me a ball park figure for what we're talking about here to build a four bedroom home, 2 baths, and 2 stories? Basically what they had?" Marty was afraid to ask.

"A similar frame house in today's market and tearing down and clearing off what's left of that one…$350,000.00. I know it seems like a lot, but about $20,000.00 of that is the tear down and clearing."

"If we tore it down, you could build a foundation and house for $330,000.00 then?"

"Marty, there's a lot more to tearing that house down than knocking down walls. It's a very major undertaking, and it's dangerous. You need someone who really knows what they're doing, and you need big equipment to do it. I'll knock 10% off to help the cause," Pat said.

"You're a good man. Let us kick this around and see." Pat climbed into his truck and left.

Lynne was drinking a cup of coffee and leaning against the entryway to the kitchen door. "I wish we could just give her a house. Wish we were rich."

"We could give her the old hunting cottage. It's a tight squeeze, but they could make do, couldn't they?" Marty asked.

"No, not for very long. Come winter it's a cold and damp proposition. It's been needing some repairs for awhile too."

Their doorbell rang. Marty went over to answer the door. He was shocked to see Grant Morrison standing on the porch.

"Grant. What a surprise. How's that bank getting along without its head booba?" Marty teased. He and Grant had worked together in various Frontier Days Committees through the years.

"I'm taking this afternoon off after the business I need to conduct with Mrs. Postelwaite. I'd thought I'd have a beer. Want to join me?" Grant asked.

"Back, up there hoss…Bette? Bette Postelwaite?"

"Yes, that's her. Is she available?" Grant asked.

"She's upstairs taking a nap…" Marty hesitated, "Uh, it's been quite a day. Did you hear what happened?"

"Heard all about it. Horrible, horrible business. Are her boys about too?"

"I think they're out cleaning out the old hunting cabin for a temporary shelter," Marty said.

"Can you send someone to get them? It's not necessary to put them to more work." Grant was smiling.

"It's not?" Lynne asked.

"No, it's not. I'm dying to tell you, but ethically, I need to talk to the Postelwaites first."

Grant kept looking at his watch.

"Are you in a big hurry?" Marty asked.

"No, like I said, I have all afternoon," Grant smiled.

Lynne went over to Marty, raised one eyebrow and crooked her head in question. Marty shrugged his shoulders.

"I'll send one of the hands to get the boys," said Marty. He took out his cell phone and called the bunk house. "Chip, can you take the truck over pronto to the hunting cabin and bring the Postelwaite boys and Demy here? Thanks."

Marty turned to Grant. "They'll be here in about fifteen minutes."

Lynne asked Grant if she could get him something to drink.

"Whatever you have made is fine with me."

"Ice tea or lemonade?" Lynne asked

"Lemonade please."

Lynne prepared two glasses and gave Grant and Marty their lemonade. She took a sip of her coffee. "I'm going to go wake Bette. I'll be right back."

Lynne went upstairs and knocked softly on the guest room door. Bette said softly, "Come in."

Lynne went in and sat on the edge of the bed. "Bette, I'm not sure why, but Grant Morrison from our bank is downstairs. Says he'd like to talk to you and the boys. Marty has sent for them. They should be here in a few minutes."

"What's this about?" Bette looked worried.

"He says he has good news, but wouldn't say what," Lynne remarked.

"I'll be down as soon as I wash my face." She had been crying.

Lynne squeezed her hand and gave her some privacy.

By the time Lynne got downstairs, the boys were coming in the back door. They stopped off and washed their hands in the laundry room sink and took off their shoes. They were covered in spider webs and dust.

Lynne took one look at them. "Boys, let's go back out on the porch. I'm sorry, I didn't realize that place was such a mess."

Bette was coming down the stairs. She had stayed upstairs a couple of extra minutes to get her composure. She had given in to a pity cry and really didn't want her boys to see her all blotchy and red eyed.

"Oh well," she mumbled, "What's someone whose husband tried to kill her whole family and then killed himself supposed to look like?" She tried to stop processing, or she was going to be a waterworks again.

Lynne caught her at the bottom of the stairs. "We're on the porch. Want lemonade, or ice tea, or hot coffee? I just put on a pot."

"I'd dearly love a cup of coffee, please. Want some help?" Bette asked.

"Would you mind grabbing those six glasses of ice water on the tray for the boys?" Lynne asked.

Bette went over and got the tray with the ice water and brought it out to the porch. She sat the tray down on the table, and Jerry got up to serve Demy and his brothers.

Grant Morrison stood up, "Mrs. Postelwaite? I'm so sorry to hear about your troubles today, and I won't infringe on you for too long. But…I have a gift for you and for each of your boys from an anonymous donor." He opened his briefcase and pulled out some papers and envelopes.

He continued. "First of all let me tell you that a motor home is being set up on your lot where the old barn used to be. The contractor was out there when the boys showed up, and he suggested that we put it there so that there would be room to manipulate around the burned structure. This is the title to it, free and clear."

Bette and the boys just looked at each other.

Marty started to laugh. "Pat was just here and didn't say one word, that son of a gun!"

"No, we asked him not to say anything until we had a chance to talk to you all."

"Who would give us such a thing? Why would they do that?" Bette looked confused.

"Mrs. Postelwaite, there's not a man or woman among us that wouldn't love to do that for you. Believe me when I say, that the person who did this could well afford to do it, and it will cause no hardship whatsoever."

"How could we possibly accept this? We can't accept this, I'm sorry."

"This is just part of the gift. I have a letter to read."

I give these gifts with a free heart and no reservations and no strings attached. Please accept these gifts from one who received help and love from charitable neighbors when I was in great need and had nothing. With the money being offered, you may feel free to build a new house for yourselves. The motor home is yours, regardless, to do whatever you would like to do with it. It should be a nice temporary home until a permanent structure has been built.

I ask only that you consider offering your bountiful love, in some form, to other families who suffer abuse and are in need. Consider what you all can teach others from your experiences. Many families are in need of a roof when they are faced with fear and abuse at the hands of people who betray their love with pain and suffering. Please do what you can to help them to rebuild their lives and have a place to go to be safe.

The trust accounts are for the boys' college education. I offer these gifts in the name of the love that you all deserve.

Blessings upon you and yours in all ways and always.

Grant handed them all envelopes. "The boys' education fund has been set up in trust. The amount of the overall trust and the provisions for release of funds is noted in the documents."

The boys all opened their envelopes and looked at the amount. They were still speechless. Jerry handed his to his ma, and she looked at Marty and Lynne, and then handed them Jerry's envelope to look at.

"Here is a check for you to rebuild your structure." Bette looked at it, and it was a cashier's check for $500,000.00. "And here are bearer bonds for your future." Bette looked at them in a daze.

"There are fifty of them in increments of $100,000.00 each. By my reckoning...that's five million dollars," Grant smiled

Grant continued, "Bearer bonds are legal in Wyoming, but you'll notice there are no names on them, so they are negotiable by the 'bearer,' whoever has them in their possession. I would strongly recommend that you open a safety deposit box and keep them secure."

Grant took a big drink from his lemonade and sat back leisurely in his rocker. "If you decide to open a safe house in the future at some point, I would also strongly recommend that you set yourself up as a non-profit organization or foundation as soon as possible to save on what they can take in taxes. Just let me know if that is your decision, and I'll help you." The boys all crowded around her and looked at the check and bonds and looked at each other in disbelief.

Bette looked down at her open hands and shook her head, "I don't know what to do? I really don't know what to say."

Marty came over to her and squatted in front of her so she could meet his eyes. "Say, thank you."

Bette looked in his eyes for a long time. She looked at the boys and they all nodded "yes."

She closed her eyes. "Thank you." She addressed Grant Morrison. "If we wrote a letter, could you get it to this person?" she asked.

"I don't have a way to do that. I don't even have a way to give the money back if I wanted to. This person's location is confidential, even from us."

Grant got up and started walking toward his car. "Marty, I'd ask you to join me for that beer, but it looks like you guys have a lot to talk over. Some other time?"

Marty walked him to his car and shook his hand. "It would be my pleasure. Thanks, Grant." Marty waved, and Grant drove away.

The boys were all huddled around their mother hugging and kissing her. Everybody was totally overwhelmed.

Jeff took both of her hands in his and said reverently. "Ma, when I look at these beautiful hands, I see and feel love and care there. Don't you think these hands could help where other hands have hurt?"

Peter added, "Ma, we would have all gone somewhere else sometimes when it was so bad if there had been somewhere to go. We can be that somewhere to go. We can do that, can't we?"

"Yes, I think we can. We'll get our bearings first for just a little while, huh? I guess we'll just have to thank God, and then we'll do what we can to help others with this money, wouldn't you say, boys?" Bette asked. They all nodded their agreement.

"Marty and Lynne, what do you think? Could we do something like that?" Bette asked.

Lynne hugged her, "I happen to think you can do anything."

Marty hugged her, "I have a name for it for you. Want to hear it?"

"Prismland?" Bette asked smiling.

"Prismland. A magical kingdom where it's safe and full of light and love and beauty. Where the surprise around every corner might be finding yourself. Finding yourselves to be worthy of love, to be worthy of being treated with simple human kindness. To know that someone is there who knows and understands, and who can teach those who are in pain to trust and love again in a safe environment," Marty replied.

"Write that down Ernie," said Blake. "Those exact words. That's good!"

Lynne smiled at Marty, and he smiled back, his eyes full of tears. "Better be careful, Daddy Shakespeare, I just might fall in love with you all over again."

"Daddy?" Martin got up and moved to Lynne. "You've only called me daddy once before!"

"When you were going to be a daddy?" Lynne smiled.

"Are you kidding, honey? You got a bun in that beautiful oven?" Marty asked while he was lifting up her shirt to look.

She giggled and let him look at her tummy. She stroked his hair and kissed him. "Just a little bun. It won't be cooked for eight months or so."

"When did you find out?" He asked.

"Spero told me this morning. Oh my goodness, was that this morning? Feels like a million years ago!" She looked at Bette in disbelief and Bette nodded. "Anyway, Spero told me I was pregnant just before he dressed in a pink satin, big top Master of Ceremonies costume, and the Fairies did the can-can for me!"

The boys looked in amazement at each other and just couldn't help it. They started cracking up just picturing it.

Bette smiled a little smile and said, "It's amazing, isn't it, this circle of life, and death, and birth."

"It's more amazing today than yesterday for me. If there can be Fairy godmothers or godfathers and Fairies and Elves, isn't the news of a little miracle of a baby possible? I'm putting my money on Spero that it is."

Lynne paused and looked around rather shyly at everyone. "I wanted to ask all of your permission for something. May I join you all in the cave? I now have an abundance of childish wonder."

Lynne turned to Marty and said, "Spero must not know what to think. I was so deep in shock, I just left without saying a word!!"

Marty hugged her. "That's my girl!" He drew back and looked in her eyes, "That sounds so much like you," and he kissed her again. "I'm sure he'll understand."

Lynne said, "I get the feeling that there's not much he doesn't understand."

Marty used his famous saying good for everything and every situation. "Boy, you said a mouthful."

✡

Spero Zezas

When Spero finished at the bank, he still wasn't finished. Bette and the boys had lost everything in the fire. The motor home he purchased was a repossession and was practically new, but it didn't have dishes or pots and pans or anything to set up a household with. He wanted Bette and the boys to be able to walk into a functional temporary home. He went by Prism, and Jo was there with Sonya going over the inventory process.

"Spero! Where did you disappear to this morning?"

Spero looked sheepishly at Jo, "That's what I came to talk to you about if you have a minute?"

Jo remembered her manners.

"A little late," Spero thought. He was really grouchy for some reason. He hummed to himself to settle down.

"Spero, I'd like to introduce you to Sonya Wallace, our new 'Prismette.' That's rather a catching job description title. Don't you think?" Sonya smiled. Spero couldn't help but to think that it was no wonder David was smitten.

"Sonya, pleased to make your acquaintance!" Spero smiled and extended his hand. Spero had a way to make every word and gesture feel and sound sincere, grouchy mood or not. Sonya was an instant friend.

"Sonya, would you mind watching the store for a moment while Spero and I go into the back room and talk?"

"No, it's fine. I'll work on this inventory until someone comes in. Then, I'll drop this immediately and pay attention to the customer!"

"That's the spirit! Remember, try to make them feel better when they leave with their purchases than when they came in," Jo beamed.

She and Spero walked to the office and went in and shut the door. Spero couldn't help commenting, "Snappy slogan. Keep it between the staff though. Tacky! Sonya is really a beautiful girl all the way through, huh?"

"I thought that too. What can I do you for? Are you all right? I worried about how quickly you disappeared."

"Remember when I told you I didn't have to work?" Spero asked. "Well, the truth of the matter is that I am really very wealthy, and I will be going home soon. There, I have no need of riches and material things." He looked at her and smiled, "No pockets and nothing to spend it on anyway. So, I have set Bette's family up with a temporary home and a future and hopefully a means of future income, if she plays her cards right. But what I don't have ready for her that I WANT ready for her, is the stuff of households and clothing."

Jo went and put her arms around him and kissed him on his cheek. "You are something, you are. That was a wonderful thing to do."

"They deserve not to struggle so hard. They would not be able to financially overcome this last disaster, and it was basically my fault to begin with. Don't get me wrong, I'm not doing this out of guilt. I had planned to distribute part of my worldly goods to them before. I'm just mad at myself. I underestimated Nels. I thought I had more time to prepare for him. If Lynne wouldn't have been on the ball, they might have been harmed, and it would have been my fault."

"What are you talking about?" Jo asked.

Spero took a few minutes to explain about his visit to the cell and the predicted outcome of Nels' violent tendencies. He stressed that Nels could have chosen to serve than to harm, and he chose the latter.

Spero was obviously in a rush. "The point is, and this is all hush-hush, I don't want them to know where the money came from, at least until we've all done what we need to do and I'm home. The motor home is being delivered, and Grant Morrison is delivering the paperwork in precisely four hours, and I'm not ready for them to come 'home' yet. I need to buy lots of stuff, and I don't know what to buy, I really don't! I used to eat out most of the time, and I don't have any idea what sizes those boys are or what kids would like to wear!"

Spero was in a panic now. "I like to wear this, and I'm apparently the only one with my sense of style. *This* is what I know how to buy, but I don't see that I'm setting any fashion trends with teenagers." He looked at her pitifully.

"You want me to go shopping with you?" Jo asked.

"Yes! Now, please. Can we go now? Can Sonya pitch hit for you for awhile?"

"That's the general idea of having an employee. Just let me let her know we'll be out awhile."

Jo told Sonya that she had some business to complete with Spero and might be gone for a few hours.

Sonya said, "If you're not back by 6:00, I'll just lock up and lock the deposit in the office, ok?"

"I'm so sorry to leave you so much when you're new at all this. I promise I'll make it up to you," Jo smiled.

Jo and Spero went shopping for "everything." Jo figured it was best to go to a "Mart" to save time. Jo had worked in a men's clothing store when she was in college, so could judge sizes pretty well. She was a "super shopper." She ripped through the store, throwing everything imaginable into three carts. They practically filled the van.

Jo stated, "Spero, we're going to run out of time. Can we bring the kids into this so they can help?"

Spero was fine with that as long as they kept his secret.

Jo called home, and David answered.

"David Selph, here."

"David, Spero and I are on the way home. A lot has happened this morning, and we'll fill you in, but right now I need you and Ariane to meet us at the Postelwaites. Don't go anywhere near the burned house."

"Burned house! What on Earth is going on, Mom?" David yelled.

"Nels Postelwaite burned their house down and would have trapped the family in the house if they would have been in there. Spero found him dead in the yard this morning. The family was at the Cresenzo's house. They knew he was getting out of jail today and arranged for Bette's family to be out of the house because they didn't know what Nels would do."

Jo took a long breath, "ANYWAY, Spero has been playing Santa Claus all day and has a motor home set up by the old barn that we need to get outfitted. We only have a couple of hours to make it look like home. Spero said to tell you this is top secret. He doesn't want anybody but us to know where the money came from."

"Spero has money?" David asked.

Spero grabbed the phone. "Yes! David, please bring sandwiches. Lots of them! And potato chips and soda too, please."

Jo was getting ready to hang up when Spero yelled, "AND COOKIES!"

Jo smiled at him. "He may not have heard the 'and cookies' part."

They were pulling into the Postelwaite place. The motor home was parked in a partially wooded area nestled beside rock bluffs. "This is really a nice location. They couldn't have picked a better spot. I'm glad they can't see the house from here," Jo observed.

They drove close to the motor home and Jo parked. Spero got out with a load of stuff and said, "It's supposed to be open."

He and Jo concentrated on getting the kitchen set up. Spero was so glad to have Jo's organizational skills. He concentrated on putting food in the pantry, and Jo did most of the rest of it. David and Ariane drove up and Jo met them at the door. "Bring in the rest of the stuff."

Spero yelled, "First bring in the food! I'm starving!"

The four of them took a moment to grab sandwiches and wash them down with pop. David and Ariane brought in six sleeping bags and then looked around the motor home.

David observed, "This is really roomy. I'm shocked! I've never been in one of these before." He looked around. There was actually room to sleep six.

"It's not a palace," Spero said, "but it's practically new, and it has a kitchen and a full size shower in the bathroom. Those were things that I thought were pretty important. We better get busy!"

Among the four of them, they got everything put away. Ariane stacked the clothes on the bed of the master suite. It was nice too, that Bette would have her privacy.

"OK, guys, let's vamoose!" Spero said, and they all piled in their vehicles and left and not a minute too soon.

✫

Postelwaites

Bette and the boys drove up alone. The Cresenzos felt they needed their space so said they would visit tomorrow. The big Cresenzo family had outfitted the boys with hand me down jeans and tee shirts. Lynne was quite a bit taller than Bette, but they managed to find a couple of things for Bette to wear.

It had been a totally overwhelming day and driving by the house was a bit much for them all. Most of them didn't want to look in that direction. Jeff did look. He was the only one.

It was a breath of fresh air to see the huge blue metallic motor home sitting in the glen. It had a pull out awning, and there were six chairs and a circular table sitting under the awning. It was very inviting.

"Welcome home, boys. Before we go in, let's sit a spell and get our breath. I feel like I haven't had one quiet moment, don't you all too?" They all nodded.

Bette sat in one of the comfortable chairs, and the boys sat in a circle around her. She reached out her hands to one boy on each side of her, and they understood she wanted to pray together. They all bowed their heads.

"Lord, this has been a hard day on this family and yet an incredibly blessed day for the gifts so graciously given and the love of our friends and family. We ask your blessing. Bless the Angel or Angels you sent to us who gave us a home and the means to better ourselves. Make us worthy of their gifts. Give us the strength to do what needs to be done in the service of your house. Please bless our new temporary house and guide us in the choices we have in the future," Bette hesitated for a moment, *".... And Lord... please try to forgive Nels what he did if you can find it in your heart... help him understand.... just help him to understand....everything. Help him to find the love in heaven that he wouldn't find on Earth. We will try to live in your love and with your grace, forever, Amen."*

The boys all dropped their hands and just sat there looking at each other. Their mother's love and forgiveness apparently knew no bounds. It was apparent that they would all have to work on that. Right now, they didn't feel very forgiving to their father, but they did feel incredibly grateful to have a secure future and a home together.

They sat there for a few minutes. Jeff asked, "Sorry, does it have a bathroom that works?"

Bette answered, "Supposed to be all set up to live in. Let's go see."

Bette opened the door and bouquet of flowers was on the kitchen table. It was a beautiful welcome. They all spread out and started opening drawers and kitchen cupboards and exploring the motor home. They were all exclaiming and yelling out when they found something else.

"Ma, they stocked the pantry," Jerry exclaimed.

Blake was happy, "Ma, the refrigerator's full."

"Hey, new dishes and glasses and silverware!" Peter was picking up one of the spoons looking at the pattern.

"Ma, there's a bunch of clothes in here. This will be your room though, it's really cute!" Jeff said.

"Here's a whole folder that tells us about the holding tank and all about the maintenance features of the motor home." Ernie sat down and immediately started reading.

Bette walked into the kitchen and opened the refrigerator and looked in there for a long time and then a slight smile came over her face. "Do you suppose Fairies had anything to do with this?" She asked as she opened the freezer and looked in there too.

Blake came and looked over her shoulder. They looked at each other and smiled, "It feels like a little Fairy kingdom, I agree," Blake grinned and said.

"All we need is candles, Ma," Jeff replied.

Peter had just opened a drawer. "Magic! Here they are!"

Jerry put the candles on a couple of holders which were also in the drawer and lit them and placed them on either side of the flowers. "There, feels like our new home already."

"I think we will have to make a special dinner in our little Fairy kingdom for the Elf responsible for all of this," Bette said. Everybody looked around at each other.

What makes you think it's Spero?" Peter asked.

"No bacon." Bette and Blake said together and everybody laughed.

☆
Vanderlin/Selph Family and Spero

Jo didn't go back to work. She called Sonya who assured her that it wasn't busy and everything was fine. Jo, Spero, David, and Ariane were sitting at the kitchen table in zombie land. It had been a very long and stressful day.

"Spero," David said casually, "How rich are you?"

Ariane said, "David, that is a really nosy and rude question to ask. He'll tell us if he wants to." Ariane looked at him expectantly.

Spero looked exasperated and threw up his hands. "Money has always been my bane. I can't get rid of the stuff fast enough. I've tried! I've invested poorly and taken huge risks, and I just keep earning more and more of the stuff. I started out with nothing and didn't need much, so I started saving and investing. Then, people kept giving me *their* money when they transformed on. I was able to do quite a lot of good with it and gave away lots and lots of it for YEARS. I finally hired a financial manager to handle everything so I didn't have to wrap my brain around it anymore." He sighed.

"In the last few years, I've been hatching plans for when I go home." Spero explained, "I can't take it with me, and there's enough to do some good, I think. When it gets closer to time for me to go home, we'll talk more about it. Even talking about it wears me out!" Spero stood up and stretched. The subject was closed.

"Jo, I can make dinner for us if you'd like?" He was offering, but he was obviously exhausted. Jo seemed to be sinking into the chair.

David said, "Let Ariane and me make it for you and mom. You guys go in the living room and watch TV or something."

Jo put out her arm and Spero took it. "Can we watch the education channel? It's really funny!!" Spero asked.

"I'm game, as long as it isn't sports or reality TV," Jo answered.

Ariane and David looked in the refrigerator and the pantry. Ariane turned to David and looked at him with big eyes, like she was having an epiphany. "I just remembered, I don't know how to cook!" She looked quite surprised.

David started laughing. "Lucky for us then, that I know how to." He went to the refrigerator and pulled out some hamburger. "Ariane, put that in that frying pan there and turn the dial for 'right front' to 5 and break the hamburger up with a turner. Just keep turning the pieces around until they're brown all the way through, ok?"

Ariane was concentrating hard and had her tongue sticking out as she was waiting to turn it over. David couldn't help but smile and think to himself, "She's a pretty cute kid."

David cut up onions and threw those into the pan and got down garlic, chili powder, and cumin. "Let me, David. Tell me how much of each one!" Ariane asked.

David told her to "shake, shake, shake" as much as she thought she should of everything but the chili, and he gave her a tablespoon full of that. "You're going to be the one who cooks the whole dinner! I just cut up the onions!"

Ariane looked deadly serious and concentrated on the task at hand. David was actually impressed that she used about the amount that he would have. The meat was fully browned. Ariane smelled it and smiled, "Now what do we do?"

David said, "We transfer the meat, not the fat, with a slotted spoon to a big sauce pan and started to demonstrate.

"Let me do it," Ariane said and out came the concentrating tongue again.

David got down three cans of chili beans and two large cans of diced tomatoes. Ariane opened those and poured them in. David continued, "Now take an empty large can of diced tomatoes and add that much water. Now turn down the heat to simmer and put this lid on it and stir it once in awhile. After about one-half hour get a spoon and taste it, and if it needs more spices, put in more. Then it needs to cook for maybe an hour more."

They could hear Spero laughing and laughing from the living room. David headed in that direction and said, "OK, you cook. I'm going to go watch Spero's comedy show."

Ariane stood over the chili and watched the clock for ½ hour. When she tasted it, it was barely warm, but it really tasted good so she decided not to add anything. "A good cook knows when to stop adding things," she told herself.

She set the table with bowls and glasses for milk and went outside and picked some flowers from her wild garden spot. She got down the crackers and the pickles. Her family always ate dill pickles with their chili. She sat in the kitchen and just daydreamed and got up to stir once in awhile. After one hour passed, she called out to everyone, "Dinner's ready!" She poured the milk and stood there grinning from ear to ear.

Everyone came in, and she asked David, "Will you serve, please?" and she sat down too.

David couldn't resist a bow. They all got a big bowl of chili, and David sat down and raised his glass in a toast. Everyone raised their glass of milk too. "To the cook!"

Spero and Jo smiled and toasted her, "To Ariane!"

Ariane looked around at everybody and smiled shyly and said, "Let's eat! Hope you like it."

Everyone did like it! Spero ate three bowls with pickles, too. David rustled her hair. "You did good, kid. I'm proud of you."

Ariane wished she could save this moment forever.

Chapter Eight
Thursday

☆

Bette Postelwaite

Bette woke up early with the Sun coming through lace curtains. How did Spero think of lace curtains for her? She had always loved them. They reminded her of her mother, and then she remembered, Spero had seen her mother's bedroom. He had been a part of her life, an integral part, all of her life. He was the reason she had a mother to cherish and a brother. She still missed her younger brother, too. He only lived to be twenty-three before he was killed in a car accident.

She just enjoyed the moment before the harsh remembrance of yesterday's ugliness snuck back into her consciousness. She couldn't get the picture of the house out of her mind and knew she would have to drive by or walk by it every day. That was just a little more than she could handle right now.

She was a multi-millionaire. She had to remind herself again. She was a multi-millionaire, and she could afford to take care of her family now without constant worry and struggle. So often in the past she didn't know where their next meal would come from, but somehow God always provided.

The Sheriff had said that the Coroner would examine the body for foul play and if none was found would release it for burial. That didn't make much sense to her, as the foul play at hand was his. She just couldn't understand how Nels could have done what he did. No matter what had happened in their lives, she couldn't understand it. She was almost ready to cry again and decided she just had too much to do.

She got up quietly and went into the bathroom and turned the shower on. She marveled for about the 100th time how efficiently organized everything was in such a small area. The shower was full sized which really made it nice for her bigger boys. She remembered that Ernie said they'd have to conserve water so the little hot water heater could keep up, so she took just a quick shower.

She opened up the medicine cabinet and smiled. There was a good supply of little essentials: deodorant, mouthwash, toothbrushes, toothpaste, peroxide, etc.

She had no doubt in her mind that Spero was her Fairy godfather. It made accepting all of this easier to handle. She didn't have to feel like a charity case with Spero. He was family. In her mind, he would always be family.

She dressed and went into the small kitchen which opened into the living room. The boys were starting to wake up and were putting their appointed beds back in place. They could all sleep comfortably. It was just amazing. Spero had thought of everything. The sleeping bags were a great idea. She started some coffee and said, "Well, shall we have our first meal in our new home?"

She said the magic words that got immediate boy attention.

"Yeah, Ma! Let's have bacon!" and they all laughed, except Jeff. He was not a morning person, and it was a moral imperative to be grouchy until ten a.m. or so.

"How about French toast and eggs?" Bette said.

They all went about getting dressed and getting ready for their day. Ernie pointed out that they would have to stagger showers to have enough hot water available, so he and Blake worked out a schedule.

Peter piped up, "And this bathroom is NOT going to be trashed like our old one used to be. Everybody wipe down the shower and pick up their towels and keep the water off the floor." They all laughed at him. "I MEAN IT!"

"So do I. I did a lot of the housekeepin' without much help. Nels always thought cleaning was woman's work, but that has to change now and forever. We are living in pretty tight quarters, and everyone needs to clean up after themselves. Everyone needs to pitch in." The boys nodded their heads in agreement.

Bette continued, "We're going to have to work things out as we go. We'll have to do laundry in town, and I need to decide where to put the dirty clothes, but those things we'll work out. I need to ask a favor of you for today. I'd like to clear the old road to the barn from the west so we can avoid having to pass the old house every time, everyday. I just don't feel like I want to face it for a little while. We can go in and out through the old gate, ok? Let's move the truck and flatbed near here. Quite frankly, we can afford to have the house torn down and bulldozed away and never have to look at it again, and I want to do that. I don't want to deal with any of it." The boys looked at each other. They felt the same way, but they were surprised that she was taking this line.

"I want to rebuild on the back part of our property eventually. We have two sections we've never done much with except timber here and there. You all have been very careful to keep our trees thinned out, and we still we have healthy wooded area all around us. Thank you for that, by the way."

Blake smiled, because he was always adamant about that, and the other boys gave him his way.

"The other thing we have to talk about is your father's funeral. I have to know what you want to do." Bette looked in all of their eyes.

The boys looked at each other and Ernie finally said, "Ma, we were talking about that last night. We all realize that you're a good Christian and all, and we try to be, but we don't really want to be such hypocrites as having a big funeral and everything with everybody talking about what a good man he is. The preacher wouldn't even know him, and it's a bit much to listen to anyone going on and on about Pa's place in heaven. We're sorry, Ma. Maybe someday we can all forgive him for everything, trying to kill us all in such a horrible way and all, but right now, there's not much forgiveness."

Bette had tears in her eyes and looked at all of her boys, "And you all talked it out and this is what you decided?"

Peter said, "Ma, we know you're awfully disappointed in us, but I tried to remember one good memory with father, and I don't have any. I wouldn't know a good thing to say about him."

Jerry said, "What we thought we could do is cremate his body and take his ashes out to the lake. I remember he used to like to fish with your Pa when I was little. I do remember that. Maybe he was happy there and would like that."

Blake said, "Ma, you could say a prayer over him. We would all be there, just our family, OK? None of us would say anything mean, we promise." Jeff nodded.

Bette said quietly, "I think that would be just fine. I think that is what should happen. We'll do that."

✼

Postelwaite Family Makes Plans

Bette called the Sheriff's office and asked if they had heard anything from the Coroner yet. Jim said the Coroner said Nels died of natural causes and that foul play had been ruled out. They could release the body anytime.

Bette then called a funeral parlor and asked that they pick up Nels' body from the Coroner and arrange for immediate cremation.

"Will you want a period of time to view the body and arrange a service?" the kind sounding gentleman asked.

"No, we just want him cremated as soon as possible, and I will pick up the ashes for a family service."

Bette finished making the arrangements and the funeral parlor said she could pick up the ashes tomorrow morning.

Bette then called Grant Morrison at the bank and arranged to come in to open up a safety deposit box and a checking and savings account. He asked her to come to him personally, and he'd get her taken care of.

Bette then called Marty.

"Marty, can you get a hold of the man you were working with for the estimate on the house and ask him to tear down the house and excavate the foundation out and then fill it with earth? I don't want any part of it left. I'd also like to talk to him about some house plans. The boys and I decided we would like to have our house separate from the safe house, so we still have a family life to go home to. I want to build a ranch style house, on one level back in the North two sections area for privacy. Boy, does it feel strange to be coming up with all these plans that involve lots of money."

"I'm loving it, Bits. I'll have Pat call you. Have you given any thought to where you would want to build the safe house?"

"I'm really leaning toward building it where the motor home is now. This area is beautiful, and I think a little more secure being backed up against the bluffs like it is. Do you think it's too selfish of me to build our house first and take it a little slow to get the safe house going? I have so much to learn, and I don't feel ready to help anyone until I'm stronger and the boys are settled and healed some."

"I think it would be doing yourself and your family a disservice to try and get it going until you're ready. Don't you feel guilty for waiting. You've got lots of time and lots of healing to do before you can take that on."

"Thanks for saying that. Is Pat a good house contractor too?"

"The best!" Marty exclaimed.

"Marty, I am so out of my element here, will you help guide me through the house building process?"

"It would be my pleasure," Marty said. "Start thinking about what you want. We'll find a plan to suit you."

"What I want?" Bette said. "How weird is that? I barely know."

"You'll be surprised when you start getting into this how exactly you will know what you do and do not want. Just relax and don't stress over it. It's a long process to get a house built, so you'll have time to regroup."

Bette explained to Marty that she was going to go to the bank today to get a safety deposit box and open up bank accounts. She said that they had arranged to pick up Nels' ashes tomorrow. She told him about their family's decision not to have a public service. He understood fully and said everyone else would understand too. She asked if he and his family would join them for dinner tomorrow night at their motor home and said she was going to invite Spero and Jo's family too.

Chapter Nine
Friday

✧

Postelwaites

Bette and the boys went into Cheyenne and picked up Nels' ashes from the funeral home. Bette gave them a check to pay for it all. It was the first large check that she had written in her life.

They drove out to North Crow Lake. It was a little known public lake, and it held a lot of memories of Bette's family fishing and camping when she was growing up. The high school crowd that Bette traveled with had a lot of parties out here, so she thought that if anything held good memories for Nels, this would be the place. She had written down what she wanted to say, and it surprised her how much she wanted to say to and about Nels that had gone unsaid.

She and the boys gathered together in a circle and held hands. Nels' cremation vessel was in the middle of the circle.

She began speaking,

"Lord, we gather together a family confused by much of what went on in our family. Nels and I started out in love and anxious to have children and a home with a future that was bright. This spot where we stand

holds some happy memories, and we bring Nels' ashes to this place to say goodbye because he was happy here.

But somewhere along the way, hard drinking, hardship, and financial worries turned Nels into someone I didn't know. The first time he hit me, I was shocked and blamed the drink. The other times, I blamed myself for not being good enough and not doing the right things to make him love me. Then I lost myself somehow. Nothing I did seemed to matter. He kept drinking and fighting and getting into trouble with the law. He kept losing friends and jobs. We almost starved. Then I finally told him I'd leave him if he didn't stop drinking. To his credit, he did stop drinking and settled down some. He was real sorry and swore he'd never hurt me again, and our lives started getting back on track.

Then Jerry was born and the other boys followed within a short period of time. Nels always worked hard when the boys were little. He was gone much of the time trying to make a living for us. We never had much, but the first few years were fine. Then Nels' dad died, and then his mother died, and something died in his soul. He took to brooding and drinking again and fighting with everyone and saying terrible mean things to me. He never opened up with what was wrong. He wouldn't talk to me. Never told me why things suddenly turned so ugly.

It wasn't long after his folks died and their house and land taken for taxes that Nels starting abusing me and the little boys. At first, it was just saying awful and unforgivable things, and then it got worse. These boys have all been really hurt by Nels when they wanted to love him. They got a harsh hand instead of a hand up. He was never a loving father, never let us love him… and apparently never really loved us back. I just have to say, I don't think he had it in him to love, and it took me a lifetime with him to figure that out. When he almost killed our Peter, I figured it out. I don't know if you can find it in your heart to forgive him for all the wrong he did. He burned our home to the ground and tried to kill us all in our beds. I haven't been able to understand one thing about all of this. Something killed the love in him, and nothing I could do ever put it right. If you can work with his soul and help to heal it, we would all appreciate it. Please help us Lord, to understand someday and heal this family of this hurt.

Amen."

The boys all dropped hands and they were all crying. Nobody said another word. Bette's eyes were totally dry.

They all got into the truck and headed back home.

"What are we going to do with the ashes?" Jerry asked.

"I made arrangements through the funeral parlor to inter them at their repository, or whatever they call it. I don't want them here. He doesn't deserve to be with us."

The boys all looked at each other. This wasn't like their ma, but Jeff seemed to understand. She was getting a good mad up and getting herself back.

When they returned to the motor home, Bette said. "We've got our friends coming over tonight. Let's get busy with the makins' of a dinner for them. We can't any of us pretend it's in honor of the deceased, so we'll say it's in honor of our Fairy godfather instead. We'll surround ourselves with the people who really love us, huh?"

☆

Friends are Family

At 6:00 everyone started showing up. Marty and Lynne brought extra tables and chairs and tablecloths, and they sat them up outside under the awning. Lynne had made flower arrangements for the tables. Jo stopped and ordered a dessert from a popular local mom and pop Italian restaurant and picked it up before she came home. It was Tiramisu.

Bette and the boys greeted everyone and after the initial tour of the motor home, everyone gathered around the table. Bette stood up and raised her glass, "Here's to friends and family and friends who are our family and here's to our Fairy godfather, Spero!"

The boys stood up with her and raised their glasses with pop in them to Spero. Spero tried to look innocent and was looking around at everyone like he didn't know what they were talking about.

"Gig's up, Spero," Jeff said. "Would you like to know how we figured it out?"

Everyone smiled and laughed and Peter said, "1,2,3" Then they all yelled, "NO BACON!"

Spero smiled sheepishly, and Bette and the boys walked over to where he was sitting. Bette hugged him and kissed his cheek and the boys all patted him on the shoulder. Everybody thanked him.

"I was kind of hoping to avoid this," Spero said. "I can't think of any one I'd rather leave my Earthly wealth to. I won't need money or possessions where I'm going, and I'm happy to be able to leave them with you and a few of your friends."

"By the way, Demy, this is for you." Spero handed him an envelope out of thin air. "Marty and Lynne, this is for you. Don't open it here, please."

Bette was wiping away her tears, "It was a blessed day when you walked into my home when I was a child in answer to my plea to the Fairies. You saved my mother and my brother and Marty, and you saved us too. There are no words to thank you for what you have done for me and my family my whole life. You are a part of us and always will be, and you'll be remembered in our prayers for all of our days. You are welcome to come visit us or stay with us anytime. Hope you can visit?"

Spero looked around at all of them. "If we're successful and I have a home to go to, I have commitments there that I've neglected for the many wonderful years that I got to live among the humans we protect. I will miss you all more than I can possibly say, and I will keep an eye out for you, but I doubt if I'll be back. When I go, just promise me that you'll all think of ol' Spero once in awhile when you have a wonderful meal…like this one. …. Can we eat now?"

Everyone laughed and queued up for a buffet style meal. Spero was first in line. He showed a great deal of restraint in not piling his plate to the ceiling but couldn't restrain himself from eating Tiramisu first. He had a blissful expression on his face as he ate it and was humming.

Everyone really enjoyed the meal and the company. They were all having coffee and dessert again when Peter asked, "Spero, you said we were running out of time. When do we need to meet again at the cave?"

"The crystals should be re-energized by now if you've all remembered to get them outside for a time." They all indicated they had. "We've all been a little busy, huh?" Everyone nodded in the affirmative. "We are in a time crunch. I'm sorry the timing is so bad with everything going on, but yes, we need to help them as soon as we can. I don't know how bad things have gotten since the alarm was sounded."

Bette said. "We have important business to take care of in helping you save your world. Let's meet tomorrow. What time, Spero?"

"How about at noon?" Spero said.

Lynne cleared her throat. "I just wanted to ask if I can be there to lend moral support to everyone. I promise not to interfere or be negative in any way."

Spero looked at her, "Did you tell everyone about your experience with the Fairies?

She smiled, "Yes, they did a lovely can-can for me."

Everyone laughed again and agreed to be there at noon. That story was never going to get old.

Jo called Tazman on her cell, and he agreed to meet them at noon at the cave.

"Spero, Tazman said a weird thing. He said to tell you he was taking his ancestor home via the sulde? What's a sulde?"

"It's a Mongolian spirit stick. Well, good, it's time," Spero said simply.

Chapter Ten
Saturday

✩

Vanderlin/Selph and Spero

Everybody at Bette's house, Jo's house, and the Cresenzo house slept in. They knew it was going to be a very draining day. They all breakfasted together in their respective homes making small talk and just enjoyed being together.

The mood at the Selph/Vanderlin household was sad. Spero might be leaving today. He looked across at Ariane pushing her eggs around the plate and not eating them and said, "Well, if you're just going to waste those, hand them here!"

Ariane smiled and handed over her plate. "I'm just not hungry. I want to help the light people, but we don't want you to leave us forever. It's hard to say goodbye to you."

"I can't tell you how hard it is to say goodbye to all of you too. You are, and always will be, my Earthly family. You are all close to my heart, and I do hope we meet again. Maybe when you're ready to all transform out of your bodies, you'll come to visit me on your way. It's very possible, you know."

"It is?" David asked.

"Yes, that is what Walkers do. They help those who have reached spiritual transformation to move up from one dimension to another."

Jo was getting concerned. "Spero, the group isn't transforming from their lives here in what they do with you today are they? They will still have their bodies and their Earthly lives afterward, right? They aren't moving off our dimension permanently are they?"

"No, in this case, no. They are being given a rare glimpse into another world, in between heavy energy and a higher lighter dimension still, to what you all term Heaven, or what we call the Soulforce Pool. I'm here asking for very special and unique help that only a very blessed and a very select group of heavy bodies can do. Because of the power humans have upon our dimension, you are our only hope."

David had been listening very carefully. "How can you be at risk, really? You're like a level of Heaven then?"

"Everything is different than people believe. It is so hard to explain. We are very often at risk, and the Creator and the Soulforce Pool handle most of the problems. They can't do this one alone. WE can't do this one alone, because man has created this problem by polluting the living organism of Earth. It is up to humans to heal it and to stop it."

"To help that end, I've built an empire on Earth of great wealth. When I leave, I will leave that wealth, in part, to the one person destined and capable of handling it. It will be his task first to fight for the Earth and work to stop the continued pollution of Earth and the space surrounding it. He will have to battle in courts and speak publicly against pollution of any kind. He is someone who has great presence and is used to great wealth. He will now be tested to distribute his own wealth of assets and knowledge and the wealth I give him now in this quest."

Ariane asked, "But Spero, who are you talking about?"

"Tazman Khan. He is the living Record Keeper of Earth. You and David together are the living Record Keepers of Rainbow World. Your mother will have half of my remaining wealth in trust for your decision to be an advocate of Earth or not. If you help keep Earth healthy, you keep the Rainbow World healthy so you honor the Record Keeper's choice and fulfill your destiny."

Spero explained further, "If either of you decides not to take on this task, and that is your choice, it goes to world environmental groups if you both decline, or to Ariane, if you decline, David. Grant Morrison has the particulars in the 'strangest trust on the planet,' as he calls it."

Jo sputtered, "Spero, I'm flabbergasted in so many areas I don't even know where to begin! I thought you hated Tazman!"

"Tazman has been chosen since birth to be the Record Keeper for Earth. He is a descendant of Genghis Khan, the first Record Keeper for Earth. Genghis left Rainbow World before understanding his true destiny, but he partially fulfilled his destiny anyway. At the time he came to Earth, he did great and glorious things to unite a people, even though he was considered a barbarian and a murderous animal while doing it. It is considered that he completed his task on Earth and it falls to his line to continue the work, but on a global scale this time, not just in Genghis' conquered lands."

"Do you think Tazman will agree to this? Aren't you afraid that he'll abuse his legacy for control like Genghis did?" Jo asked. "And, quite frankly, this is putting an awful lot on David, and Ariane, and me, too. I'm not sure how I feel about that."

"I don't blame you, but I don't think the crystals choose lightly. Tazman, David, and Ariane will fulfill their destiny. Whatever they decide to do, it is their destiny to do that. Don't worry too much about it. It will all fall into the natural order of things."

"Spero? Why did the Record Keeper choose us?" Ariane asked shyly.

"Because you are both of true and pure hearts, the very purest of the pure. It has been my deep pleasure to have gotten to know you both and your mom and to be able to call myself your friend. I will always be watching out for you all, I promise." Spero's eyes were filled with tears.

"What will you tell the others? Will you tell them what you've told us?" Jo asked.

"No. This isn't easy to tell anyone. It hasn't been easy to tell you. Tazman will have to stay with us for a time to understand what he is doing. He won't be coming back to the circle. Jo, you'll need to step into the circle when his body disappears. This will all be explained to the group in Rainbow World. Depending on what is going on in Rainbow World, you should all be able to stay with us a day or so, even though it's thirty minutes on Earth."

"Tazman will be back in sixty of your days. He will, in fact, spend a great deal of time with us. At the point that he returns to Earth, he will decide whether or not he will take on the task assigned. If he decides to, he will have one-half of my remaining wealth available to him over a ten-year period. If he refuses the task, it all comes to you, Jo, in trust for David and Ariane."

"David and Ariane and Jo. You will keep, regardless, the separate fortunes I have arranged for you all. David and Ariane. When you both reach the age of twenty-four, it is for you then to decide if you will do the ten-year task. If one or both of you decline the ten-year task, it will fall to Jo to either shift the wealth to the other, or to donate to various world watch organizations, or hire a manager to handle the distribution. You all still have choices."

David had been very silent trying to get a handle on all of this. It was way overwhelming right now. He felt he would understand more when he actually had time to think and maybe it would be more meaningful when he got to Rainbow World.

David needed to bring something up to Spero before the group gathered in an hour. "Spero, I built this for Ariane to wear on her forehead. I believe that it will help her best on her third eye." It was a phylactery made of a soft white leather pouch with two long white leather strings attached. "I thought one of us could whistle to Mom when we were ready to cross over, and she could remove the crystal from Ariane's body at that time."

Spero looked at David in wonder. "David, how did you possibly think to do this?"

"I am gifted in very strange ways and fascinated with all things spiritual and mystical. It just seemed the logical way to handle this," David said.

"Ok with you, Ariane?" Spero asked.

"Oh yes. I've been wearing it around the house since David made it for me to get used to how it feels. It makes things really clear, and I can hear all kinds of things I didn't before. One of the things I heard was that we needed as many crystals as we could possibly get, so David and I have gathered all we could buy or find. We've been cleansing them and asking them to help. We have the ones ready who want to help in this bag."

"So that is who bought the bag that was in the store," Jo said. "So you guys are the crystal buyers who bought all of Prism's crystals from Sonya when I was out, huh?"

"Yeah, it was a really terrible experience," David smiled. "I may run entirely out of money trying to think of more things to buy when you're out, Mom."

✫

Into the Light

Demy and his family opened Spero's letters, and he had given Demy a trust for his college education. He gave Marty and Lynne enough money to build the dude ranch. They were really grateful. Ranching was land rich business; cash was hard won.

Marty had been out after breakfast in the truck. He and the ranch hands had been checking out the horses' feed and water consumption. If the horses didn't drink about ten gallons of water a day at least, they got dehydrated. Marty would often add a tablespoon or so of salt from their salt bag to their special yummy grain to make them thirsty so they would drink the water they needed. They were just finishing up when Marty looked at his watch. It was 11:45. He tore back to the house in the pickup he'd been driving. Lynne and Demy were waiting on the porch.

"Cut that a little close, didn't you slick?" Lynne said. She was clearly annoyed.

"Sorry, pile in here, and we'll skedaddle," Marty said as he was throwing ropes and gloves and junk on the floor. He turned to Demy, "Got your communicator, son?"

"Yep, you son?" Demy responded.

"Yep, you son?" Marty bantered.

"ENOUGH! You sons," Lynne replied testily.

He drove to the cave and they were all waiting at their cars. "We wanted to wait for you all to get here before we went in," Bette said.

"Spero here yet?" Lynne asked.

"They'll be here shortly," Bette replied, "Jo called and said they were on their way."

Tazman had been standing there silently. He had slung a bando-lier sling arrangement across his back holding a really ancient looking wooden and metal staff with odd symbols and patchy fibers of some sort...horsehair, maybe.

"What's that?" Demy asked pointing to the staff.

"My great, great, great... well, lots of greats, grandfather," Tazman replied.

"Oh," said Demy stoically. When he turned his back and only Peter could see him, he rolled his eyes. Peter tried to be cool and not burst out laughing.

Spero and the Selph/Vanderlin tribe drove up and disembarked. "Sorry, we're late. We were having lunch."

Jo said jokingly, "We may have to roll Spero in there."

Martin and Lynne and Demy took the opportunity to go shake Spero's hand and thank him for his generous gifts. He touched fore-heads with them all and didn't say anything.

Spero said, "Well, the first thing is to re-build our circle again. Let's all do the same as the first time. Ariane has received a message that the circle needs extra crystals for white light help, so we will place those last."

Demy and Peter came alongside Ariane, "What's that on your head?" Demy asked.

"David made me a phylactery to put the Rainbow World crystal in so I can hear better. When we get ready to go through the light, I'll whistle and Mom will take it off because the Record Keeper can't go through. David thought of the idea!"

The Postelwaite boys patted David on the back good naturedly. Ernie said, "That's really purdy. You should wear one to school next year, David."

"Yeah? Will you beat me up if I do?"

"Yeah. We'll beat you up so we can wear it too, so we'll be purdy too," Blake joked. He looked at his mother's scowl, "Ma, don't worry, we're just kidding! Our beating up people days are over. Besides that, David is our buddy. You gotta let us joke once in awhile."

"You have a reputation to overcome and those types of comments are still aggressive. You need to re-evaluate what you call a joke. Lots of intimidation goes on in the disguise of a joke." Ma wasn't backing off it.

Both of the boys apologized to David and to their ma.

Marty said to the group, "I've brought along a few of the torches my dad made. These last quite awhile Jo, and fit in places in the wall. If they start to go out, you can light one with another or with this." He gave her a long pilot lighter.

Spero and David and Ariane started placing the stones back in the circle.

Spero explained, "I'm working with my spare crystal to determine placement. It can tell us just as well as the Record Keeper. We need to keep the Record Keeper as strong as possible."

Once all of the stones were placed and Ariane was happy with the circle, they lit a good size fire in the fire pit and everyone started to enter when Jo stopped them. "Don't forget to place the crystals first."

Ariane said, "We have twenty-four crystals. I really don't know where they should go."

Tazman suggested, "Make a crystal outer circle. It helps to keep the energy and us safer within the stone circle. Place the crystals in between where the stones are, so there is a continual path of protection all around."

"That sounds right," Ariane said. She put her hand in the bag and drew out one crystal at a time, placing the crystals in the suggested pattern going clockwise around the circle.

Jo said, "I brought along blankets this time. You'll be gone a long time, and your bodies need to stay as warm as possible. Everyone take a blanket and some water."

They all queued up and got their blanket and water bottle. "Why water?" Marty asked, "Just curious."

Jo answered, "I honestly don't know why. I just had a feeling it was really important."

Spero answered, "Then we'll go with that, and here's a lesson for us all. Trust those kinds of instincts because they are generally there for good reason. Ok, Tazman, tell me if you agree with my instinct here. Ariane, before you place the last crystal, hand it to me, everyone go in through the gap in the North, and I'll go in last and seal the outer circle?"

"Sounds right," Tazman said.

"Sounds right," Ariane agreed.

This time, when Spero sealed the crystal outer circle and took his place, the energy was already starting to build on its own. Last time they felt the circle gently come alive. This time, it felt like a strong living entity.

Spero reiterated, "Remember, the circle must have twelve at all times, understood? Jo, it will be up to you to make sure."

Spero looked at Lynne. "Don't worry, Lynne. Remember what I told you." Lynne nodded.

Spero went on to explain. "What we are doing today is visiting the Rainbow World, assessing the condition and what is needed and returning to our bodies when we hear Jo's whistle, understood? Remember that Ariane will be whistling to Jo just before she enters so that Jo can physically remove the phylactery."

Spero thought of something else. "Oh! Jo, I didn't tell you this before, but come in from the North and move clockwise to Ariane. Ariane, you must not move through the light until Jo does a short whistle back to you indicating she has the crystal. Jo, put the crystal in front of Ariane but totally away from her body. It's ok for the crystal to be close to the fire and that would probably even help. Move back out of the circle clockwise back to the SOUTH, I didn't tell you guys last time, you enter from the North and exit from the South." Tazman nodded that he agreed.

"Everybody on board, everyone ok? Everybody got their communicator?" They all held it up. "Put it safely in your pocket so your hands are free," Spero said.

Jo started her guided meditation and very soon, everyone's head dropped. Jo started her stop watch for thirty minutes.

They all moved up into their astral bodies. Looking down, they saw their bodies and Jo and Lynne walking around the circle. The astral group gathered together and looked toward the light. It was not as bright as before. Spero indicated that they should follow, and he seemed to be speeding back. The group kept up with no problem, but not having the experience of actually moving very far before, they weren't prepared for what felt like the scenery changing and them barely moving forward. Still, they willed themselves forward at the same time.

Then, Spero held out his hand to Ariane behind him, and she offered her other hand to the person behind her, and they all joined hands. The tunnel whizzed by even faster then. The colors around them became a blur. They were closer to the light at the end of the tunnel than they had ever been. Spero slowed up and stopped and extended his astral hand with the palm out for a "stop" signal. The scenery around them became the rolling crystal prism shades again. He pointed to Ariane's phylactery, and she pulled the communicator crystal out of her pocket and whistled a short whistle to her mom. The phylactery disappeared, and they all heard Jo's short whistle back.

Spero grabbed Ariane's hand again, and they all joined hands. They all heard a psychic message: "Close your eyes through the door. It's too bright at first. Don't open them until I say to." Everyone did as he asked, and they went through blindly, trusting Spero to lead the way.

They felt the motion come to a complete stop and heard Spero sigh, "Oh, no!" They all tried to see what he was so distressed about but Spero cautioned quickly, "No! Don't open your eyes, yet. First, shield your eyes, and open them slowly behind your hands. Don't remove your hands until you've acclimated to the light."

When the group had their eyes closed, the brightness was evident even through closed lids. They shielded their eyes and opened them slowly. The stark clarity and brightness still overwhelmed them, but gradually a great shape came into view. It was a horribly injured and what appeared to be, chemically burned, Dragon. His eyes were closed, but he was breathing.

Spero got down on one knee and bowed to the Dragon, and the rest of them filed suit. The Dragon opened one eye and said, "Took you long enough to get here."

Spero smiled and walked over and hugged the Dragon. "Are you going to be ok?"

"I always am, but look around you, Prime," the Dragon snapped.

The group looked around them, and it looked like a war zone. Words can't describe what they saw. Creatures of unimaginable beauty and creatures that appeared almost like bugs or monsters being helped by the resplendent or by more things that appeared even more monsterish, alien, and foreign.

There were giant elusive long limbed semi-opaque rainbow colored creatures with big black slanted eyes. It was apparent that they usually dressed in soft, floaty attire, but that attire was burned in places and blackened and torn and dirty. Many of these beings appeared to be injured and were being nursed. Spero said these beings were called "Rainbow Creatures," and they worked in our skies too, moving moisture where it was needed. When they rejoiced, they made rainbows.

There were thousands of disk creatures of various sizes, from the size of a dime to the size of a big dinner plate. They had brightly colored backs and thousands of tiny tendrils surrounding the disk. They moved in any direction lightning fast. They darted in and out of the blackness trying to keep it from consuming the survivors. So many were lying on the ground upside down and appeared to be dead. Countless more of these creatures appeared to be working over the injured, even moving in and out of their mouths to work internally. Spero said they were the Minervans, who made the twin cloud spheres and helped to make clouds and move the air currents where they needed to go. They were the artists of the sky, telling stories in their cloud pictures. They had taken the biggest death toll here because they consumed the pollution, and it often made them sick or killed them. Spero said they had been giving their lives to us forever on Rainbow World and on Earth and deserved our respect because not only did they work in the sky, but they were learned healers also.

The Fairies were flitting everywhere and were showering the group with kisses. There were more on Earth now, then here.

There were so many different kinds of creatures. It was hard to even see them all. There were fantastically huge giants who seemed to be working in groups in circles on the ground, blowing at odd places onto a holistic floating sphere of the Earth that had cloud cover which was being affected by the blowing. David said, "I've seen their faces in the sky, blowing." He moved over to them to say hello. Spero said that those were the Directional Beings. They move air currents around the Earth to try to give moisture and cloud cover where it was needed. They primarily created wind currents, but that was also helped by the other Rainbow World workers.

They saw dolphins, whales, salmon, manatees, and jellyfish swimming and jumping out of a perfectly clear sea and noticed rainbow trout in lakes. The colors in the water can't be described. There were the blue and green and turquoise colors of the sea brightened by white light behind it, but on closer inspection, great dark patches could be seen in the waters, too. Additionally, there were mermaids and mermen lying on shore in sand that looked like crystals. Many of them were clearly hurt as well. Many of the water beings seemed absolutely frantic and panicked. Spero said that the Water Beings sang healing to all the worlds and worked diligently in the seas to help contain the pollution as well. Many of the Water Beings didn't look very healthy. Spero said their numbers are fewer and fewer, not only due to the work they did but because of Earth beings over fishing or mass harvesting in their feeding grounds.

There were Fire Beings too. They were surrounded by what could be described as the light of a fire, but not actual flame, here. They seemed to be surrounded by blue and red and orange auras. They were graceful and flowing, all of their movements seemed to be a dance. Spero called them "Astanaga People."

There were beings that at first glance appeared to be trees, but they were forms that David said he sometimes saw in trees or hidden among the leaves. They were the Wood Beings.

There were many characters that almost appeared like cartoon characters. Squat and funny faced, all different colors, but dressed primarily in Earth colors. Spero said they were inner Earth beings and lived around the Inner Sun of Earth and in vast cave systems.

Spero had said that the Lemp were beautiful and life-sized, but nothing prepared them for seeing their first Lemp. They had pink translucent bodies and even pinker hair. They were exquisitely hand-some. The males and females were slender and graceful. Their limbs were long and their fingers long and elegant. All of them wore black frame, nerdy glasses. Spero said, it was their running joke.

David asked who the Dragon was. Spero said, "He's called Senti-nel, and his real name is sacred and cannot be known. He is the old-est among us now. He is responsible for everything and everybody basically. He is, in fact, the Creator energy in form, called "Lifeforce Energy" which is VERY hard to explain or understand. I barely under-stand myself, and I'm the second oldest here," Spero sighed.

They had all been so fascinated, it took awhile to figure out that when they looked at each other they didn't just hear voices, they were starting to be able to see each other's bodies. It took awhile for them to notice a stranger walking along with their group. He was stand-ing beside Tazman. They all stopped suddenly and looked at Tazman. Tazman turned and looked at the stranger. He was mesmerized and was apparently at a loss for words.

The man said, "Hello, Grandson. Thanks for bringing me home."

Spero crossed to him, and the man got on one knee and bowed to Spero, and then bowed to the Sentinel and said, "Forgive me. I ask that I be allowed to come home. I will spend the rest of my days doing whatever is asked of me without question. I do not deserve your forgiveness, but I ask for it anyway."

The Dragon spoke, "Temujin, you have been a long time away from home. You may stay. But as to whether or not you will be forgiven, well, we'll have to see, won't we?"

The Dragon was clearly in pain and spoke after a long pause. "You will be tested. Your first task is to help your grandson understand his duties here and on Earth 1. He will stay with us for this period of time." The Dragon took a pocket watch out from behind a scale and handed it to Temujin. The watch had many hands and concentric wheels and symbols that turned within the face on small spheres.

Sentinel waited awhile longer before he seemed to gather the strength to speak again. "Your second task is to help your grandson go back safely to Earth 1 at the end of his time here, provided the humans here can help us clean up this mess. If they are not successful helping us, then Earth 1 is also finished. You must move your grandson and the crystal to safety. Do you understand these tasks as I have assigned them to you?"

Temujin got down on one knee and dropped his head.

Sentinel continued to speak, "NOW! Do you understand now just how misguided you were in stealing the wrong crystal?"

"The wrong crystal?"

The Dragon held out a crystal. "Yes, the wrong crystal. You stole the Rainbow World Record Keeper crystal which did not belong to you. THIS one belonged to you and your line. It is the Record Keeper for Earth." The dragon handed him the Earth Record Keeper. "You were meant for greater things up here. Vanity and power and pride were your premature downfall. Have you learned to deal with your insignificance yet, Genghis Khan?"

"I…I think so, finally, living in the sulde. I am only Temujin. I wished to come home to throw myself at your mercy and couldn't return. I accumulated wealth on Earth, yes, but always meant for it to be used to better advantage than it has. I accumulated the wisdom of many people that I meant to be used for better advantage than it has. I left these things in the safekeeping of my family to the day when we could give back. I tried to live the Walker life, even though I was unworthy. I hoped that my descendants would be more worthy." He turned and looked at Tazman and spoke, "It appears, Grandson, I was mistaken. We have a lot of work to do together."

Tazman lowered his eyes. The conflict within him was apparent. He was reacting very strangely to this speech. He seemed ashamed, but at the same time proud.

The Dragon looked from Tazman to Temujin, "I see you have your work cut out for you, Temujin."

"Yes, sir," Temujin turned to Tazman and looked him fiercely in the eyes. "Tazman Khan, I've watched you your whole life as I have watched our family before you. You have no secrets with me, and you do not fool me. You will stay with me here to begin Walker training at the very lowest level. I desire to begin again, with you, at the beginning."

Tazman raised one eyebrow and looked to Spero, and Spero nodded, "yes."

Marty interrupted the group, "I'm sorry to state the obvious, but have any of you looked up?"

As a group they all looked up. In the sky, they saw great angry looking black clouds, with lightning flashing in waves across the sky. There were several rolling tornados moving sporadically through the mass. It seemed like blackness was trying to consume what was left of their rainbow sky.

"Welcome to our World," said the Dragon in a tired voice. He closed his eyes and seemed to be sleeping. He said very weakly, "See what you can do about that, will you?"

As the Dragon said that, all of their communication crystals whistled with Jo's whistle. The Dragon smiled and said, "Clever that. Prime, you must stay too."

Spero obviously wasn't expecting that. He looked at them all for a moment before he bowed to the Sentinel. He walked over to the Postelwaite boys, Marty, and Demy, and hugged them and touched foreheads to each of them, thanking them and whispering encouragements. He hugged Bette for a long time, and she was crying. He went and stood between David and Ariane and pulled them into a group hug. He whispered, "I'll always be with you. Just think of me, and I'll see you and you'll see me." He touched foreheads to each of them.

He addressed the group, "I guess this is goodbye. Sooner than I thought, but…" He pointed up at the rolling blackness and shrugged his shoulders.

"But Spero, what do we do?" Ariane asked.

"Do what you did for the little one. It's just bigger this time. So THIS time, use more power!"

The Dragon whispered, "Matrix."

"Oh, and as you send it away from here, weave the hole it made and close the door behind it. You will probably not be able to get rid of it entirely, but surround it with a light weave and contain it until it becomes as small as you can make it in its own container." He was pushing them towards the light door to go back home. "I'm sorry you couldn't spend more time with us. It's obviously not safe here."

He hesitated and just looked longingly at them all one last time, memorizing all of their faces. He was crying and could barely speak. "Thank you guys for everything. I have every confidence that you can handle this."

He pulled David and Ariane close to him and gave them extra hugs and also gave an extra hug to Bette. "Lynne is going to need this," and he handed Ariane a crystal. "You have to go now. Jo will be worried. Give her my love."

"How do we get through the door?" David asked.

"Hold hands and close your eyes through the door and then follow your cording home. Stay together and don't let go. Remember, if you can conceive a thing, you can do that thing. See yourselves as successful and you will succeed."

The group grabbed hands, closed their eyes and walked through the Rainbow Light door.

Back in the cave, Lynne and Jo were getting worried. Jo had been whistling, but they had not returned immediately. "How long did it take for them to get to the door?" Jo asked.

"Shorter time than this. What can we do to help?" Lynne asked. She was really getting anxious.

"The only thing I keep thinking was that Ariane said they needed more crystals. She and David gathered a bunch, but I keep asking myself if they need more…wondering if they need more power or something now?"

"Wait here!" Lynne cried out and ran outside to their truck. She picked up the bag of salt that they used to mix with the grain and ran back into the cave. She started pouring the salt in the circle with the crystals. "Salt is crystalline structure. This should be like adding thousands and thousands of tiny crystals!"

Within seconds of the salt crystal being complete, everyone's eyes started fluttering, but their physical circle bodies were fading and flickering. Lynne and Jo watched helplessly as Spero's and Tazman's bodies became totally transparent and then disappeared entirely.

Jo yelled, "There have to be twelve in the circle, Lynne, go in the North and take Tazman's place, and I'll take Spero's."

As the women took the empty spots, the group's bodies became more substantial, and their eyes began to flutter. As their bodies came solidly visible, they all jumped up. Their clothes were smoking. The people who regained their bodies immediately doused themselves with the water Jo had forced on them.

They all looked at each other and laughed. Demy said, "Oh boy! The trip back was a lot faster than the trip there!

"Where's Spero?" Jo asked.

"He had to stay. Mom, we don't have much time. We have to help them, NOW," Ariane said and everybody nodded. "Mrs. Cresenzo, this crystal is from Spero. You'll need one to help us." She passed it to her, going clockwise around the group.

Ariane noticed that David was still sitting, smoking slightly and had his eyes closed. Marty leaned over and doused him with water.

David appeared to be concentrating hard on something, but other than that, he seemed ok.

Ariane elected herself to describe briefly what they saw and explained what they needed to do. "Spero said to do the same thing we did for the black tornado, but we have to send more power. Their sky is almost totally black, and there are several black tornado things, and there is a big hole in their...uh..."

"Matrix," the others chimed in.

"Yeah... matrix, which is invisible, but Spero said to weave the matrix closed with light and trap the blackness that we can't turn to white light in its own container outside of the closed hole...I don't understand what he wants, do you guys?"

Ernie said, "I was thinking it would be best first to build a big light sack, like a balloon that expands but won't break to contain the blackness, then push all of the blackness out the hole into the balloon and seal the hole. At that point, the Rainbow World is safe, and we just have to deal with the balloon outside. Then we concentrate on blasting the balloon with white light and turning it as light as we can, and then envision it shrinking and shrinking until it is as small as we can make it."

"Yeah, let's do that. How will we know if we are all doing it? How will we know when one part is sealed so we can go on to the next?" Jeff asked. They all looked at each other.

"I can tell you that. I don't know how I know, but after being there, I see them still, and I feel everything they feel, here." Ariane touched her forehead. "I don't think I have to have the crystal to see anymore."

"You are the crystal, Ariane," David said.

Ariane looked at David, and he nodded "yes." Her eyes were starting to adjust, and she looked around the circle and noticed the salt for the first time.

"Where did the salt come from?"

"You said you needed more white light and crystals. Salt is crystal." Jo said, "Mrs. Cresenzo had the brainstorm to add salt for more white light."

The group looked at her and smiled. Marty and Demy were beaming at her.

"Thank you so much for thinking of that," Bette said. "It feels powerful in here. Even more than last time. I really think that will help a lot." Everyone agreed.

"Maybe that's what helped us go into burn your clothes up super speed when we were coming back!" Jerry laughed, and everyone chuckled.

Ariane looked at Lynne, "You weren't here last time, so what we're going to do is concentrate on building up white light in the circle, moving it like the clock moves until it feels like it's ready to bust loose. You might even feel a little woozy; some of us did. Then we hold our crystals in the air and point them above the fire pit, and then we all VISUALIZE the energy in the circle going up through the crystal like a laser, meeting together, and then we send it to where we want it to go. Last time we even heard it, huh?" The group all nodded in an affirmative.

"The first visualization," Ariane smiled at the big word, "Let's do exactly what Ernie said. Make the pouch outside the hole, weave it together with light and attach it firmly to their outside matrix with lots of light legs that weave in and out of their sky matrix. Know what I mean? No gaps, no holes." Everybody nodded in agreement. "Make it really strong so it can't escape from the bag or bubble, ok? I'll tell you when we have that done."

Ariane continued, "When I say, 'Push, push, push,' send some of your own energy along with the white light so there is lots of power behind the white light from us. Visualize turning as much of the gunk as we can white. I'll tell you when it isn't shrinking anymore and then we'll seal their sky matrix quickly, ok?"

Ariane looked around. There was something she was forgetting. She suddenly remembered. "Oh, is everyone ok with this? I should have asked you first." Everyone nodded yes and smiled. Spero's spirit was still with them.

"Begin," Ariane said. Lynne was really not prepared for the amount of energy the group was generating. She tried to just keep it rolling so she wouldn't get sick. It was palpable and so heavy she thought she would get sick anyway. Being pregnant didn't help.

"NOW!" Ariane yelled and everyone held their crystals up over the fire pit. This time they could see what they were doing. They all actually saw the light meet and intensify. "NOW SEND IT TO THE RAINBOW WORLD!" The light traveled down the rainbow tunnel to the door and blasted through the blackness to the hole in their matrix.

Those who were in Rainbow World stood back and watched the light weaving the balloon through the hole in the darkness it had created. The weaving was going very quickly. Spero was proud of them that they thought to reinforce the attachments. He watched and knew that Ariane was seeing through his eyes. When the balloon became a white light sphere, he lowered his head and touched his third eye and said, "Now Ariane, push the blackness in."

Ariane heard Spero clearly although there was a loud static electricity noise reverberating in the cave. She yelled, "WE'RE READY TO PUSH THE BLACKNESS INTO THE LIGHT SPHERE. SPERO SAYS KEEP IT LIKE THE SUN AND THE WHITE SPHERE ITSELF WILL TURN WHAT IT CAN LIGHT. CONCENTRATE NOW ON MOVING THE BLACKNESS IN! PUSH, PUSH, PUSH…..NOW!"

The group was physically sending its energy along with the light and it became so bright in the circle and the cave they could barely see each other across the circle.

Ariane was screaming over the roar of the static, "SPERO SAYS IT'S WORKING, KEEPING PUSHING THE BLACKNESS IN THE LIGHT SPHERE!" The energy that the group was expending was exhausting them, but they kept sending as much as they could.

"IT'S IN. THE BLACKNESS IS MUCH SMALLER, AND THE REST IS JUST KIND OF MUDDY NOW AND IT'S ALL IN. WEAVE THE HOLE CLOSED!"

Bette started moving her hands like she was weaving, and the rest of them followed suit.

"SPERO SAYS WHATEVER WE'RE DOING IT'S MAKING A VERY PRETTY PATCH!" Everyone smiled weakly.

"IT'S DONE. WE'RE DONE!!!" The energy died down substantially, but the circle had a sphere of white light encasing it.

"No, we're not," said David. "We have energy here that can be sent to all of those who are hurt and dying to help heal them. This can be a soft sending, and you don't have to get more tired. Just wish them healing and VISUALIZE their wounds healing and the white light we have surrounding them and going through all of their bodies, down through meridians, and see them as whole and healed and healthy. I've been working on the Dragon. He's still really hurt. Everybody, let's help heal them, ok?" Everyone agreed.

"1, 2, 3. Please send your healing energies now."

The group was really quiet, and the white light became green, like a green Sun, and this green Sun moved toward Rainbow World. Their whole land was bathed in the healing energy. The green could be seen most brightly around those who were the most hurt.

"Spero is crying, I think. He says they didn't expect that from us, and they are so grateful for our help. He says that the big chicken is much better, and he sends you all his blessing." Ariane looked confused and then smiled, "I think he means the dragon!"

The brightness in the circle faded away. They sat looking at one another. They were too exhausted to speak or move yet.

Bette broke the silence. "Sorry, I seem to be setting a pattern here, but I have to go to the bathroom!"

Everybody chuckled and moaned. It was about all the energy they had left.

"Remember to exit to the south guys, and then come back in to clean house," Jo said. "There's lots of extra water and some fruit and granola bars in the cooler."

Everyone started to move, but Ariane stopped them. "We've forgotten something." They all looked at her. "We need to thank the stones and the salt for their help and bless them for the hard work they did too!"

Everyone took a moment silently thanking the Stone People. Everyone was sincere and serious, and the fact they were all thanking rocks seemed perfectly natural and right.

Ariane heard something from Spero that she didn't pass on. He said, "That's my girl."

Chapter Eleven
Sunday in August in Wyoming

Life went on without Spero, but it just seemed rather dull without him. He had brought magic and wonder to their lives and experiences that they could never forget. Even now it felt like a dream rather than something that really happened. Ariane thought that she would continue to hear him talking to her and see more visions of Rainbow World, but it wasn't working that way. It made her feel sad and disconnected.

Demy, Peter, and Ariane spent a lot of time during the rest of the summer at Demy's ranch riding horses and working with the cattle. Ariane had never ridden before and it became her very favorite thing to do. She fell in love with a small mare named Roxanne, a really gentle chestnut colored quarter horse. The boys always teased her when she always wanted to ride "Roxy," saying it was because the horse matched her hair.

Peter's birthday was coming up soon, and it seemed like everyone had just forgotten. There was mad, frantic activity going on at his house planning their new home, and he tried to stay out of the way.

He was having the time of his life with his two best friends. Ariane had become someone he was just as comfortable to be around as

Demy. He would have never thought a girl could be a best friend too, but she was.

David was spending most of his time between helping at his mom's business and helping the Postelwaite clan build their new house. Ariane had barely seen him all summer.

The Postelwaite's burned house had been completely removed, foundation and all, and rich earth filled in the hole. Grass and wild flowers had been planted there.

The Postelwaite boys had decided that they needed to learn everything about building their own house so they could build the Prismland Sanctuary or "safehouse" themselves. Blake had been working with the architects and had actually designed a lot of the safehouse already. Ernie seemed to be the one watching the money and making sure everything was within the budget they decided on. Blake seemed to have a natural talent for design and all aspects of construction. He was busy all summer trying to figure out how to change the house plans which drove the contractor nuts. A lot of his suggestions had gone into the design though.

Jerry was more interested in keeping the lumbering business going and taking care of the Christmas Tree Farm. He planted a huge garden and spent most of his time there. Jeff actually seemed to have more interest in how they would set up the rules for the safehouse, and how to administer it and structure it as a non-profit business. He was going to be the social worker of the group it looked like.

Bette was just walking around watching the flurry of activity. Her major wish was that there are three bathrooms, one of which would be hers alone. She was adamant that the house be ranch style, and that there were several exits out of the house and emergency exit windows. She said all she really wanted was a big kitchen, painted white and yellow, and an open, airy design with lots of windows and hardwood floors throughout the house.

Bette had talked to Jerry about going to college next year. He asked if he could take a year off to get everything established and give himself a break from school. He really didn't know what he wanted to major in anyway. Jeff suggested that he major in forestry, and that got Jerry thinking more in the direction of college as a possibility. Jeff looked into the forestry program at the University of Wyoming at Laramie for Jerry. Laramie wasn't that far away. He was really pushing Jerry to at least take a couple of classes starting in the fall to "get his feet wet." Jerry was starting to be more open to it.

All the boys were really getting in shape working outside on the house all summer. Their blond hair turned almost white and they all tanned deeply.

David was tanning too, and Ariane noticed one day with surprise that David was actually handsome!He was shaving and combing his hair for a change and dressing really cool. He actually started dressing a little like Spero. Ariane couldn't believe how much he had changed since he started seeing so much of Sonya Wallace. They really liked each other, and Sonya spent a lot of her spare time helping the Postelwaites build the house too. Ariane had never met a girl who did the things Sonya did. She wasn't afraid to try anything. Ariane wanted to be just like her!

David had a lot of confidence in himself now, and it showed in so many ways. He had decided he should study International law so he could take on big business and even countries if he had to. He was already on the computer every night, learning what he could about the biggest pollution offenders and the types of pollution that did the damage they all saw. Sonya was just as interested, and they worked together quite often. He was a lot nicer to Ariane and talked to her, and that's what she cared about most. It was like they were friends now. Ariane hoped so much that it would always stay that way.

Peter's birthday was today. He was pretty bummed out that nobody apparently remembered. Demy and Ariane were really playing up the "everyone is just too busy and forgot part," being all indignant that they really must not like him at all and stuff.

Ariane made cupcakes, and they lit one candle, "The three of us will just celebrate your birthday without them," Ariane said.

Demy hammed it up, "Uhh…here's a spare set of poker dice to play at school. Maybe you can earn enough for a better present."

Peter tried to seem happy, but it was pretty evident he was disappointed.

Ariane and Demy had conspired to keep Peter busy and away from his house as much as possible all summer. Jerry and Jeff had been busy building part of Peter's surprise. It was really rough to keep Peter from finding it! The three of them had wonderful adventures all summer just being outside working with the stock at Demy's ranch. It had been a dream come true for Peter and Ariane. It was old boring work to Demy. To satisfy Demy, they had been playing fantasy games until they all three decided that it was a poor excuse for the real thing, so they lost interest in it.

They started learning poker instead. Demy was the school's poker master. He earned money at school playing poker with five dice on the playground. He would have really gotten in trouble if the teachers would have figured out the kids were playing for money most of the time. Fifty cents a hand and twenty-five cents to re-roll three or fewer dice, winner take the whole pot. Demy was rarely beat.

He had taken his poker winnings and his allowance and talked to his dad about buying a horse for Peter. Marty knew, without asking, which horse Demy would choose for him. Annie was a grey and black paint with blue eyes and black mane and tail. Her full name was "Apple Pie Annie," but everyone just called her Annie, except Peter. He loved the story of her full name and never called her anything but Apple Pie Annie.

She was named Apple Pie Annie because she had eaten a whole apple pie that had been cooling on the porch once. Every time Peter rode horses with Demy at the Cresenzo's ranch, he rode Annie. Annie actually seemed to love Peter as much as he loved her. Even the ranch hands noticed how happy the horse always was to see him. Marty was pleased to set the price so it was affordable for Demy to give Peter to Apple Pie Annie and vice versa.

Ariane and her family were buying the bit and bridle. Bette and the boys were buying the hay and grain and water trough, salt blocks and setting up the corral and small barn. Jeff had purchased a brush and curry comb set. Blake bought a few other tools Peter would need. Marty and Lynne were pitching in Peter's favorite saddle as their gift.

The surprise was going to be sprung tonight. Ariane and Demy were having fits trying to keep Peter inside for awhile so Jock could move Annie into the trailer to her new home.

Jerry drove up in the pickup to take Ariane and Peter home for the evening. Demy was really playing it up that he might not be able to see them tomorrow because his dad was going to make him work for a change.

As Jerry exited the ranch, Marty, Lynne, and Demy quickly rolled into their car and followed out of sight. "Feels like we're spies tailing our mark," Demy said. He was so antsy he couldn't sit still in the back seat.

When Jerry pulled into the motorhome parking, everybody was standing outside. There was a table and a cake and lots of food and presents on the table. The whole family was there and so were Jo, David, and Sonya. The Cresenzos drove in behind them.

Peter was speechless. He turned to Ariane and said, "You guys! You really had me feeling sorry for myself. The cupcake and candle were a pathetic birthday cake. They tasted good, though."

"Well, you really aren't supposed to eat the candle too!" Ariane laughed.

"Well, it made it chewier!" Peter smiled. They got out of the truck and Demy immediately walked toward them.

"I wonder if I could give you your real present now?" Demy said. Peter came over and put his arm around his shoulders. Demy was about ready to cry, you could tell.

Everyone was totally silent. Jock came around the bluff leading Apple Pie Annie.

Peter just stood there with his arm still around Demy. "Oh man. You're kidding. You're really kidding!" He hugged Demy hard and went over to Apple Pie Annie and wrapped his arms around her and buried his head in her neck. He tried to hide the fact that he was crying. Everyone gave him a few minutes to get his act back together.

"Come on, shrimp." Jerry said, "We'll show you part of the rest of your presents."

Peter took Annie's reins and walked with Jerry and Jeff. The whole group followed, walking over to the corral and small barn. Peter was totally shocked to see it there. "How on Earth did you guys pull this off without me seeing it?"

Ariane said, "It wasn't easy! We had to distract you for the whole summer! You almost did see it a couple of times!"

"You and Jeff did this for me, Jerry?" Peter asked shyly.

They nodded "yes."

"You guys must have been planning this for awhile!" Peter smiled at everyone.

Bette said, "Why don't you try out the new corral, put Annie in for now, and come see the rest of your presents."

Peter led Annie in and took off her bridle and reins. He went into the barn and saw that they had thought of everything. There was a tack area with hooks for the bridle, and a saw horse for the saddle, and an area to keep the hay and grain, and a stall for Annie.

Jeff brought over the curry comb and brush set. "Here, this is from me. We built you a shelf to keep them on."

Blake gave him the tool kit which included a hoof pick and shedding comb, "And these are from me."

Peter took his gifts shyly and looked at each item. "These are really nice. Thank you, Jeff and Blake! Thank you, everybody!"

Bette said, "Mr. and Mrs. Cresenzo gave you your favorite saddle and a bag of salt." Everyone looked at each other and laughed. "And Jo and her family and Sonya gave you the bit and bridle."

"And Spero gave you the saddle blanket."

Everyone turned around in shock. Spero was standing in the door with a brand new saddle blanket. They all exclaimed happily and rushed toward him. Marty and the boys were talking and greeting him all at once and pounding on his back. Bette and Ariane and Jo all rushed in to hug him and about knocked him over.

Sonya was standing back slightly, watching them all with a big smile. Spero caught her eye and greeted her as well. She smiled at him and shook his hand.

"Well, I couldn't miss the party. Can we eat now?" Spero asked hopefully.

Everybody totally cracked up.

Jo put her arm through his and said, "Thank you so much for coming back to us. It was really, really, REALLY, boring without you."

"I decided that there was no reason I can't have a family too and be with them on special family occasions. I can't tell you how much I've missed all of you too! I want to be with you once in awhile when I can possibly get away. I want to have a real family life outside of my responsibilities, so I decided to have one! Now can we eat?"

Everyone walked back together to eat and open more presents. Spero was already humming.

Chapter Twelve
Summer's End

The rest of the summer went by very fast. Spero didn't stay long but promised to be back soon. He said everybody in the Rainbow World was recovering nicely, and they had been working hard cleaning things up and repairing everything and rebuilding the Lemp Tower of History. Most of those who had been evacuated had returned. Tazman was still in training, and he was spending his evenings rubbing sore muscles and doing every little thing his Grandsire Temujin demanded without complaint. Spero said Tazman seemed to be in his element and had actually been caught smiling a couple of times.

The problem that had caused the hole in the ozone of their world wasn't gone, but it was contained for now, and the containment was holding. Spero was worried that the corruption that was already building would cause another hole, but everyone was working on it. He asked them to gather periodically as a group and send white light to them. Spero said that Sentinel had recovered fully and was out exploring the Universe again.

Before anybody knew it, it was the first day of school. Demy, Ariane, and Peter stood at the 6th grade class roster for Mr. Finch's room and read down the list. They were all in the same class!

"No way!" Ariane said. Peter and Demy both said, "WAY" and did a high five "ALL RIGHT" jump. They both patted Ariane on the back.

They went into the classroom and sat in the back together. As the kids started coming in there were a lot of happy smiles and the usual put- down comments from the snobs who thought they were better than everyone else. Demy loved imitating them and had Ariane and Peter thoroughly entertained. Ariane had never had friends like this before. She was really happy.

Peter knew Mr. Finch had a reputation for being strict but fair. He was a really good teacher according to the Postelwaite boys. He wouldn't take any of their stuff, they said, and they actually learned something.

The bell rang, and he called roll. When he got to Peter's name, he smiled widely and said, "Oh no, not another Postelwaite," and the whole class laughed.

Mr. Finch was really funny and nice. He looked up after he called each name and said something to each person. When he got to Ariane's name, he asked how to pronounce it. She said, "Air-e-ann, but everyone can just call me Ari."

"Air-ee it is," smiled Mr. Finch. He winked. The class laughed.

He finished the roll and turned to the board and wrote,

> *1ˢᵗ ASSIGNMENT – DUE BY*
> *THE END OF CLASS TODAY*
> *WRITE A TWO PAGE ESSAY*
> *ON WHAT YOU DID THIS SUMMER.*
> *WHAT YOU ACCOMPLISHED*
> *OR LEARNED BY DOING IT,*
> *AND WHAT YOU DID, OR*
> *DID NOT ENJOY*
> *ABOUT IT.*

Ariane, David, and Peter just looked at each other in shock for a moment and tried to keep themselves from busting out laughing.

It was no use.

They just totally lost it.

Dedicated to the memory of the real Prism that we all miss and the real Spero, DeJon, wherever he may be.

Bless the wonderful friends my partner, Jeannie Sexton and I made at Prism and bless those who helped out and were always there for us. Special thanks for their time and generosity to Sunny, Bobby Maes, the two Jacks, Marvyn Syferd, Carolyn Rowe and Chuck Short (the famous Yo-Yo man, who is my brother too.)

Hail to the real Wordsmiths, a wonderfully talented group of very fun writers.

I also want to thank my sister, Shirley Anderson, who kept urging me to write faster and provided much needed encouragement, and my husband and best friend Tom, who hasn't been killed… yet.

Blessings and thanks to our family - daughter, Shannon Heidelberg and son, Ryan Heidelberg, and to Tyler David and Riana Nicole Strohbehn, who are, and will continue to be, my inspiration.

Blessings to the angel on Earth who raised us and keeps always a sense of childish wonder and play alive in us all, my mom, Gwendolyn "Gwen" Short. Sorry, I said you were dead in the book, I don't give that any energy… because you're not dead…in case you wondered.

Blessings forever to my dad, Lloyd Short, a real angel in heaven. He gave me my punny, quirky sense of humor. We miss him every day.

Oh yeah. We can't forget Clueless, the cat, who keeps lying on my keyboard editing the book! He hates to be called "Kitty" too.

And last, but not least, to Spirit, who has guided these hands teaching me to see and hear and keep open to the miracles all around me. Thanks for being patient for your teachings to be published.

References and further reading

Genghis Khan and the Making of the Modern World; Jack Weatherford, Three Rivers Press, an imprint of the Crown Publishing Group, a Division of Random House, Inc, New York, 2004.

Genghis Khan and the Mongol Empire: Miriam Greenblatt, Marshall Cavendish, New York, 2000.

Genghis Khan; R.P. Lister, New York: Stein and Day 1969, Reprint, Lanham, MD: Cooper Square Press, 2000.

Life in Genghis Khan's Mongolia; Robert Taylor, San Diego, CA, Lucent Books, 2001.

Truth, history and Politics in Mongolia: The Memory of Heros; Christopher Kalonski, Routledge, London and New York, 2004

Internet sites:
Wikpedia
http://en.wikipedia.org/wiki/Genghis_Khan
Encyclopedia of World Biography: http://www.notablebiographies.com
About.com
http://asianhistory.about.com

About the Author

Johan Adkins lives on a "dang yuppie wannabe cowboy ranchette" outside of Cheyenne, Wyoming and is the former owner of the real Prism in Cheyenne. She has a historical educational background. She loves to write, however, and enjoyed the writing workshops of Tacoma Writer's Guild and "Wordsmiths" at Prism. A voracious reader and writer for years, she has kept her writing on the shelf until now. She has an extensive metaphysical background based on nature and "light work" and has acted for years as a teacher and student of metaphysics. She still keeps a metaphysical hand and an "open" ear. Word has it, she once had a friend named DeJon, who was the inspiration for Spero Zezas.

Excerpt from Prismland

David stepped out from where he had been standing and confronted Spero. "What did you just do?" he demanded, "I followed you because you took the crystal, and I watched the whole disappearing act."

"I know," Spero said quietly. "I was aware that you were there. I thought it might be the easiest way for you to swallow what you and I need to talk about if you saw for yourself that I'm not a nutcase."

Spero looked straight in David's eyes, and David noticed for the first time, how different Spero's eyes were. They were deep green and slightly slanted. He had really dark eyelashes and eyebrows, but white, white, hair. David had noticed when they were swimming that Spero's ears were slightly pointed and wondered about that.

"You're not from around here, are you?" David asked.

Excerpt from Prismland's sequel, <u>Earth One</u>

Spero woke up early and disassembled from Bette's house and re-assembled in Peter's room in the hospital. Peter was sleeping. Spero did a quick scan of the condition of his body and his injuries. He put his hand on Peter's head and sent healing energies to the puncture wound. He could tell it was deep and would result in infection. The doctors would take off the dressing this afternoon and pronounce him ready to go home, and his fever wouldn't climb, and the wound wouldn't become septic like it would have a few minutes ago.

Peter opened his eyes and saw Spero standing over him. He looked down at his leg and back up at Spero. "What did you do?"

"Just sent a little extra healing your way. What did you do?" Spero looked at him solemnly.

"Stupid stuff. Ma called you, huh?"

"Yes. She was pretty upset."

"Well, I didn't want to upset anyone, I just....I don't know... I felt like I was going to explode if I didn't do something."

Spero looked deeply into Peter's eyes and his look was sad. "I want you to promise me something, Peter. I don't want you to hurt my really great grandson ever again."

Peter said slowly, "Whaaattt??"

"My grandson, Peter. I don't want him hurt, even by himself. Would you like to hear a story?"

Bette had come to the hospital early too and was just outside the room. She had been there long enough to hear what Spero said. She leaned against the wall outside the room so that she didn't interrupt their conversation. She wanted to listen too, so she hugged a comfortable wall and stayed there.

"Once upon a time there was a lonely God. He had a lot of names, but one of them that the Greeks liked was Zeus. Zeus existed alone and got tired of talking to himself, so he visualized the most perfect mate and all of the attributes he could possibly wish for her. He wished and wished and "whooosh" he extended enough of his lifeforce, elemental, visionary, and dream energy to create a lovely mate. He named her Diana. The mythology books say "Dione" but it was really Diana.

He and Diana loved each other so much and together created an expression of that pure love in the form of a baby daughter who was the most beautiful baby in the whole world and her name was Aphrodite. Aphrodite didn't grow up like most children; she was alone because Zeus and Diana were busy visualizing and creating other deities to rule various aspects of the World they envisioned. They wanted to populate and rule their new world, Olympus which is now called Rainbow World. They had long discussions about ruling it wisely and together as regent and co-regent. Zeus visualized many creatures that you saw there and they have stayed the same through the years.

Aphrodite was always surrounded by multitudes of strange creatures who kept a watchful eye. The woodland creatures known as the Oreads or nymphs, adored the child and cared for her every need.

She grew up wild and free but was kept separate from the other gods and goddesses. Because she was so beautiful, it was feared by Zeus and Diana that she would introduce an aspect of love that their creations had yet to experience and were not mature enough to deal with. She would teach them jealousy and cause strife because every man who looked into her eyes would fall in love with her and would do anything to have her.

So to keep this from happening in their new world and to allow her a normal childhood, Zeus and Diana sent her to Earth to live alone there surrounded by and constantly doted upon by her beloved nymphs as well as by the Earth People, Tree People, Fire People – the Astanagas, Air Beings, Fairies, and all the sea creatures you met and more.

Aphrodite loved the sea best and she was always safe there, because everything in the sea loved her back.

She was natural and wore no clothes and the sun even seemed to kiss her skin, never burned or discolored it. She had long white-gold hair like your family and large blue eyes.

Now remember that the water element shares dimensional space on Earth and in Rainbow World. Sea creatures on Earth can exist simultaneously on Rainbow World.

Aphrodite was happy until she was fully grown and then she became aware that she was one of a kind on Earth. She had nobody who looked like her.

One time when she was riding her very young dolphin friend and swimming in the sea, they followed a beautiful mermaid to a sunken kingdom that Aphrodite had never seen before. It was named Atlantis. The mermaid entered an archway and there was a bright flash and she disappeared.

"Take me there, Bontitu."

"It is too deep, mistress." the Dolphin replied.

"Then go very fast!"

Bontitu was very young or he would have known he was not supposed to take her so deep and never was he supposed to take her to the portal for it led to Olympus.

They both took great breaths and Aphrodite flattened herself against the dolphin's back so they could go even faster. The Dolphin rushed through the doorway and there was a "flash" and they came out on the other side in a sea cave.

Aphrodite arose from the bottom of the sea in a great rush of water and foam on the back of her dolphin friend. The mermaid who had just come through was beside herself. She didn't know what to do because Zeus had entrusted all of her people to guard that Aphrodite never found her way to Olympus, and there she was. Aphrodite had to go back right away before someone saw her.

But, there was a catch. Now that Aphrodite was here, she could never go back. If beings came through in their heavy bodies, they split themselves into two entities who existed simultaneously in both places. They were aware of their split apart self for the rest of eternity, existing in both places, but never again could they re-unite. The portal that brought the beautiful Aphrodite here would not open again to take her back, because now there were two Aphrodites.

The Aphrodite on Earth would age and eventually die and the Aphrodite on Olympus would stay young and live a long, long life because, as you know, time passes differently there. The Aphrodite on Earth became known as Persephone. More about her later.

In that cave, a group of Olympian gods and goddesses were bathing and having a picnic. Among them was a God named Hephaestus, who was the God of Metal or they say of "Smithing." He wore a beautiful golden torc that he had crafted himself. Contrary to myth, he was not ugly. He had bronzed skin and was tall and muscular and beautiful. Aphrodite was drawn to him instantly. Also, she had never seen anything crafted of such shiny metal glistening in the sun before. She seductively and unashamedly walked over to Hephaestus and touched the golden torc. She met his eyes and he was immediately in love.

The problem was, any man who looked into her eyes was also immediately in love and this was the problem Zeus and Diana hoped to avoid. The gods fought among themselves and when Zeus became aware that Aphrodite had returned, he placed her in seclusion in a palace of women.

Remember I said that Aphrodite was natural? Well, she taught all of those women to enjoy their beauty and their bodies and their sexuality. She was rather a bad influence, and as a result of that, was known as the Goddess of Sexuality and Carnal Love.

Hephaestus crafted beautiful jewelry for her and an intricate golden cestus or girdle that caused even more stir among the males of Olympus. Zeus decided to marry her quickly to Hephaestus and they were sent to live in seclusion. They eventually had a son, Aeneas.

Aphrodite was restless and she missed the women's court and the company of other adoring men. She had been banished too long already to her friends on Earth and she hungered for social company and gaiety.

She bribed her blind guard with heavenly touches and kisses and escaped back to the women's court. All of the priestesses and hand women were happy to see her and they disguised her as a hand maiden. She was able to attend all of the parties and orgies and her identity was not revealed because she kept a veil over her face which kept anyone from directly looking into her eyes.

Now, mythology tells that she found a baby named Adonis and raised him and eventually fell in love with him. That isn't how it happened. Adonis was created as an adult, an energy extension of Zeus and by Zeus alone, as a younger version of Zeus, but with a different personality. And different ears, Adonis' ears were pointed. Adonis was to be a right-hand- man, a totally loyal friend and companion who would be immortal and would stand beside Zeus and only Zeus for all time. Zeus wanted someone with joy and imagination to help him design and create creatures for Earth and other planets and dimensions. Zeus was the God of all, the Creator, and he was bored with his own ideas.

The gods and goddesses he created as an experiment in Olympus were mostly Diana's idea of a perfect world. Zeus became unhappy, and living with them was becoming a bore. Also, now, because of Aphrodite, jealousy and strife were causing problems in this perfect world. The gods wanted her and the goddesses hated her because she was more beautiful than they were.

Some of Zeus' creations worked and others didn't, so he was always busy creating things and destroying them as well. Everybody tried pretty hard around at that time not to make him mad, or 'ZAP.' Anyway, Zeus built Adonis to be oblivious to Aphrodite's charm, but he didn't count on Aphrodite falling in love with him.

Adonis was spending most of his re with Zeus. When Aphrodite saw him in the court at a celebration, she removed her veil and expected him to swoon over her like everyone else. He didn't. In fact he seemed repelled by her. She couldn't believe it. His rejection just enflamed her to have him and her pursuit of him was merciless. He was bored with her shallow and immature efforts for she thought that just being pretty was enough to get her anything. Adonis was more interested in studying and getting to be friends with intellectual people and interesting creatures who had something to share with him. Something to teach him.

Aphrodite set out to recreate herself into an interesting and stimulating companion and in the course of doing this, she found great joy in learning and becoming her own person again. She reconnected with the person who was wild in the woods of Earth and in the seas. She started to be moody and sullen and then became desperately lonely for what she had grown up with.

She lost interest in her child Aeneas and she had long ago lost interest in Hephaestus and barely spent any time with them. She became depressed and ill and seemed to lose the will to live. Zeus and Diana watched their daughter deteriorate in despair. Nobody understood what was wrong. She was pining for what she could not have and everyone believed, as she did, that it was her old home, but Zeus was wiser than they were and thought he understood she wanted Adonis.

Zeus relented in an effort to save Aphrodite and planted a flame of passion for Aphrodite in Adonis, not so much to make him a slave of her, but enough to make it possible for them to be *partners. Enough to make it possible for him to love her for herself. Zeus wished this change in Adonis and it was done.*

Because Zeus made Adonis a physician too, he called upon him to treat Aphrodite. Adonis showed such tender care that Aphrodite soon started to recover. They spent enough time together laughing and talking about everything that they soon realized they had become fast friends. That friendship grew to love.

Eventually Hephaestus found another love and released Aphrodite from her commitment to him. They still shared the child Aeneas and Aphrodite eventually became a better mother to him.

Now Aphrodite was free and she and Adonis became lovers. They produced a child, a beautiful little girl named Gwendolyn with pointed ears like her father, who later became Queen of the Woodland Creatures and your ancestor.

Aphrodite loved Adonis, but still missed her Earth home too much. She soon became ill again and seemed to be dying. Adonis and Zeus and Diana didn't know what to do. She asked to be able to return home to Earth to die there. Because of the split apart, only one could be in one dimension at a time. Zeus bent the 'rules' sufficiently to allow the dying Aphrodite to enter a portal to Earth at the exact time Persephone entered the sea portal to Olympus. He sent Adonis to Persephone to explain what was going on and to entreat her to exchange places and identities with Aphrodite. When Persephone saw Adonis, she fell in love with him too and so agreed to go to Olympus thinking she would be closer to him.

But Adonis stayed on Earth to take care of Aphrodite and their child who was to accompany her. They were all happy and free in their Garden of Eden, but she still sickened and died. She was the love of his life and even Zeus couldn't stop her from dying. Nobody at that time understood why she died, least of all the man called Spero now, who loved her more than anybody ever loved anyone.

His beautiful daughter Gwendolyn was all he had left of her, and in his final goodbye, he promised Aphrodite to always take care of their daughter and her family for the rest of time."

"And that includes you grandson." Spero put his hand on Peter's head. He looked toward the door, "And you granddaughter."

Bette came around the corner and she was crying.

Spero hugged her and handed her a handkerchief, "Blow."

Bette blew a big loud honking blow.

"My dainty flower!" Spero and Peter laughed.

www.ingramcontent.com/pod-product-compliance
Lightning Source LLC
Chambersburg PA
CBHW070842250626
47159CB00003B/893